DESTINY COMES DUE

BY PAPER LANTERN WRITERS

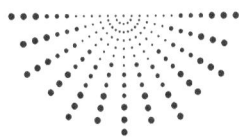

ANNE M. BEGGS   ANA BRAZIL   EDIE CAY

REBECCA D'HARLINGUE   MARIANA GABRIELLE

C.V. LEE   JONATHAN POSNER   KATHRYN PRITCHETT

VANITHA SANKARAN   LINDA ULLESEIT

PAPER LANTERN
WRITERS

First paperback edition November 2024

First digital edition November 2024

ISBN 979-8-9871222-5-9 (paperback)

ISBN 979-8-9871222-4-2 (ebook)

Cover design by Jillianne Hamilton

Published by Paper Lantern Writers

PAPER LANTERN
WRITERS

CONTENTS

STAR-CROSSED

KATHRYN PRITCHETT

LOS ANGELES, 1952

J uli Lynne removed her gloves and set them near the gold-rimmed tea setting. Royal Albert. Nothing less than the best for the Countess.

"Sugar?" offered her mother-in-law as she poured a thin stream of Earl Grey into the bluebell-and-thistle-patterned cup. Juli Lynne noted that the flowers' shapes were simple enough to reproduce in felt. The turquoise background was *au courant* as well. Something to consider for her spring line.

"None for me," she responded, reaching down to place her chocolate-colored dachshund Zeppo on the floor. "Trying to slim down a bit."

The Countess nodded discreetly before plopping two cubes into her own cup. A naturally thin woman who lived primarily on tea, Marlboros, and grapefruit halves topped with maraschino cherries, the Countess kept the kind of youthful figure Juli Lynne envied.

After a round of polite conversation about the oppressive, ever-sunny weather, the Countess brought up the topic at hand.

"I understand these skirts of yours are experiencing brisk sales," she said in her clipped British accent. "How clever of you."

Juli Lynne let down her defenses and chirped. "Yes, it's not only Bullocks Wilshire that's placed orders but also Neiman-Marcus in Dallas and Bergdorf Goodman in New York City!"

"My goodness," said the Countess, raising the teacup to her thin, beet-hued lips. "And they all think women, grown women, will wear these skirts with poodle dogs on them? Whatever for?"

Juli Lynne should have known that the compliment was too good to be true. Praise from her mother-in-law was as rare as summer rain here in the City of Angels.

"They don't all have poodles on them, though those have been a big seller for us. Some have trees or flowers or even fairytale scenes. I insist that each skirt tells a story. One of my first designs featured three dachshunds chasing each other—a boy pup in search of his true love." Even though she knew it irritated the Countess, she picked up Zeppo bringing him dangerously close to the plate of stale Lorna Doones. "It was so popular the shop owner requested one with French poodles. All things Parisian are a hit."

The Countess sniffed, as she slipped a cigarette from the pack hidden behind the squat teapot, lit it, and took a deep drag. "Philip's father's family came from Paris, you know."

Of course, Juli Lynne knew her husband had French lineage, even though he'd been raised in England. Part of what attracted her to him was the European elegance sorely missing in her first husband or the other Tinsel Town Tommies who pursued her. Philip was a cut above the rest. He even had the title to go with it. Just not the fortune.

"I'd like to have met the Count," said Juli Lynne, scratching Zeppo behind the ears.

The Countess tapped her cigarette on the ashtray. "He was a gentleman amongst gentlemen."

Juli Lynne's eyes wandered to the backyard grapefruit tree. She tried to focus on the golden orbs rather than the window frame's chipped paint. Her father-in-law might have had a title, but he was no better breadwinner than his son.

PHILIP'S INABILITY TO find a new job was what spurred the circle skirt business. Once they'd married, he'd insisted Juli Lynne quit working. He'd take care of her now—no need to sully herself performing for others. Twelve years her senior, he was an established film editor for Paramount Pictures. It was a fine job befitting a man with a wife who waited for him at home beneath a grapefruit tree offered as a wedding gift by his mother. But then he'd been let go—*for no good reason*—and found it surprisingly difficult to secure another position.

She'd done her best to rectify things by chatting up her remaining friends in the business. One of her social calls had turned up an invite to a Christmas party where there were sure to be some promising connections. She accepted, keen to help secure another film editing position by wearing an especially eye-catching ensemble. It would be like going out on audition again. Only now she'd be trying to land the part of film editor for her husband. Alas, there was no money to spend at Bonnie Best, so she'd have to make something herself. If only she hadn't refused to learn how to sew.

Her mother had sewn for hire ever since they'd moved to America from the old country. "Better than doing laundry," she'd said whenever Juli Lynne (then Shirley) had complained about the mounds of fabric littered around the apartment. Once they'd moved from New York to LA, her mother had started her own seamstress shop—a factory, she called it, though it was just two small rooms in an old warehouse.

Three days before the Christmas party, Juli Lynne borrowed the Roadster—Philip would be driving the "company car" that day—and headed west to Mama's to see what she could rustle up for a party dress.

Elegant ingénue pickings were slim, since most of her mother's creations were for children. But past the candy cane and Santa prints, a snowbank of white felt caught her eye. She remembered the costumer for the traveling Marx Brothers show saying that she never dressed anyone but the star in white, since white drew the camera's attention. But attention was just what Juli Lynne needed if she was going to secure a new job for Philip.

"Mama, mind if I snag some of that white felt?"

"Felt? For a dress? Too stiff. Better for quiet books or storyboards to entertain church-going children. Women don't wear *felt*."

Juli Lynne slumped down in the old desk chair that listed to the right on account of a missing caster. Her eye landed on the turquoise flocked Christmas tree plopped into an old bucket. Mama should have covered the bucket with some left-over fabric, made a tree skirt. A tree skirt!

"What about a skirt?" she said. "A skirt made out of felt would work, wouldn't it?"

Her mother shrugged. "Guess so. Easy to make. The yardage is so wide you won't need any seams. But a white felt skirt—what's so special about that?"

Leave it to Mama to point out the obvious flaw in her plan. There was nothing that special about a plain white skirt made from fabric better suited to a craft project, but Juli Lynne would somehow turn it into something special. She shoved the white bolt of fabric and some bits and baubles from the trim drawers into the Roadster and headed home.

Back at the bungalow, she kicked off her heels and spread the white felt out on the living room floor as she hummed along to "Jingle Bells" playing on the kitchen radio. Cinching her waist with her hands, she thought how a circle skirt would emphasize the curves that Groucho had loved to ogle during their tour of army bases.

But how to make an exact circle, both for the waist and the skirt edge—which thankfully, due to the felt's inability to unravel, wouldn't need to be hemmed? She rummaged around in the top drawer of the kitchen and unearthed her brother's old slide rule—a gag gift when she'd graduated from Hollywood High. "You never had much of a way with numbers, thought this would help," he'd said with a laugh after she opened it. "Good thing you're a looker."

The gag was on him since life had given Juli Lynne a pretty good grasp of numbers that only got better when she tried to make it in show biz. Singing with the Civic Light Orchestra and performing bit parts in the movies had earned her some steady income. But she still had to watch every penny to make ends meet. She hadn't needed a slide rule to manage her budget, but she'd hung on to it just in case. And now its time to shine had arrived. Paired with a measuring tape, it produced the numbers she needed to draw a waist-sized circle in the center of that snowy felt field, then a second set for the hemline. She got down on her knees and wielded a pair of old scissors to cut out her very first circle skirt.

Up on her feet again, she wriggled through the center opening, smashing her ample breasts and praying that the edge would hold. When it did, she twirled, and the stiff white fabric lifted off her legs like angel wings taking flight. She felt downright hopeful.

But her mother was right—the expanse of white wasn't remarkable enough on its own. She opened the bag of trim and pulled out some scraps of emerald felt as well as two packets of green and red sequins.

The night of the party she didn't reveal her creation until Philip had honked twice for her to join him in the Roadster. Only then did she trip down the bungalow stairs in the red blouse that matched her favorite lipstick color, Revlon's Cherries in the Snow. The white skirt embellished with sequined green trees floated just above her ankles. A no-sew showstopper!

"What in God's name are you wearing?" said Philip.

"Our ticket to success," she said. "Now drive."

THE COUNTESS STUBBED out her cigarette and, with shaking hands, poured another cup of tea. "This skirt business has been a charming episode in your very colorful life. But now it's time to put it aside."

Juli Lynne grabbed a cookie and offered half to Zeppo. "Why would I do that? We're turning a tidy profit. The factory is up and running and I have orders from around the country."

"Yes, you continue to tell me that you're quite the success."

"So, why would I quit?" She willed herself not to stuff more short-bread squares into her mouth.

The Countess slammed the cup down, spilling tea into the saucer and onto her second-best tablecloth. "Because your damn doggy skirts are killing my son."

PHILIP WAS everything Juli Lynne had ever dreamed of—tall, dashing, with an authentic British accent, not the posh put-on of every actor who aimed to be the next Cary Grant. No, he was the real McCoy. Not an actor, but an exacting editor with a knack for splicing images into an artful whole. Much more technically demanding than acting, his work required the discipline of a former military man. The way he commanded a room, it came as no surprise that he had been an officer in the Royal Navy. He still fit into his uniform; the double row of gold buttons neatly fastened over a trim figure; the band of colored ribbons telegraphing his valor.

But the Christmas when she'd debuted her sequined circle skirt at that holiday party, Philip had worn a different uniform to his day job. To make ends meet, he, too, was dressed in white—the white shirt and trousers of a Good Humor ice cream truck driver. No longer sailing the high seas, Philip captained his frigate full of frozen confections through the suburban streets of LA.

It was a good job. Something to tide them over. Even though he had to sit through three days of "courtesy training"—tip your hat to a lady, salute to a gentleman— to earn the sprightly captain's cap that was a mockery of his braid-embellished Navy hat. Working his way through the British military ranks, he'd already learned to comport himself with the decorum befitting a royal audience. He could have taught every man in LA something about respectful behavior, and yet he was forced to mimic the affected manners of a beach bum from Burbank. This was one of the indignities that caused him to flinch even now whenever an ice cream truck passed by broadcasting a tinkling *Turkey in the Straw*.

Not that Juli Lynne couldn't have returned to auditioning for movies or picked up some singing gigs at the club to spare him such humiliations. But Philip continued to insist he'd take care of her. Ever the chivalrous knight, he'd refused to let his wife return to work, even if it meant he must pilot the company car through Hancock Park to dole out popsicles and sprinkle-covered swirly cones. At least he'd not been forced to park in front of the Paramount lot as a Good Humor publicity stunt. What if his old chums had seen him dispensing change from the coin holder on his belt, rather than expertly handling a small firearm as he'd done in his military career? Or bowing to a clutch of harried housewives, instead of casting his elevated eye on a mishmash of footage and turning it into a box-office smash?

Once when she fancied a late-night soft serve, she'd popped into the truck after Philip fell asleep and discovered a flask beneath the chocolate jimmies. She carefully tucked it back where she found it. Didn't say a word. She'd tolerate whatever it took to keep their little ship afloat.

JULI LYNNE CLEARED her throat and stroked Zeppo's ears before replying to the Countess. "My skirts allow Philip the opportunity to pursue his art."

"Pshaw. Surely you don't mean those tepid watercolors he sells to tourists on the boardwalk?"

"They're lovely."

"They're mediocre at best. Perhaps if he was sober when he created them, they could be better. But your blind pursuit of fame and fortune has driven him to drink. He was always a man who could hold his liquor until you insisted on pursuing this fashion folly."

Juli Lynne bit her lip. It was her "folly" that got Philip out of the truck and away from the flask. Her folly that kept him from nearly running half-soused through a gaggle of children, and stopped the drunken rages that vanquished her own good humor.

"He's happier now than he's been in a long time." She bent her head to stroke Zeppo's silky ears so her mother-in-law wouldn't see the forced bravado in her eyes.

"If he's so happy, then why does he seem so diminished?" said the Countess, her voice breaking in a rare display of despair.

"He's forty-two years old. He's earned a respite," said Juli Lynne emphatically.

"He's a man in his prime—a prime you've stolen from him." The steel had returned to her mother-in-law's voice.

Juli Lynne swallowed hard, then whispered, "I've restored his life."

"If you truly want to restore him to the superior man he once was, you must put these silly skirts aside. Allow him to resume the role God bequeathed a man. Let him care for you in order to find himself. Return home–where you belong."

Zeppo nipped at the crumbs remaining on her fingers before jumping to the ground.

"I appreciate your advice, Countess," said Juli Lynne, choking down another Lorna Doone. "You know we both only want what's best for Philip."

AND WHAT WAS best for Juli Lynne? She'd been blessed with a big, coloratura voice, one that lent itself to her mother's Slavic folk tunes when she was a child, Mozart and Rossini as an older teen. She'd won the title of Miss Hollywood at age sixteen and sung with Xavier Cugat's orchestra before she'd even graduated high school. But her classmates quickly lapped her. Lana wore those tight sweaters, skipped class, and got discovered sipping soda at the ice cream parlor around the corner. Now her name was shown in big letters on the marquee. Judy had been cast in that children's movie with a cracker-jack song about a rainbow and ended up with an Academy Award. And Miss Hollywood 1938. Well, she made a few so-so movies that no one came to see.

Except Groucho. He'd seen one, had his people call her to offer her a spot on the Marx Brothers' tour of military bases. Wasn't long, though, until he was asking for more than a song. Thank goodness his baby brother Z had run interference a few times, convinced her she could and should do better by leaving the show. So, she did.

And then she met Philip who convinced her she didn't need to chase the stars anymore. He promised to take care of her, keep the ogres away. And he did, for a while. But when misfortune found them, she had to step up, didn't she? Oh, she'd kicked herself then that she'd burned bridges in the business and couldn't even sew herself a snazzy party dress. Some smart cookie she was—so high and mighty about men behaving badly and mothers who made their living with a needle and thread.

But her star quality refused to stay hidden. It had surfaced again, in of all places, in a fashion phenomenon made from felt and sequins. How could she turn her back on the gift of the poodle skirt?

She dusted off her hands, grabbed her gloves, and snatched Zeppo. "Philip will be home soon. I should go."

JULI LYNNE PLOPPED Zeppo onto her lap, yanked on the gloves, and grabbed the steering wheel as she roared down the Countess's cracked driveway. How dare her mother-in-law tell her how to run her marriage? As if she had any idea how much she took Philip's needs into account. She pressed the pedal and sped along, enjoying the rush of warm air through the open window. Depending on how his water-color sales had gone that day, Philip might already be waiting for her at home. She hoped he'd made at least one sale. That would call for just a small celebration. If he hadn't, it would be a longer drown-your-sorrows kind of evening.

She turned onto Mulholland Drive and the Hollywood sign on the hill came into view. That towering beacon had called to both her family and Phil's, promised a more benign place for the impoverished. They'd all hoped that the glimmer of the Golden State would turn their golden dreams into reality. But nothing had turned out exactly as they planned. Still, didn't those types of stories—the dashed dreams, the near-misses, the almost-rans—make the happy endings all the more satisfying?

Passing by a balconied storybook cottage near Griffith Park, she recalled her high school production of Romeo and Juliet. Already too buxom to play the virginal lead, she'd been cast as the old nurse—a "smaller but meatier" role, said Mr. Melton, the drama coach, when he found her crying in a corner. Sidelined from center stage, she observed how the young lovers cut a swath of destruction wherever they turned, finally destroying each other.

Peeking around the curtain in a nun's costume sewn by her Jewish mother, she heard the audience gasp when Romeo took his own life after finding a sleeping Juliet who he mistakenly presumed dead. Only to have her awaken to find her Romeo gone where she could not go—until she did. Juli Lynne had thrilled at the collective breath-holding as everyone willed the young lovers to reveal their secrets before it was too late.

She turned onto Wilshire and envisioned how she'd recreate the star-crossed lovers in felt. Her mind flitted over the most well-known scenes and landed on Juliet crying from the balcony for her Romeo. He, of course, would be hidden in the evening shadows of the garden below. Where the skirt flared over the hip, she could stitch a curvy Juliet leaning over the railing. Then near the hem, she'd place Romeo in a medieval costume that just screamed Shakespeare. Classy.

But how to depict the anguished cries of true love? The inflexible nature of felt demanded that the designs be simple. But love, as Juli Lynne had discovered, was anything but simple. She passed a faded billboard where Susan Hayward and Rory Calhoun danced in the sky above her. With a Song in My Heart, was one of her favorite movies. She could almost hear the exquisite Rogers & Hart music over the honking traffic. See the beautiful songstress singing her heart out to the handsome WWII officer. Aha! That's how she'd convey young love, through a torrent of hearts flowing from Juliet's mouth as she showered her love with song.

Then she'd embellish the rest of the skirt with flowers from that doomed garden, the floral imagery layering in extra meaning just as it did in the play. Mr. Melton had taught her how Juliet is convinced upon first meeting Romeo that their love is destined to bloom. How Romeo is compared to a bud until he kills Mercutio and becomes a flower with a serpent's heart. How the bridal flowers eventually blanket a coffin.

As she drew closer to home, she sang *With a Song in My Heart* just like the woman who had dubbed it for Susan Hayward. A friend had told her about Jane Froman, an actress with a beautiful voice who wasn't cast in the role because she stammered. But oh, could she sing —as Juli Lynne sang now–about the love that manifests as a song in the heart. Like Susan/Jane, how could she not help but rejoice at such a love?

She always felt happier, more secure, after conjuring up a new design. Much like what she'd felt when she'd first met Philip. The thing she'd loved the most about him was that he made her feel safe. His handsome maturity, plummy accent and refined ways gave him the air of a fairytale prince (and that was before she knew he sort of was!)

But now, seven years into their marriage, she chafed at the walls he'd raised to keep her safe. She'd had to leave them after all to fight the ogres that continued to threaten them. And when she'd won the battle, she resented Philip's reluctance to recognize her triumphs. Even as their bank account swelled, he refused to acknowledge that Juli Lynne was responsible.

As a good wife, it had been easier to leave things unsaid. Like how much she loved coming up with new designs, and how much she loved making money. The combination of cash and creativity was intoxicating. Despite what she'd told the Countess about wanting the best for Philip, she wasn't willing to give that up.

Her stomach dropped as she turned up their cul-de-sac and roared past a ghostly display of pale hanging blossoms, her neighbor's gorgeous but deadly Angel's Trumpets. What was it that Friar Lawrence said about how the most beautiful blooms could either harm or heal? "Within this ... weak flower poison hath residence and medicine power." Poison or power. Could the design work that was a

11

"remedy" for her also be toxic to Philip? Was the Countess right after all?

The little beach buggy purchased with poodle skirt money hunched in the driveway. Philip was home. Whether he was celebrating a sale or self-medicating after a disappointing day remained to be seen.

Juli Lynne turned off the engine and applied a fresh coat of Cherries in the Snow in the rear-view mirror. She opened the car door and Zeppo raced up the stairs past two rose bushes aflame in the same brilliant crimson. She'd send over a lipstick tube to the dyers so they could custom dye a bolt of felt for the star-crossed flowers.

Opening the front door, she squared her shoulders. "Phil? Philip darling? I'm home."

From the next room, she heard the clink of ice in his glass.

"Philip, we need to talk."

HISTORICAL NOTE:

Dress designer Juli Lynne Charlot was best known for inventing the poodle skirt. Her husband Philip was a former Royal Navy Officer, a viscount, and a film editor whose fallen fortunes spurred Juli Lynne to create her first circle skirt made from felt and adorned with Christmas trees. She divorced Philip after her mother-in-law told her that the poodle skirt business was destroying her son. Yet Juli Lynne always maintained he was the love of her life. Along with the poodle appliqué, Romeo and Juliet became one of her more iconic motifs. Her most famous client–a young Queen Elizabeth–was photographed dancing in the star-crossed lovers skirt.

ABOUT THE AUTHOR

Kathryn Pritchett writes about strong women forged in the American West. A journalist by profession, she has written for numerous print and online publications. Her popular first-person column "Things Elemental" ran for many years in a large daily newspaper and evolved into a lifestyle blog. She is seeking representation for her debut novel, *The Casket Maker's Other Wife*, which was inspired by her polygamous great-great-grandparents tempestuous marriage. Her work-in-progress, *To See the Love-Light*, features Gilded Age actress Maude Adams, a closeted lesbian and Broadway's original Peter Pan. She earned her BA in English from Brigham Young University and is a founding member of Paper Lantern Writers. Connect with her at thingselemental.com or on Instagram @klooslip.

TASTES LIKE DIAMONDS

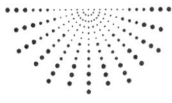

EDIE CAY

NEW YORK CITY, 1863

Prudence did her best not to gape at the rich damask wallpaper that glowed in the low candlelight of Delmonico's restaurant. *Comportment,* she heard Mrs. Talley admonish her in her head. They had worked on this, planned for this. Bought an extravagant dress for this.

She smoothed her gloved hand over the cream printed silk. In Delmonico's, one mightn't realize there was a protracted war on. Until one looked around to see no man without silver whiskers occupying the tables amongst the bustling waitstaff. She was the youngest person in the room, though not by much. The women her age were mistresses or new brides of those silver-whiskered men who were too old to be drafted into the ranks of either the Union or the Confederacy.

The war that made widows of young women didn't touch her as it had others. She felt guilty about her removal from the wider world at the country idyll her husband had set up for himself after his doctor admonished him to rest more and work less. That his health couldn't handle the toll of sleepless nights any longer. While he had the tele-

15

graph installed at the house to keep doing business, being far from the bustle of cities and commerce kept them insulated from the hardships the rest of the country experienced.

On their small farm they kept hens for eggs, and a tidy kitchen garden plot with plenty of vegetables for their limited household. Neither of them added sugar to coffee, nor was there an occasion for a specialty dessert that would require more butter or flour. They ate simply, and their routines were undisturbed.

But tonight, Prudence had taken a room at the Fifth Avenue Hotel in New York City. Alone but for her maid, she was here to prove her business acumen. To acquire as men did, to peacock with her peers as men did, and ultimately, protect and grow the finances of her family, as men did.

Prudence was fifteen minutes early for the dinner meeting at Delmonico's, the restaurant institution that brokered deals of both a business and social nature. She spotted the three railroad men already seated, looking like they were well into indulgences.

"Your party is waiting, madame," the maître d' said with an outstretched arm.

Prudence knew it wasn't an accident that the men had convened before she arrived. Now they could insist she "catch up" both in drink and in conversation. As if they needed more exclusionary tactics. Mentally she smoothed the wrinkle between her eyebrows, trying to keep her expression neutral, even pleasant.

"Mrs. Cabot!" The slim, bearded Mr. Didario exclaimed, getting to his feet. He was younger than the others, but not by much. At least he had threads of brown left in his hair, where the others had none. The other men also stood at their places. They were all similarly dressed in black coats, black trousers, white waistcoats. The cigar smoke was thick enough to turn her stomach. Stifling a gag, she gave them her best Minnesota-sized smile.

"Gentlemen," she said, willing her voice to be as cheerful as when she'd picked up baby Benjamin after a skinned knee. "Thank you so much for having me."

They all chortled some kind of affirmation of her right to have dinner with them, as she was a proxy for the devilishly clever railroad baron Gregory Cabot–her husband. What they didn't know was that Gregory's first apoplexy had occurred two years ago, and she'd been communicating for him ever since. The first attack had only caused one-sided paralysis, but it was enough that he taught her Morse code so that she could operate the telegraph for him. By the time the second stroke occurred, he'd taught her more about business than any school ever could. It was then that he reinforced what her father had taught her: knowledge was power.

Now, Gregory was barely Gregory anymore. She and Mrs. Talley cleaned him, rolling him from side to side every morning and night. Mrs. Talley spoon fed him beef broth and applesauce three times a day. Prudence would sit with him several times a day, between telegraph sessions, correspondence, and the careful analysis she made based on the movements of the war.

Prudence forged Gregory's signature on documents. She traded stocks in his name. Mrs. Talley fretted that what Prudence was doing was fraud, but Prudence insisted that in the eyes of the law and God and everybody, she and Gregory were one. And when her trades proved profitable, her acquisitions of more railroad track in the West were lauded as clever, and her speculation on the grain harvest came true, Mrs. Talley stopped all protests, and instead began bringing her afternoon coffee and buttered toast in Gregory's study. Never complaining as she delivered the stacks of newspapers, broadsheets, and journals to Prudence's elbow.

But she could read every scrap of information that came her way in her dressing gown. Tapping out the telegraphs didn't require her hair to be done. She didn't have to charm anyone or make anyone believe she was not a mere twenty-one-year-old girl from Minnesota. Well, twenty-two in another month.

A movement over her shoulder startled her. But it was only a waiter filling the empty crystal coupe glass at her place setting with champagne. She let out a subtle, steadying breath. This dinner was but business and champagne, and Prudence was prepared for both.

Just as Prudence proved to Mrs. Talley her business acumen,

Mrs. Talley prepared her for a Delmonico's dinner. They'd practiced drinking. How Mrs. Talley came to this talent, Prudence didn't know nor wanted to ask. But when the meeting had been proposed, a summit of interested railroad owners to discuss the acquisition and divide of the Southern railways ravaged by war, Mrs. Talley told her to keep her head, and that those kinds of men drank like fishes.

So most nights, Prudence and her housekeeper drank two glasses of wine. At first, Prudence had to run outside and heave over the railing. Mrs. Talley was there with water and a cool rag. It got easier over time. But Prudence was grateful for her days of rest—when her digestion could settle in the face of a fine vintage.

But then she acquired a taste for it. They'd made a healthy dent in Gregory's vast cellar, tidied away and hidden underground from prying eyes.

"You look a vision, Mrs. Cabot," Mr. Brown commented. "What a sight for men like us to gaze upon a beauty such as yourself."

It was vacuous flattery, and Prudence made herself preen as if she cared about his opinion. "I had this frock especially designed by Mrs. Keckley. She dressed Mrs. Lincoln."

"My wife lives by her designs," Mr. Verruch said, daring to reach over and touch her gloved fingers.

She snatched away her hand and turned her gaze elsewhere. Anywhere besides Mr. Verruch and his small, beady eyes that looked at her as if she were for sale herself.

"And we are all very sorry to hear of Mr. Cabot's sudden illness. He is one of the very pillars of the industry." Mr. Didario's heavily-furred eyebrows inched together like albino caterpillars in a show of regret.

Which Prudence knew was their glee. With her husband out of regular contact, there were already opportunities not presented until they were gone. They informed him by telegraph after the fact. But Prudence, too, knew that information was valuable, giving her the chance to lay her own trap tonight.

"Thank you for allowing me to bargain in my husband's stead. I know it's highly irregular, but—" she shrugged her nearly bare shoulders. "—Needs must, and all."

"We understand," Mr. Verruch murmured, smoke from his cigar wafting over, curling around her hair as if it were an extension of his wandering fingers.

Her eyes watered, but she didn't dare wave it away. She gave a brilliant smile instead and sipped at her champagne. To her surprise, it was rather good champagne. She wouldn't have minded if Mrs. Talley made this their evening drink. And if tonight went well, they could afford it.

"Oysters, lads?" Mr. Brown boomed from across the table. When his gaze landed on her, he smiled sheepishly. "And lady, of course."

The urge to giggle bubbled up in her throat—the effect of the champagne—but Prudence tamped down the reaction. Alcohol was already lacing through her bloodstream, potent and purring.

When the waiter returned, they ordered a vast array of oysters, canapés, and more wine. While Prudence listened to the men opine and smoke, the waitstaff refilled her champagne glass every few minutes. It was never less than half-full.

"Well John, are you going to buy a hunting license now that they make you pay for your own kills?" Mr. Didario grinned at Mr. Verruch. "Benefits of living in New York, they say. Ha! That wouldn't stand in Virginia, let me tell you."

They discussed hunting for a few minutes, though when it came time to give specifics of guns and game, none of them had enough expertise to discuss the topic, and it was dropped.

"How do you like the permanent location of the New York Stock Exchange building?" Verruch asked Brown.

"It's so far away from everything," Brown complained.

"I find—" Prudence tried to add, but Didario cut her off.

"You Yanks are so concerned about distance! How many blocks is it, how many hours is it? Write a letter! Things happen in their own good time. In the meanwhile, enjoy yourself." The men raised their glasses to toast, the crystal coupes tinkling as they touched.

They didn't even look in her direction, but her exclusion was nothing new. The few times she thought to interject her opinion into the conversation, the men spoke over her, ignoring her as if she weren't seated at the table at all. When the room felt as if it might tip, she realized she'd imbibed too much and excused herself to the ladies' lounge.

They smiled and waved her off, as if they didn't need her at all. They didn't—it was true—but she would insist on her place. They had either already discussed their business, or wouldn't discuss anything of note until the main course, so she had time. She weaved around tables, and the hazy gas lighting made the adventure seem pleasant and distant, even if it was just a walk across the dining room.

Inside the ladies' lounge, she yanked off her gloves and drank the cool water from the tap. Uncouth perhaps, but she had to maintain her sobriety. A woman in a scarlet red dress entered, catching Prudence hunched over the gleaming faucet, sipping from her cupped hand.

"Oh." Prudence straightened and shook the water from her hand. "Good evening."

The woman in red was the most alluring woman Prudence had ever seen. Her hair was the color of fire and her dress the color of a hot ember. She wore rouge and lip coloring and kohl around her eyes. The dress exposed her shoulders and almost all of her décolletage, which was all creamy white and practically glowing. The woman pursed her shiny red lips in amusement at Prudence's desperation.

"Good evening," she purred. There were two mirrors, and the woman in red sashayed to the unoccupied one. "Too much to drink?"

Prudence could do nothing but nod. This was the kind of woman that inspired men to do silly things: sign over fortunes, abandon their families. What Prudence wouldn't give to have that kind of power. Any power at all right now would be helpful. She was out of her depth.

"I didn't see you in the dining room." Prudence cleared her throat. Because no one would be eating their dinners, they'd all be staring slack-jawed at her.

"I don't eat in the dining room. Private party on the third floor." Her voice was smoky and flat. Not angry or depressed, just bored.

"You are very distracting," Prudence said, unable to keep her mouth shut, even though she was normally very good at it. The pleasant heat of champagne still buzzed through her system.

"It's my job," she said with a wink.

"How do you do it? The men I'm with need to be distracted, but I'm married. And I'm not...you." Prudence had money to make tonight. And not a nice deal, the kind her father would approve of, but the kind of rug-slipping-out-from-underneath kind of money. Well, it would take three or four more moves to make that fortune, but this was the first step. And if those men out there were worth their salt, at least one of them would see the opportunity she was presenting, but didn't have the ability to move as decisively as she could.

"It depends on the man. Some like this kind of woman." The red-clad woman gestured to herself with her dainty red-gloved hand. "Some prefer women like you. Ladies. Respectable types." She pursed her lips into a faux kiss at the mirror, as if exaggerating her wantonness. In a moment, she snapped her attention back at Prudence, her sultry demeanor vanished with the moue. "What kind of distraction are you needing?"

Prudence chewed on her lip. The best way to keep a secret was to not tell anyone. But there was something about this woman she liked. And the champagne made her want to dissolve into giggles for no reason. Prudence leaned in to whisper: "I want to take their money."

"As in, knock them over the head and run away kind of take?" the other woman asked.

"No, like doing a business deal in my incapacitated husband's place kind of take."

The woman let out a husky chortle. "That's not *take*, hon. That's *earn*. A man would call it earning, and so you should too. If they aren't smart enough to outbid you, that's their fault. You just have to be modest about it and act like you're surprised when the money rolls in."

"How could I act surprised if I made the deal happen?" Prudence frowned, even though Mrs. Talley had expressly told her not to frown at all. Men don't respond to churlish women. That was the trouble. She was supposed to distract them with her girlish charm. Her seductive body. Except she didn't know what that would even look like. Admittedly, this plan was flawed.

"Like this." The woman in red straightened her shoulders and closed her eyes. When she opened them again, it was like seeing an entirely different person. Even her voice was higher: "What luck! My husband is simply a genius." Then she ended with the largest, toothiest smile Prudence had ever seen. Which was saying something coming from Minnesota where the Scandinavians settled. They smiled enough that New Yorkers found them unnerving.

The woman in red shrugged her bare shoulder. "Try that."

Prudence nodded.

"And they'll try to get you drunk. Pretend sips. Don't swallow any booze if you can help it." The woman in red winked at her.

Prudence took a breath. "Thank you. Pretend to drink and act like I'm incompetent."

"Precisely." Out of the small, red silk reticule, the woman took a compact of powder. "Go on, now. Remember, they're fools for trifling with you."

Prudence nodded. She took a breath, trying to rid her system of the bubbles that flew through her veins. The other woman tended to her appearance, and Prudence headed back to the table, packed with men in tailored coats, hunched over the table like black bears.

"Mrs. Cabot, you are back in time for the last of the oysters!" Mr. Brown's cheeks were pinked with the flush of alcohol. "And I know we would all be interested in you partaking of this bounty!"

Prudence smiled thinly. She was a married woman, so she knew the marriage bed, but these comments were designed to see how loose she was, how satisfied she was in that bed, all the while giving them plausible deniability if an angry husband showed up. It gave them a way to claim innocence for their wretched behavior, their wretched thoughts.

"Thank you, but I can't eat shellfish," she said with a feigned pitied pout. She sank into her chair with an ease she hoped looked graceful.

Mr. Verruch snatched the last two oysters and before slurping them down, looked her dead in the eye and said, "I love the salty sea taste of them."

Prudence was too naïve to understand that reference, but she still hated him for saying it. Because it had something to do with her being a woman, and something to do with bedsport, and she did not appreciate it. She curled her gloved hands into fists in her lap and wished she could be a man for just a night. Put on his skin for an evening, like buttoning into an elaborate dress. What a relief to not be an obvious intruder in the group. But that wasn't going to happen, so she had to accept who and where she was and move forward with her plan.

"More champagne?" Mr. Didario asked, gesturing to the waiter holding the bottle.

Prudence smiled and offered up her glass as if she were most impressed with his gallantry.

"So, Bill, what do I hear about your needs?" Mr. Brown asked Didario.

"Money to get back on my feet. As you know, most of the track was blown up or scavenged for parts." Didario focused his watery blue eyes on the other men and Prudence felt herself vanish into invisibility. They all now ignored her completely. She might as well still be in the ladies' lounge.

The railroad track in the South was more valuable to the Confederacy as its parts than as its whole, and to the Northerners, track represented the possibility of escape by their enemies. Around this table though, they did not discuss the war as a clash of ideologies or soldiers, but like an uncontrollable catastrophe that could not have been avoided. There were murmurs of sympathy for the state of the railroad, but not for the thousands of dead, starving, and injured. Not for the war. Not for the enslaved. Not for families who lost every member, their blood lining the ditches where the scavenged steel tracks once lay.

"We've all had to make sacrifices," Mr. Brown continued. "But none so much as you."

Prudence, who admittedly had been relatively untouched by the fighting, couldn't believe how completely callous these men were to the actual circumstances of the civil war.

"Rebuilding will be considerably more difficult in the South," Didario said. "As you can imagine."

Prudence blinked. And then realized what he implied: that he would now have to pay workers, instead of using slave labor to lay track. Granted, the conditions in the West and the Chinese labor being used was despicable, but there was a way to lay the foundations of something without needing to make mountains of money every single day. Ethical working conditions might be more costly, but none of them at this table had need of that extra penny.

Her father had taught her that, and she was proud of him for retaining his ideals as his fortune grew. It was how they communicated, sending clippings back and forth, writing sheaths of letters to each other on labor practices, philosophies on ethics, as well as gossip on the men who sat at this very table.

Last April, the heads of the Southern railroads had come together, Didario included—none of the other railroad presidents knew what was said in the meeting as far as Prudence knew. Though she wouldn't put it past Brown and Verruch to have wheedled out the details from Didario before she arrived at Delmonico's. But one thing the business people of the Union understood was that ideology didn't make money. It didn't put food in bellies. It wasn't practical. The agrarian way of life the southern states had enjoyed was losing its ability to keep up even before the war. Now, the inferiority of the agrarian ideology was lethally obvious.

"I'm happy to loan you the sum you require in return for shares, and minimal interest, of course." Mr. Verruch leaned in on the table.

"What rate?" Didario asked.

The waiter brought another round of canapés. How could they even eat after all those oysters? And was this dinner? Were they not ordering a main course?

"Same as a bank, but with a better guarantee." Verruch smiled at Didario, then winked at Prudence. Verruch owned the Western railroads. Prudence's father had worked with him, connecting the transcontinental track. There were still some minor players, and Verruch was muscling in on Prudence's father's territory, clearly wanting to buy him out when the time was right. Currently there were hundreds of small players like her father, but that wasn't going to last much longer. Monopolization was the way to fortune, and Prudence knew Verruch saw the world solely in terms of his pocketbook.

Still, his attention to her was unnerving. She kept her mouth closed, waiting to hear the rest of the offers at the table. Prudence and Gregory had discussed the future of railway ownership.

"Let's not ignore the real issue here, lads," Verruch said. "In the future, there will be fewer and fewer owners to deal with. As we are the largest holders in the area, it makes sense to keep things pleasant between us. The transfer costs are high to go from line to line, so it makes sense for us to keep civil and work together." He grinned again, showing a mixture of yellowed and ivory replacement teeth.

Prudence heard what Verruch didn't say: *It makes sense to consolidate*. There were few industries that needed copious amounts of steel and lumber as well as the technological information to maintain both engines and track. While none of them at this table understood the engineering portion of the trains, they all understood the ledger books.

The back of Prudence's neck prickled. Suddenly, Verruch's leering interest in her made sense. Once Gregory was dead, Prudence would control their holdings, and Verruch could bypass any taxes by marrying Prudence. He could get the right-of-ways he wanted and a young bride to boot. She shuddered.

Brown leaned back in his chair and looked at Verruch, sitting next to him. He nodded and then said, "No interest. I loan you the money, and I get forty-five percent share."

Verruch winced. Didario visibly relaxed, considering. Prudence realized he didn't think he would get this good of a deal. No interest was of great value when discussing sums such as these.

"Can I buy you out of shares later on?" Didario asked.

Brown drummed his fingers on the table, glancing at Verruch, clearly wondering what his counter offer would be. "We can discuss it when it comes time to draw up the contract. Something fair for both of us."

The Union had access to over twenty thousand miles of track. At the outset of the war, the Confederates had nine thousand miles. Now, there was no telling how much remained, but it was drastically reduced.

Verruch was clearly stewing, trying to think of some way to sweeten his proposal. But it was the first time there was a lull in the conversation. It was time for Prudence to lay out her trap—which was clever only because they didn't know her, they didn't read the papers as closely as she did, didn't watch the death counts of both sides of the war, knowing that fatigue was a powerful peacemaker.

"My husband told me to give you the money," Prudence said, hoping she sounded as incompetent as the woman in red told her to be. Her heart beat hard in her chest as she began her gambit. "And in exchange, you give us the company."

The men all laughed. "That's just buying me out," Didario said, as if telling her something she didn't already know. Didario owned the right-of-way and whatever track was left in the crucial Virginia corridor. While it was unlikely Didario would sell now—while the war still raged—promises could be made.

This was one of the reasons Prudence had made the trek down to Delmonico's. She'd hoped to obtain the land and have a reason to begin amassing the supplies needed to build immediately after the war ended. Of course, newspapers had been claiming the war would be over in a month for nearly four years. Why was it any different now?

Because Prudence could see the fatigue. The food prices were high, and everyone knew someone who'd served or had died. Sometimes on both sides of it. And well, because of General Sherman. He understood supply lines more than most, and he'd taken over the Confederate ones.

Despite how Sherman had burned the towns he'd taken, Didario, and many businessmen, believed themselves above war and its aftermath. That somehow, their money was God-given and immutable. But Prudence listened whenever anyone spoke, regardless of station. The exodus of working people from the South was steady. Those women who had been housekeepers and cooks, the women who had already lost not just their homes and their employers, but their brothers and fathers, they came north. Free and formerly enslaved. And they all had stories.

The wealthy were not untouchable, despite their beliefs. Didario likely believed that he would recoup his money, and his life would keep on as it had been, largely unchanged. But Virginia was a battleground. Prudence firmly believed that the key to post-war life was that stretch of land that Didario owned. And she wanted it. She could employ workers with fair wages and decent hours. She could atone for the sins of her colleagues by doing better for those they had wronged. It wasn't perfect, but it was something.

She nodded, all smiles for the three men at the table. Her hands sweated inside her gloves. More than anything she wanted to throw back all the champagne in her glass to quench the overwhelming throb of anxiety she felt.

But she didn't. She required clear-headed sobriety.

Instead, she said, "My husband says that after the ceasefire, it is extremely likely that the government will come in and *take* your company from you. Completely and without recompense as punishment for supporting the Confederacy." *You own people, Mr. Didario, and you expect them to work for free and be grateful about it.* She bit her tongue to keep herself from saying that outloud.

Didario shook his head. "I didn't expect your husband to be some damned abolitionist. No real businessman would be. Labor costs more than any other sector, and if it were your husband sitting here and not you, he'd know that."

Prudence cocked her head, thinking back to the woman in red's advice in the ladies' lounge. "I thought we were doing business, not discussing ethics," she said in her sweetest voice.

Verruch sat back in his chair hard, emitting a disgusted harrumph.

Brown sighed hard and signaled to the waiter. "More wine," he called.

If she could sit at this table long enough, she would get a very big glass of champagne in her room at the hotel, where it was safe. Instead of fiddling with her gloves or the coupe's crystal stem, she concentrated on not frowning and not clenching her teeth.

"I won't sell my company," Didario said. "I built it and I intend to keep it."

"Is your stock in dollars or Confederate bonds?" Prudence asked, already knowing the answer. Three years ago, at the beginning of the war, when there was a surge of visible loyalty to the rebellion, Didario proudly proclaimed in a Confederate newspaper that he'd converted his entire holding over to Confederate currency. *Sounds like you only read gossip pages*, she thought to herself. "Because everyone knows the Confederate dollar is already worth nothing."

"Yet these fine gentlemen are willing to—" Didario gestured to his dinner companions before Prudence cut him off.

Fine gentlemen! She wanted to huff and throw something. Prudence could show him what good men looked like, and it wasn't anyone here. "These fine gentlemen expect payment in American dollars. Gold-backed Union money," she said, desperate to keep her expression neutral. Didario had what she wanted, and she intended to get it, one way or another. Though it appeared more and more evident she would have to play a longer game.

Didario finally turned to face her. Deep lines were etched on his face as he tried to control his temper. "I don't need a lesson from a child-bride! We included you here out of respect—"

"Is it respectful to try to oust my husband at every turn, despite the fact that he gave every single one of you favorable rates when you needed a loan?" She looked at Brown. "Sold you the land when you couldn't get the right of way for your track through the Dakota Territory?" She looked at Verruch. "Or gave you a lumber supplier with his own discount?" She stared down Didario. The lumber supplier had come from her father's contacts. There went her attempts at being light and incompetent. She'd showed her hand, and now she definitely wouldn't get past the first round of wrangling. This had not been part of her plan.

"That was a long time ago, girlie," Verruch growled.

Prudence batted her eyelashes just to irritate him. Maybe she could salvage her act of incompetency? "I'm offering you a chance, Mr. Didario. My husband has authorized me to purchase your company here, tonight, in gold-backed American dollars. You evacuate your family before the Union Army occupies your house and eats the food from your children's plates. It's enough to land on your feet and start anew in a different business." Prudence opened her reticule and pulled out a small paper that she'd already written the purchase price on.

"That's absurd! I wouldn't sell my shoes for so low a number!" But Didario didn't throw the paper back at her, as she expected he might.

"These two gentlemen won't offer to buy your company." She looked at both the other men, ready to spill their secrets. "Both of them took risks in the war, and as a result, are waiting for the Union government to pay out their contracts. They'll get their money eventually, but for now, they are cash-poor."

Prudence sipped her champagne and then dabbed at the corner of her mouth with a napkin. She could taste the money in that champagne. Sparkling and near, as if each bubble were its own diamond. "One of the benefits of having to live in the country as my husband recuperates is that we were unable to engage in war profiteering."

Both the other men puffed up as if they were insulted.

"While we rusticate and shore up our existing business, my husband and I have funds available to make you an offer. A decent, kind, generous offer that expires as soon as this meal ends. The next time we offer, that number will be considerably less."

"You brag about having cash on hand, but there's no way you can rebuild. The cost is high, given the lack of workers," Verruch grumbled.

"Or do you mean the lack of workers willing to work for free?" Prudence challenged, looking from Verruch to Didario. "I've done my best to make sure we pay a decent wage to every single person who works for me."

"Your husband," Brown snarled his correction. "No one works for a trumped-up ruffled hussy like you."

If this was how she was talked to, Prudence didn't want to know what men said to the woman in red. "Of course. I forget myself. But do not despair, Mr. Didario. Once peace is achieved, we have lumber and steel waiting on the task."

"You cannot have steel waiting, that's for the American government!" Verruch argued.

"That is true," Prudence agreed. "The steel we have is still in its component parts, not yet rendered. But I trust my supplier. Relationships are so important, aren't they?"

None of the men spoke, since none of them had ever bothered to write a personal note to their suppliers. Nor arranged for a piano teacher for one of their suppliers' children. Or sent a physician for an ailing mother. Or remembered birthdays and anniversaries. Gifted linens for a wedding, a silver cup for a baptism, or a Christmas ham during lean times. Loyalty could not be bought, nor achieved overnight. And during her hours at Gregory's sickbed, lonely and in need of connection, Prudence had written dozens of letters and made arrangements even when the cost was dear.

She thought of the gifts she'd wanted to give to her brother, a medic in the Union army, who was too young to have ever held another human at riflepoint. He worked at the northern clinics well behind Union lines, knowing he would go to medical school once the war was over. She thought about baby Benjamin, who would barely remember growing up during a war.

And she thought about her sisters, unmarried, dancing in Minnesota church basements with whatever men might be available. Prudence had been spared all of this by virtue of her marriage—and then by Gregory's personal tragedy. They'd convalesced in peace, and while she felt guilty for her luxury, she was grateful for it all the same.

Relationships formed the backbone of Gregory's company, even when Gregory could no longer speak. Many believed that they'd made no changes or moves to expand due to the war. But now, Prudence knew she could take control and not just improve Gregory's company, but make it grow.

Post-war starvation was not uncommon, especially in the ravaged landscape where blood was spilled—that had been easily learned from the Prussian wars. A functioning railway could supply foodstuffs at rapid rates. And blankets, and fuel, and freedom. There would be plenty of people in need of paying jobs. Ones that paid more than a pittance. And Prudence would be happy to provide that.

The three men were hunched over, refusing to look at her; still, she gave a bright smile. The kind that one might give to a neighbor in Minnesota, thanking them for a jar of honey or a basket of eggs. "Thank you gentlemen, for this instructive evening. Mr. Didario, I will be staying at The Fifth Avenue Hotel tonight, and leaving in the morning. Remember what I said, that number changes the moment I leave Delmonico's."

Didario gave a small laugh, as if she were making a joke, but he couldn't or wouldn't meet her eyes. She'd rattled him and that sense of security.

"Good evening." She said one last time, then stood up and left the table. True, she hadn't gotten the outcome she'd wished for, but the line was in the water, baited with the very best offer. Words, in the end, were meaningless. And no one knew what to expect in the coming months of war. Gambling was sometimes the cost of doing business.

As she pulled on her coat at the doorway, she saw the woman in red already outside with a few gentlemen. The men were inebriated, swaying and red-faced. The woman pulled her head back and laughed, throaty and showy, just as intoxicated as they were. But when she caught sight of Prudence, she winked.

That woman had a secret power, to be what they wanted her to be, but never compromising herself. Prudence hadn't thought it possible to possess such a power, but more than once that evening she'd wanted to throw champagne in Didario's face, or chuck the oyster platter at Verruch. But she didn't. She'd smiled, laid her cards on the table, and left when it was clear that none would engage with her out of stubborn pride.

It was very likely that Didario wouldn't take her up on the offer. She didn't blame him. His pride was under fire, and if the Confederates had shown the world anything, it had shown their pride was worth more than their lives, or the lives of their children.

She'd hoped he would take the offer tonight, her first plan. She'd hoped to cajole with sweetness and charm, but ultimately, Didario was too stubborn to sell. But caring for someone as incapacitated as Gregory taught her patience. She learned to bide her time, and lay the groundwork ahead of her, hoping for good outcomes, and keeping pathways open for the future. Why, she was only twenty-one! There was so much life left to discover.

A cab was ready at the curb for her and spirited her back to the hotel where Mrs. Talley's young niece waited for her. Georgie Pendansky looked up from her book as Prudence entered. The farm-girl was quiet and slow, but competent.

They didn't speak as Prudence handed over her fur coat, her satin slippers. She sat at the vanity table, unclasping jewelry and sliding out hairpins. Georgie returned with a hot towel for her face. Georgie tucked her fingers into Prudence's locks and massaged her scalp, and Prudence felt the tension melt into the steaming towel.

The evening had not gone as she expected in so many ways. She would not consider it a success nor a failure, but rather something else. There was still her trap that she would spring if her predictions came true. Not so much a trap, she supposed, but being poised to take an opportunity when it was presented. Much like the lesson she learned from the woman in red. Ultimately, however, Prudence had to be true to herself, and she couldn't play the fool when she wasn't one. She wasn't a good enough actress.

But she did like the idea of wearing red dresses.

By the time Prudence was in her nightclothes, sliding into the bed heated with a warmed brick wrapped in the softest wool, sleep was there, ready with open arms.

⁂

NOT SIX MONTHS LATER, Prudence bought what had once been Didario's Virginia railway company and the scorched land that still bore the long scar of railroad track for pennies on the dollar from the cash-poor United States government. What she had predicted came true so accurately that Mrs. Talley covered her mouth with a gasp when Prudence read the news story aloud.

The Union Army did take over Didario's mansion, eating every last scrap of food in the pantry. The enslaved peoples had disappeared shortly before the Army's occupation, and the Didario family had no other place to go.

Wedding bells were expected soon with Didario's eldest daughter and the captain of the occupying Union force. Prudence smiled. That must be the real bitter pill for Didario.

The business deal, such as it was, left Didario out completely. Since it was little more than right-of-way through undeveloped land, the Federal government took over the worthless company, which had been valued in Confederate bonds.

"Looks like you didn't need to go to the City after all," Mrs. Talley said, throwing her towel over her shoulder. "You got what you wanted in the end."

Prudence shrugged, not wanting to say Mrs. Talley was wrong. That what she had learned about negotiating was invaluable. That the woman in the red dress had given her a confidence she hadn't possessed when she'd first walked through the doors of Delmonico's. Even if her advice was something Prudence ultimately couldn't adhere to, it was another piece of information in a business where personal strategy made a difference. "It was still a good experience."

"Learning to make business deals, I suppose," Mrs. Talley said, gathering up their plates of afternoon coffee and cake.

She'd learned that she couldn't help how others looked at her, but she could help how she saw herself. Being married to Gregory meant she'd been an afterthought at the social gatherings they'd attended, understood to be the baby maker he'd bought, a tool for a specific purpose.

But Prudence knew that she'd gained his respect when she had learned his trade. When she sat at the dinner table with Gregory and her father, asking questions and contributing an idea here or there. When she brought humanity and compassion to the cold business of numbers and lines on a ledger.

"Hello, Gregory," she cooed as she entered his room. There was a wish she had suddenly, to call him a pet name. To make him a *darling* or a *dearest*. But that wasn't the kind of relationship they'd had. It was far more professional, more educational than beloved.

Gregory opened his blue eyes. He was there, she believed. He saw her, knew her. But he could barely move one side of his body, and couldn't speak with any intelligibility.

"We acquired the Virginia line," she said, unable to keep the pride out of her voice.

He blinked with both eyes twice and purposefully so.

"Remember what I said to Didario at Delmonico's? How I'd buy it later for pennies?"

Two blinks.

"Well, it turns out the Union Army also occupied his estate, as I thought they would. An estate like that in Virginia must have been perfect."

Prudence couldn't tell anyone that Gregory smiled at her, but he did. It wasn't a smile so much as a shift of emotion. But she felt his approval.

"And his eldest is marrying the captain that's living there, too." Here in this room, just the two of them, Prudence let herself chuckle with childish glee. "Serves him right."

Two blinks and a wheeze that Prudence thought was a laugh.

Prudence picked up his hand and threaded her fingers through his, squeezing it, the only affection she gave him. The only kind she knew how to give him, which was still more than he'd been able to give her with the lights on. Theirs wasn't a traditional love match, which was fine. She had more than most, and she wouldn't take for granted the lessons she'd learned. Not like those men she'd sat at the table with, who couldn't see the world already changing before their very eyes. Men who were nowhere as smart as Gregory. Or, if she could be so bold to say, even herself.

"We make a good team," she said, with another squeeze.

Gregory blinked twice and Prudence felt a faint squeeze of her hand. And while that wasn't love, it was still success.

HISTORICAL NOTE:

This is a work of fiction, but the impact of the railroads during the 19th century cannot be overstated. The north did have over twenty thousand miles of track, and the south had nine thousand. But the numbers weren't everything. The southern track was not laid out to bring supplies like food and passengers, as the agrarian lifestyle much preferred roads for carriages and horses. The railroads were meant to bring high yields of cotton to seaports, where it could be exported. Also, the individual railroad owners of both sides numbered in the hundreds. In the north, these individual owners would eventually be bought out into larger and larger corporations, the largest player being Cornelius Vanderbilt. In the south, each track had a different gauge of size, meaning that cars could not be shifted from line to line. The railcars would have to be unloaded from one sized track to empty cars on another line. Due to the non-standardization of the railway, the Confederacy could not transport food, supplies, and soldiers at the pace the Union could.

As the Civil War wore on, much of the Confederate track would be blown up to prevent a battle advantage by one side or the other. In later years of the war, track would be scavenged for steel to make bullets and lumber for fires to keep warm.

Delmonico's Restaurant was, and still is, an institution of high society in New York City. So is The Fifth Avenue Hotel that Prudence stays at. It was a place of networking both politically and socially. Prudence announcing her stay there is a power move that those men would have understood.

***

READ MORE of Prudence's story, after Gregory, in the historical romance novel *In the Money with You* published by Dragonblade. Prudence brings her financial prowess to bear on the expedition accountant Leo Moon in the second installment of *The Ladies Alpine Society* series.

***

ABOUT THE AUTHOR

Edie Cay writes award-winning historical romance. Her When the Blood Is Up series about historical women's boxing has won the Golden Leaf Best First Book, the Next Generation Indie Book Award, the Best Indie Book Award (twice!), and has been a finalist for the HOLT Medallion, Chatelaine Award (twice), and Lambda Literary Award.

She is a member of The Regency Fiction Writers, the Historical Novel Society, and a founding member of Paper Lantern Writers. Her latest series, The Ladies Alpine Society, is from Dragonblade Publishing. Connect with her at ediecay.com

AUTUMN ANGEL

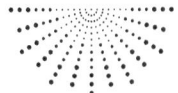

A SAILING HOME SERIES NOVELETTE

MARIANA GABRIELLE

Note: This story contains significant discussion of crimes against women and children.

Prologue

THE ENGLISH COUNTRYSIDE, 1835

Madeline Swift cleaned the knife with salt and a dry cloth after she cut dried berries from leaves and stems. Then, she used the mortar and pestle to crush them into powder. She twisted a piece of foolscap into a small funnel and coated the insides of two wineskins. Later this evening, the cook would fill them and pack for the hunting trip Antonin would set out on tomorrow.

With great good luck, and the wisdom of the grandmothers, he would both suffer and never return.

Once the wineskins had been doctored and set aside, she tidied the workbench she'd been gifted when she left her foster family. She kept her tools and medicines and herbs packed away in the false bottoms of two drawers, covered by sewing supplies and Antonin's shirts for mending. There was no reason for anyone to know what she had learned from the wise women in her village.

She left out a basket of yarn and needlework on the workbench, and a pile of more darning and mending. Better Antonin and his friends think her a poor housekeeper and a simple country girl, rather than what she was: a woman desperate to keep the one child she had left.

Chapter I

London, 1835

"John, you said you would be at Ostelbrooke Farm," said Bella, Duchess of Wellbridge.

"Ostelbrooke!" The duke called out. "Glad you could make it, after all. It's not every day your nephew celebrates his twelfth birthday."

"Shall I have a place set...?" Bella rose as her thought trailed off, dropping her napkin next to her plate. The footman stepped forward to pull back her chair, and she met her brother halfway across the dining room, drawn by the intensity in his gaze. "What is it, John?"

John had fought a hard war, and an even harder homecoming. Any such drastic change in his demeanor could portend a breakdown, and if that happened, he might do anything to escape his demons.

"Bella, it's..."

His eyes darted about the room, taking in the others who had all fallen silent. The duke, now standing; their young son, David, the Marquess of Abersham, who had followed suit; his sister, Almyra, still young enough to require a pillow to bring her chest level with the table. Strictly speaking, Almyra would be far too young for the formal dining room, were it not for a special occasion.

John stopped short and pulled himself back. "I'm interrupting." His eyes roamed ever faster.

"You've not interrupted," Bella spoke in a quiet, grave undertone, "but the children are in the dining room this evening, and I can see privacy is needed. Come with me." She took in the way his shoulder twitched and how he jerked back from her, eyes looking around to mark the exits. "You are safe here with me, John Smythe. There is nothing to fear."

Grasping his arm, pulling him toward the anteroom, she held off incipient questions from anyone else with a wave, but murmured to the butler on the way out, "Please send a fast buggy for Lady Ostelbrooke at their London residence, and if you can find either the dog or the cat, please bring one or both to the Conservatory."

As they crossed the threshold, Bella heard her husband say, "Abersham, take your seat. I was about to regale you with sage advice about your recent troubles at Eton."

"The Conservatory, do you not think, John? We can have tea and a bit of quiet while we sort through whatever this is." She was prattling in a way that might equally soothe a troubled toddler or a tortured soul—which was to say it might not work on either at all. But John breathed easier among the trees and flowers; it had been true since they were children. And while Bella was not as skilled at resolving his fears as his wife would be, she had learned a few things from Rose over the years. She also had a voice he had trusted since she spoke her first word.

"Here," she said, physically directing John to a loveseat in a niche close to the drinks cart, where she poured him a very short brandy. "Drink this."

She sat next to him across a small table and held his grasping hand as he tried to slow his frenetic eyes. He threw back the brandy in one swallow and put the glass down on the tea table, shoving it away hard enough to tip the glass. Bella made no move to pour another and used both hands to hold his.

"What is it, John? What's happened? You look as though you've seen a ghost."

The ragged sound that emerged might have been ripped from his throat with a dull knife.

"Indeed, a ghost. Miss Bairstowe..." He stopped to clear the emotion clogging his voice.

Oh, dear heavens.

"Miss Bairstowe? Angel Bairstowe?" He nodded and sat back, his shoulders loosening just slightly now that someone had said the dreaded name aloud.

No wonder John was regressing so dramatically. Bella had never seen him this bad; only heard stories of the days after Rose found him, before anyone thought he could reclaim his life, when Bella still thought him long-dead. While she had been traveling the world with her first husband, her older brother failed to outrun two wars, one external, one internal.

It had been thirty years since Miss Bairstowe's death, following swiftly behind John and Bella's father, Jasper, and brother, Jeremy, and John's flight into the army as a private. Almost twenty years since he had taken leave from the army to repair his battered mind enough to acquire a wife and be offered a training post. Fifteen since he was bestowed a barony for service to the Crown. It was then he resigned his commission and began Ostelbrooke Farm, a different sort of service to his country.

John had been deeded a manor house and 500 acres with his title, which he and Rose had grown into a substantial township, populated entirely with veterans, all wounded in one way or another, and military widows and orphans. John had added to his original acreage by four times since he started and held the tenancies of no fewer than two hundred families, adding more every season.

Even so, his mind had never fully recovered from its injuries; his faculties were occasionally yet fragile, given the right set of circumstances. All these years later, anything to do with Miss Angel Bairstowe might be enough to finish Bella's brother, depending on the news at hand, and whether he'd suffered any other recent emotional blows. At the very least, Rose would tell Bella to contain John, not to allow him to leave the house. The Conservatory might not have been the best plan, given all the windows. It was a good thing she had sent for Rose.

John tapped his fingers, one after the other, slowing gradually, as though he were counting—onetwothreefour... one two three four... one, two, three, four... one... two... three... four.

"What's happened, John? Please, take a deep breath and tell me what's happened, so I can be of help."

The excess energy he was holding at bay expressed itself ever faster by a wild twitch in one knee shaking the table. But for his left knee and right hand, though, his face and body were in strict control.

Finally, he took the deep breath she had prescribed and said, in a voice so low she had to lean forward to hear it. "It is as though I have seen a ghost. She has the Smithson eyes, Bella. Just like yours, like mine. She has Papa's jawline and his chestnut hair."

Bella tried to follow him. He seemed both lucid and logical, but when he was disturbed like this, his mind and conversation wandered. One never knew if one was speaking to John Smythe who was fifty-one years old, or John Smithson at twenty, or, occasionally, the Johnny she remembered at age six, just after their mother had died. Nor was it ever clear when a shift might occur or what ordeal he might be reliving, even when he seemed to be quiet and contained, just staring into the distance. And it could not help that Bella was, herself, beset by the same slight tremor in her hand that appeared whenever the ghost of their father permeated a room.

"Who has Papa's jawline, John?"

"Angel Bairstowe had a daughter, Bella."

Bella sat back and sucked in a breath. "She had a..." She sat speechless for a moment. "Jeremy's child?" She wasn't sure why she felt speechless. This was hardly the first girl who had turned up with a baby who looked like Jeremy. Decades ago, when she had much less influence than she had now, Bella had even arranged for one to be apprenticed in a family friend's stables.

John winced at Jeremy's name and looked away; the shaking of his knee gained speed. Bella considered everything he'd told her ten years ago, when he'd made several hours' worth of confessions to Bella at Rose's behest, about the incident with Angel. "Jeremy's child or Papa's."

He dropped his head into his hands. "Or mine."

She sucked in another breath. "Yours? But John, you told me—"
No. Whatever he had told her, he had needed to believe it to keep himself from running away from his life, or worse. Bella was not going to say anything that would take him back to those days.

"I told you what I remember, Bella. But there is so much of that night that is naught but black, and what I know to be true has been fragmented and splintered so many times. I cannot trust my mind for truth in this. But I—" his hand started reflexively making and releasing a fist again and again. "I know everything Papa and Jeremy did. I can't ever stop seeing it. But—I—I can't say for certain what I did or didn't do."

Bella sat back and reached out a hand to hold her brother's. "Surely... after all Jeremy did for a fortnight after the... Surely, it is far more likely he was the..." She stopped and shook her head, grasping his fingers a bit tighter. "That poor girl."

"The poor girl she whelped."

"There is sympathy enough for two." They both sat silently for a time, each lost in their own thoughts of their brother and their father and their horrific misdeeds.

"Do you feel you can answer questions, or would you like to wait a bit?"

John's knee jerked hard before going back to the same shuddering. He swallowed hard. "Did you send for Rose while I was gone?"

'Gone.' That was how he spoke of his incidents afterward, because he couldn't count on remembering any of it. Good. That meant he was coming back to himself.

She nodded. "Yes. If she is at your London house, I expect her any minute now. Since you are in London, I am hoping she is, too."

"Yes. We were to leave for the farm, but we had a... a visitor. Two visitors. I stayed as long as I could, but I couldn't manage the... I left the house while Rose was wrangling the boys."

Bella sighed. She would get to the question of these visitors who had driven her brother from his house, but the higher priority was his wife's peace of mind. "So, Rose is worried sick about you right now. Or will be until my footman reaches her."

The bleak depths of his eyes worried Bella sick, too, and the brief bob of his head before he hung it, presumably in shame or guilt or just overwhelming sadness.

"Well, with luck, she will be here shortly. Blakeley is gathering up an animal or two who would welcome your loving attention. I cannot remember the last time anyone brushed Blue."

As if on cue, Blakeley arrived, leading the duke's spaniel, Blue, and carrying a basket of grooming implements and a large soup bone. He quietly settled Blue on the empty half of the settee, then lifted a brow to ask Bella for further instruction. John shifted to make room for the dog, who responded by laying his head and the bone in John's lap immediately and settling into being brushed.

"Please bring us tea, Blakeley." With both brows, she signaled to the butler to bring the special tea Rose had provided for their pantry, which would do Bella no harm, but had a beneficial effect on John when he was agitated. It had been several years since Bella had needed it, but Rose kept all the family's houses faithfully stocked.

"And cream cakes, if Cook has any set by." Cook always had cream cakes set by; on Bella's order, she made them daily with the morning bread and had since John had returned from the dead, once Bella understood the depths of the hell he had been living in. Anything that reminded John of his childhood, bleak as it had been for both of them, was better than reminding him of the horror that came as soon as his father judged his sons old enough to bring along in the family's illicit businesses: card sharping, thieving, blackmail, and swindling.

Bella waited patiently for John to settle, busying herself with arranging and pouring tea when it arrived, and setting a plate of cakes close at hand for her brother. Once he had sipped a bit of tea, eaten a cream cake, and calmed into the rhythm of brushing Blue, he finally cleared his throat and told her what was happening.

"She came to the house just as we were putting on our coats to leave for the Farm. Just turned up on the doorstep with a six-year-old child. Apparently, Angel gave guardianship of her baby to her father before she died, and Bairstowe farmed the child out. She's fully grown now, of course, with a child of her own. She turned up wanting information about her supposed noble heritage. I don't know more than that, because I... I had to leave the room."

Of course, he'd had to leave the room. Bella was only grateful he'd left the room and not exited the whole of England, given his historical reaction to any such seismic shift in his safely ordered world. "Does the woman have a name?"

John scratched Blue behind the ears, eliciting a delighted doggy growl. "Madeline. Miss Madeline Swift. She looks enough like Angel to... to send me into a state. But Bella, she is a Smithson. The eyes, the hair. There is no doubt in my mind."

"I do not doubt you, John. I am sick at heart for her, for her mother, and for you, and I am once again livid at our unconscionable male relations, but I do not doubt you. Where is she now?"

"She is still at the house. She told Rose outright she has nowhere else to go. Nor should she go elsewhere, for she is my responsibility."

"Does Rose know you've taken on this duty?"

"She is in agreement."

If Rose was in agreement, she did not sense more threat than John could handle, but the fact he was here might prove her instinct was wrong.

"That is kind of Rose." Bella clucked her tongue. "And not just a little bit rude of you to run out on her and your guests."

"What was I to do, Bella? I cannot be trusted near her. I cannot be trusted near women, especially not women who look like... like Angel Bairstowe."

"That is a truth long past its time. You have been perfectly safe around women for years now. You are a loving husband to Rose and father to three girls and two boys and uncle to your niece and nephew, and this young lady will be no exception. You are overwrought by the enormity of it, but you are not a danger to her, John, especially not with Rose at your side. Do you understand me?" Rarely was she harsh with her brother, especially when he was feeling fragile, but she had too intimate a knowledge of John's past sins against women to let this particular delusion lie.

"Bella, I—"

"No. No, John. I will not let you take responsibility for every horrible thing Jasper or Jeremy Smithson ever did in their miserable lives. You may claim your part in it; you may even discount the coercion and extortion Papa used to gain your compliance, but you are not Jeremy. You are not Papa. Whatever dastardly part you played in that unimaginable incident, you did not rape Angel Bairstowe, and I would stake my life on it."

"I wish I were so certain."

"Yes, I know. And I wish I had evidence, but I have only my faith and trust in you."

Hadn't John been the one who always tried to protect her when Papa and Jeremy took out their anger and drunkenness on her? Hadn't he snuck her food whenever their father withheld it from her? Hadn't he helped her escape to sea with Baron Myron Holsworthy when Jeremy and Papa threatened to sell her to a brothel? Hadn't he been the one to save Bella's young cousin from a madwoman? John could be trusted with a person's life.

"Do you know why she has come now? And how did she find you? You have not been a Smithson for many years." John had changed his name to Smythe when he entered the army as a private, to outrun his father's and brother's ghosts and debts and the criminal legacy of the now-defunct Smithson baronetcy.

"Why now, I have no idea, for I could not stay to hear her out. I could not think through the... the noise... the chaos of it."

Noise and chaos, indeed. She doubted her brother could hear himself think now, through whatever voices and impulses drove him when he started running. "I hope it was no mention of my Smithson connection in the newspapers," she surmised. "I cannot seem to stop them reviving old scandals for publication. One would think two exemplary husbands' names would erase the stain of one father."

"No one will ever erase his shame, Bella. We will carry it for a lifetime. But as to how she found me, it was nothing to do with you. I sent Bairstowe a bank draft when I was paying Father's debts twenty years too late, so he knew where to find me, and that I had been a Smithson. He gave Miss Swift my direction and told her—his own granddaughter, mind—he didn't know which Smithson had defiled her mother and didn't care, but he had paid out to my foster parents for years so he would never have to see the—" His voice broke, and he took a sip of the tea before he finished, "—the bastard daughter of a whore and a thief. He shut the door in her face."

"He said that to his own flesh and blood? His own daughter's child? Dear god, what a monster."

"It is true, though, is it not? All three of us were thieves, and I saw Angel in the brothel myself. That was all she could ever be after Papa and Jeremy finished with her. Her daughter would have been better off never knowing a thing about her mother. Or her father, for that matter, whichever one of us it was."

When Angel Bairstowe had declined the dishonorable Jeremy Smithson's honorable marriage proposal, he'd been as furious as John had ever seen and was bent on revenge. Papa had gone along because the two of them egged each other on in their schemes; John had gone along, as ever, under threat of being taken up for common thievery.

"I cannot help but wonder if that is true. But it is irrelevant now, for she knows about her parents now, and we must find a way forward for and with her. At least she is safe at your house."

"She is," Rose said from the doorway, "at least for the moment and while she remains there. Blakeley told me you were back here; I hope you don't mind." John scooted over on the sofa to give his wife a place to sit on the other side of him from Blue, and she took it, brushing the hair out of his eyes and giving him a kiss on the forehead. "You frighten me when you run off like that, my love. Thank you for sending word, Bella."

Rose picked up John's teacup and sniffed it, and a bit of the worry on her face dissipated, but only a bit. "Has he told you what's happened, Bella?"

"Yes, I have," John answered for her. "What I know, anyway."

Bella assumed Rose knew more, for she had assuredly spoken at greater length to Miss Swift after John left, but it wouldn't do to press. Better to let her take the lead in telling what she knew, for she could manage John's reactions to unsettling news even when no one else could. Bella poured tea for her sister-in-law instead and passed her the plate of cakes.

"While I am never pleased when my husband decides to go gallivanting across London in a state without leaving his direction, it is fortuitous he came here, for Miss Swift needs assistance, and I am afraid it is not the sort a minor baron and baroness can provide."

The duke followed close on Rose's heels. "Please, Rose, tell us what's happening, and how we can help. I've sent Abersham and Almyra to bed."

Bella rang for more tea, and Wellbridge poured himself a brandy after a quick shake of Rose's head warned him not to offer any to John. John only ever had one brandy if he was having an episode. More than that, he said himself, and he might bury himself in the bottle.

Bella provided her husband a rough outline of the conversation thus far, and he took a seat and fell silent, waiting to hear from Rose how he should proceed.

"I've just left Miss Swift, and she is well enough, though rightly frightened for her prospects. She is not a Mrs., you see, but a Miss, with a child, and one without any means of support. She's been a kept woman for ten years, but her... gentleman friend has died and left her nothing. No one has been willing to so much as talk to her, much less offer her help of the sort she needs."

John stood abruptly, only taking the effort required to move Blue onto the seat he vacated instead of dumping the dog on the floor. "I—I need... I... I have to go."

"No, John," Rose said quietly. "You can stay here. You are safe here." The faraway look in John's eyes receded just slightly and he nodded, but added, "If you will excuse me... another room, perhaps..."

Wellbridge was closest to the bell pull, so he summoned Blakeley to take John and Blue to another room, and requested that Abersham's tutor attend John and keep him occupied.

Once he had gone, Rose drained her teacup and refilled it with sherry. "I've tried to ease Miss—Madeline—as well as I can, and have settled her daughter, Beth, into the nursery, but her troubles are dire. She needs the most powerful of protection and at least solicitors, probably barristers—and a touch of ducal ire would not go amiss."

"Perhaps you can help me understand how best to help John in this," Bella said, far more concerned for her brother than a woman none of them knew.

Rose sighed. "I suspect it will be better for John if I am his filter for information for the time being, and better for everyone to keep all of this as private as possible for the moment."

"Better to keep all of this private into the afterlife," Wellbridge growled.

"Better," Bella said, placing a restraining hand on her husband's arm, "that we do not cause that poor girl any more grief or harm than the Smithson men already have, with the understanding we wish no harm to John either. If the Wellbridges are cast in a poor light for a time, we shall accept it as the price to rectify a terrible wrong and seek only clarity of conscience as reward. It can be no worse than any of the other incidents that have landed the duchy in a Fleet Street frenzy. We will hear her troubles and learn who she is and what she needs from us, *her family*. And *as with any member of our family*, if we can help her, we will. There is no other course of action to be considered, if any of us mean to retain our honor."

Wellbridge sighed, and his nostrils flared, but he didn't argue.

Rose spoke quietly in agreement. "Nor if we wish John to retain his faculties. He has been under a good deal of pressure anyway, with the new houses nearly complete and expanding the wool operation. He always struggles when it comes time to choose who will be offered a tenancy; he hates to turn away deserving men and women, and the closer he comes to the end of the list of available houses, the more agitated he becomes. We cannot accommodate a tenth of the people who apply. And now this? If the woman could only have waited until after the harvest, after we have the new tenants settled... He would have been in a much better position to absorb the shock."

She swirled the sherry in her teacup. "I have not seen him so fragile since the first weeks I knew him. And in only moments. One minute, he was helping the boys on with their coats and arranging the disposition of our trunks for the move to the Farm; the next, he was trembling like a leaf, mumbling about angels and hell, and leaving orders she be made perfectly comfortable on the other side of the house from him. He stayed long enough to ascertain she needed a place to stay, and then ordered it and disappeared with the carriage. You have seen it; he is not ready to see her again, nor even discuss her at length, but he is determined she will not be left to fend for herself."

Bella went to the hearth to pick up her needlework bag before she returned to her seat. "I do not wish to seem overly dramatic, Rose, but can he survive this?"

A knock at the door revealed Blakeley with a tea service, followed by a footman with a tray of sandwiches and more cakes. "I took the liberty, Your Ladyship, Your Graces. And I've sent a tray in for Lord Ostelbrooke and Mr. Bunson."

The servants bustled about setting up the refreshments while everyone else in the room sat staring, waiting with a deepening sense of fear and horror, imagining the worst possible answers to the question that couldn't be discussed before the servants, no matter how likely it was they already knew everything.

Finally, Bella said, "You may leave us. I can pour and serve, thank you."

Rose added, in the quiet, inflexible tone that had kept John from running every time he had taken the notion since the day they spoke vows, "Please do not disturb us further until you are asked."

Bella had settled into a comfortable position on the couch, her shawl drawn close, embroidering an altar cloth. "Will he make it, Rose? Would we be better to take him back to Ostelbrooke Farm directly and keep him there? Or take her away somewhere?"

"He will not stand for either, Bella. He is not incapacitated, and is fully capable of making his own decisions for himself, his family, his residences, and the Farm. I beg you recall, he led the troop of soldiers that kept you alive, Bella, when that was not a certain thing, and in the years since, has built an entire town from a 500-acre barony. He simply has an injury that flares up when he is faced with emotional blows, and this is a large one."

"We don't mean to suggest—" Wellbridge started, but Rose waved him off.

"You mean well, both of you. And in truth, I am not sure how we will manage it if he cannot accustom himself to her presence. But he will not allow anyone to remove her from our home unless she wishes to go, nor will he be gainsaid. Major the Honorable Lord Ostelbrooke, late of the Coldstream Guards, gave the order to our butler before he vacated the house, not John Smythe, my loving husband and caring father to our children."

Wellbridge cleared his throat. "We have plenty of land and properties of every size available. I would be pleased to settle her somewhere and provide her with an income. If we haven't anything suitable, we can buy or build something. John needn't imagine his roof is the only one in England under which she will be safe. She can live as close or far away as she'd like."

"More to the point," Bella said, stabbing at her needlework, "as close or far away *from John* as *you* would like. While respecting both of their wishes and requirements, of course, to whatever extent we can."

"I will put my husband and children before that woman, Bella, no matter what hold she has on the Smithsons."

"The same is true of me, Bella," the duke agreed. "I will put you and Abersham and Almyra before a stranger, no matter how closely related or how much responsibility you feel for your rotten brother's poor choices."

"That is thoroughly understood, my dears, and so greatly appreciated by all concerned," Bella said in a soothing tone that would reassure Rose, but grate on her husband, who was acting entirely too ducal for her liking, and should not be so quick to overprotect a woman who could more than protect herself.

"We will learn something of who she is before we decide on any course of action for anyone, do you not agree?" Bella sat forward and poured another cup of tea. "And on that note, my dear, please summon Blakeley to fetch John. I suggest we all go to bed, for we will need our strength in the morning when we speak to Miss Swift. Rose, you are welcome to stay here, should it please you."

"No, Bella," Rose said, "As unfeeling as it may sound, I'm afraid my husband must learn to be under the same roof as Miss Swift if he is to order her housed with us."

"That is a good start," Bella replied, then asked Blakeley to ready the Smythe carriage. Upon his exit, the duchess continued, "I am quite anxious to meet my new nieces, and I am certain we can find a path forward."

Chapter II

Miss Swift walked into Bella's drawing room the next morning, dressed head-to-toe in black. Bella sucked in a breath so fast she might have choked, had her teacup been any closer to her lips. She did, indeed, look like Bella's vague memories of Angel Bairstowe, but the shape of Jeremy's cowlick in their father's gilt-chestnut hair, and the jawline that had seemed feminine on Jasper Smithson, brought back the tremor in her hand.

Invoking every ounce of steel her first husband had ever instilled, Bella smiled and rose from the chair when Rose did, setting her teacup down on the table. Wellbridge rose and made a short bow. John rapidly excused himself, but Bella's attention was riveted on the small girl holding Miss Swift's hand. She looked exactly like Almyra had at the age of six, which is to say rather like Bella's cousin Charlotte, but with Bella's own eyes staring back from this familiar-but-unfamiliar face.

Rose made the introduction, "Their Graces of Wellbridge, may I present Miss Madeline Swift and her daughter, Miss Elizabeth Swift? Elizabeth is called Beth, Your Graces."

As Miss Swift made her curtsy, she said to her daughter, "You must make your bow, as we practiced."

Bella swept across the room. "No. No, Beth, you needn't make your bow today, nor you, Miss Swift. We shall discuss bows on some other occasion. For I am your aunt today, not a duchess."

"Your Grace?" Miss Swift stared, stopped halfway, rising from her curtsy. Bella took her hand and pulled her upright, then crouched down before Beth, holding out both hands. After looking up for agreement from her mother, she placed one hand in the duchess's, but held on to her mother with the other.

"Look at you. What a beautiful girl. She is lovely, Miss Swift."

"She is illegitimate, Your Grace," Miss Swift stated flatly.

Bella pinched Beth's cheek and smiled, then rose to address the assertion.

"I assumed as much when I was told your situation. Will you sit and take tea with us?" Bella gestured to a chair. "Beth, Lady Ostelbrooke told me you can read story books with pictures; is that true?"

With another glance at her mother, Beth said, "Yes, Your Grace," and reflexively curtsied again.

"That is a very good bow, my dear, and shall surely gain you the favor of kings and queens in years to come, but you needn't make it again today, and you may call me Aunt Bella, if you'd like, as Lord Ostelbrooke's children do. I have a daughter only two years older than you, and I know Almyra will be longing to meet you."

"Your Grace, do you not need—?" Miss Swift swallowed hard. "I've brought what proof I have of our familial connection."

Wellbridge took a step forward. "I will be happy to see your—" Bella reached out to hold him back.

Bella smiled. "I need only look at the two of you for proof of our familial connection, and I am also your Aunt Bella, Miss Swift. I am sorry the circumstance is such that—well, be that as it may..."

She held up one finger to Miss Swift and returned her attention to Beth. "Since you can read picture books, my girl, I've had a selection brought with a tea table from our nursery and some company, so you may have tea with new friends while we do the same." Bella gave Beth a stack of books and settled her just outside earshot in a child-sized chair at a child-sized table, where cakes and milk were already waiting on child-sized china to be shared with new dolls and spilled on the picture books.

As Bella returned to her seat and invited her husband to take a position beside her, Miss Swift said, "Beth is usually shy of strangers, Your Grace. You are very kind to her. I am quite overwhelmed by the care you have taken, before you had ever even met us, and the thoughtfulness with which you—" Miss Swift's voice broke, and she had to stop and swallow tears. "I had been quite at my wit's end until Lord and Lady Ostelbrooke asked us to stay."

"My dear," Bella poured tea for Miss Swift and handed her a plate, passing a cake stand of pastries. "Pray, tell me what brings you to us? And you may start your tale as early in your life as you like. I've nothing else planned."

Taking a deep, fortifying sip of tea, Miss Swift started with, "You must call me Madeline, if you please, if you would have me call you Aunt Bella, for what we shall speak of will surely be more intimate than any two strangers have a right to share."

With a slight slackening of the ducal mien, the duke conceded the informal name he used among family and friends, "Wellbridge."

"I am overcome by your courtesies to me, Your Graces. I will do my best to remember, and I thank you for the consideration." With another sip of tea, she took a deep breath and began, "My mother was Angel Bairstowe, as you know, and when she died shortly after my birth, my grandfather was made my guardian—Squire Bairstowe."

"Yes, his landholding was near enough to ours to walk," Bella said. "That's how Jeremy met Angel."

"I was told only that I had been orphaned at birth and was raised by foster parents. It wasn't until I was much older that I learned my foster mother had been my mother's former nurse, and Squire Bairstowe had paid her well to keep me out of his sight. It was not so bad a life. They cared for me at least as much as the monthly stipend. I was fed and clothed and educated to some small degree, and I learned how to run a farm, so I can always feed myself, given a plot of land. I was not handed over to the workhouse, or worse."

"That is lucky, indeed," Rose said with a pointed glance at Bella. They both knew how lucky a woman was to have a trade.

"When I grew old enough to fall in love, I met a boy at a fair, Danny Woodruff, from a neighboring village, who was a farmer's son and would inherit his father's holding. Danny asked my foster father for my hand, and it was only then I learned he was not, in fact, my guardian. At the suggestion of my foster father, my beau wrote to Squire Bairstowe, whom I had never met, asking for permission to marry. He was summarily denied.

"We made plans to run away together, but before we could, I received a visit from Mr. Antonin Ballard. He said he had bought my services from my guardian, and he had contractual paperwork to prove it. I would be paid a quarterly stipend to keep house for him. He offered to take me by force from the house where I grew up, if I did not come willingly. It was only after we arrived at his home some fifty miles from anything that he produced the real terms of the contract, my intimate services outside the bonds of marriage."

"Good god!" Wellbridge exclaimed, sloshing his tea into its saucer as the cup slipped from his fingers and clattered on the saucer.

"Oh, you poor girl," Rose said.

Miss Swift continued, "Well, you can imagine how I reacted to that."

"I should say!" Rose snapped. "Did the people who raised you do nothing?"

"When the man who paid them decided he would no longer pay for my support? No, they approved of anyone who would remove me as their responsibility, and thought housekeeper a fine trade. There was naught I could do about it, save throwing myself on the mercy of the nearest workhouse. But, before I could even consider that seriously, Antonin told me his intentions would be carried out no matter my wishes, but how difficult my life was, and what happened to me afterward, would depend on my compliance and my ability to produce handsome boy-children.

"I resisted, of course, but what was I to do? I didn't even know my guardian when he signed my life over to Antonin—I never clapped eyes on him until a few weeks ago. So, I left with Antonin ten years ago and bore four of his children." Madeline's eyes shuttered in a way that made Bella sit up straight, which made Wellbridge take notice, even if he didn't know what he was seeing. "Beth is the only one left."

Bella's hand covered her mouth. "My word. I am so sorry."

"Your... Antonin... died recently?" Wellbridge asked quietly.

Madeline took a sip of her tea before replying, "He was taken ill last month while he was out hunting with friends."

"I see," Bella said, and she likely did, for she had witnessed more combat—domestic and otherwise—than most women would in a lifetime.

"He left you in a bad way, then?" Wellbridge guessed.

"I—I am so grateful, but I do not wish to impose my troubles..." She stopped herself speaking, looked over at her daughter with a longing glance, as though she wished to steal her away through the French doors to the terrace. "He left me in debt and under suspicion of murder, Your Grace, though exonerated at the inquest, and of course, I've no claim to respectability left even before I was accused of murder. But that is not the worst."

Wellbridge sat forward, now paying close attention, seemingly tallying in his mind what favors might need to be pulled in to help this unfortunate woman.

She did not seem able or willing to continue. The silence itself marked the urgency of what she needed to tell them. She glanced over at her daughter again, and lowering her voice to a near-whisper, said, "He's left Beth's guardianship to one of his... one of the friends with whom he trades... He wished boy-children, you see, but there are others who prefer..." Her voice trailed off.

"My word!" Wellbridge exclaimed, standing and pacing to the hearth. "That will not happen. Not on the weight of my duchy will that... Never! I swear it. If I must make petition to the king himself!"

"Wellbridge!" Bella snapped. "While I appreciate your enthusiasm and share your sentiment, do not start throwing around your ducal consequence until you know where it will best be aimed. And please do not throw it anywhere when there are children in the room. You will terrify the child. Everything is fine, Beth. The duke is just a bit over-excited. Go on, Madeline, my dear, if you can continue."

"I am nearly certain that's what he did with our other three children. He told me the two older girls were at school, and the eldest, a boy, was taken into service in a marquess's household. But they have houses... clubs, really... you would call it a brothel were the residents not all so young. And they take on wards and guardianships and trade orphans of the lower classes amongst themselves. You must forgive me, Your Graces. You see why I had to take her and leave, but now I am a notorious woman running from trustees sworn to carry out my husband's last wishes, and most likely Bow Street Runners now, as the man who wants her is... well, he has more money and influence than I do, and the law on his side, and he has assuredly realized by now we've gone. It's been three days." Madeline absently tore a piece of bread from a finger sandwich into confetti, littering the plate with it. "I went to my former guardian first, whom I had just discovered to be my grandfather. I had hoped he might feel something in the way of conscience for having sold me as breeding stock and his great-grand-children as fodder for the grossest perversions."

"I suspect he did not," Bella said.

"No, he did not. He said a whore's daughter was lucky to have had a living at all, and he would call the magistrate if I did not remove myself and my child from his property. He told me how to find Lord Ostelbrooke, most likely out of spite, without knowing what he had confirmed."

"What has he confirmed?" Bella asked quietly.

"It is this..." She opened her reticule and retrieved several sheets of folded paper. "This document. It was written by my mother and left with solicitors just after my birth, meant to be given to me when I turned twenty-one, but Antonin put the solicitors in his pocket and didn't care to pass along anything they gave him for me. I did not find this until he died, and it is clear he never read it. If he had, he would have used it to blackmail some or all of you."

Wellbridge sat up straighter.

"That is not my intent, Your Grace. Please allow me to make that

56

perfectly clear. I never intended to use this for… this document is… it is rather… well… I have run out of options. I had no choice but to present myself, on even the slightest chance Beth might be saved by some unknown familial connection."

"And so, you have been," Wellbridge said, clearly softening. "And grateful we are to have been here when you appeared. It is a lucky thing, young lady. You may be certain your new family can overcome a great many obstacles on the weight of my name alone, and when that does not work, I have vast resources with which to reach my required ends. And my wife can say the same, even were she not married to me." With a hand on his wife's arm, he added, "If you would be so kind, Miss Swift—Madeline—I would like to see your documents. I do not doubt you; I merely wish everyone to understand all the facts."

"Of course, Your Grace." She handed over the papers without looking up, but as he took them, the duke chucked her under the chin, raising her eyes to his, and said, "Am I not your Uncle Wellbridge, young lady? Now…" He pulled out his spectacles and adjusted them on his nose. "You ladies enjoy your tea, and I will see what we have here."

"Alas, perhaps the duke is losing his faculties," Bella said, "as he cannot tell there are women with minds in the room with him, one of whom could likely explain every line of what he thinks to read."

"I heard that well enough, Bella."

"Did you, Your Grace?"

He looked at her over his spectacles, and she met his one elevated brow and raised him another, plus pursed lips. "You've made your point, Bella. Would you care to explain what I am to read, Miss Swift?"

"No, Your Grace. I'd prefer to know your opinion of the facts in their entirety, if it is all the same to everyone concerned."

"Well, then." He gave Bella a smug smile which she answered with an indulgent grin. "Bella, shall I read aloud or paraphrase?"

"Your summation will be sufficient until I have time to read it more closely myself."

"Very well." The duke adjusted his spectacles again and began to read, while Bella called in a nursemaid to take Beth to the nursery for a nap, ordering rooms to be made up for both Madeline and Beth as soon as possible, so they might feel at home in both family's houses. Besides, Rose had whispered to Bella on the way in that Madeline's presence had caused John's nightmares to return for the first time in years.

"Aha!" Wellbridge exclaimed after the maid had left with Beth. "This is excellent news!" With an apologetic glance over his spectacles at Madeline, he amended, "Well, perhaps 'excellent' is not the appropriate word, but do allow me to explain."

"Go on," Rose said.

"John can set his mind at ease about the worst of it. He was not... er..." He looked over at Madeline again. "He abetted the thing, but he was not a perpetrator. At least not according to Miss Bairstowe herself."

"What?" Rose asked without thought. "He did not... Oh, my. That is excellent news." In fact, Rose now seemed on the verge of tears.

"Nor was your father the primary villain, Bella. This is sworn testimony from the lady herself that Jeremy was the only Smithson who performed the worst atrocities. Not for lack of threats or trying, mind you, and they all had a hand in the execution of it," Wellbridge added with a decided downturn to his brow. "The act itself, and then her ruination, and the sale. And Jeremy's awful... Bella, your brother was an absolute monster. It's no wonder John has such a hard time—"

From the doorway, John said, "He was a monster and for too long, I was a monster alongside him. I must make amends to Miss Swift on behalf of myself and my father and brother." His hand was steady on Blue's neck, the dog seeming to patiently wait for him to have the strength to enter the room. "For they cannot—and assuredly would not—acknowledge the need, and my opportunity to redeem myself passed with her mother, to whom I owe the far greater debt."

"Darling, are you—"

"John, you needn't—"

"I say, Ostelbrooke, I can manage—"

John held up one hand, while the other held ever tighter to the scruff of the dog's neck. "And if I cannot make recompense Miss Swift deems adequate, then I shall take myself to Newgate to stand trial."

"You cannot mean—"

"No one will be—"

"I'm sure we needn't—"

Ignoring all of them, John entered and bowed once to the room, then made his bow to Miss Swift. "I hope you will excuse me for making myself scarce, and I do hope you will call me John."

John flinched when Bella said firmly, "Your *Uncle* John."

John took a seat next to Rose, who fussed until he grasped her hand, the dog sitting at his feet, resting his head on John's knee. "Miss Swift, I do not wish to alarm you, nor give you reason to fear for your safety or your daughter's, but I feel it only fair to warn you that I have… starts… since the war, since…" He stopped and gathered himself. "…since my brother and father and I violated your mother, for which I cannot ever express enough sorrow and regret. I relive the shame of it on at least a daily basis."

"It seems, Ostelbrooke," Wellbridge said, waving the papers in his hand, glancing at Bella to silently offer up his regret for upsetting John, "you have rather less need of sorrow and regret than you have assumed. Miss Bairstowe left an account of the incident with her solicitor, on the assumption your brother might ascend to the baronetcy, or her progeny might find some other use for the information."

"She did what?" John barked. "Let me see that."

"Listen to this, Ostelbrooke." Wellbridge adjusted his spectacles and read aloud, "'Mr. Jeremy Smithson, heir to the Smithson baronetcy, was the only gentleman to reach his completion during the rape. Mr. John Smithson declined to participate, but for holding my arms down and whispering to me to be silent so they would cause me less damage. Sir Jasper Smithson was unable to adequately perform, so beat me instead, taking care to tell me he was avoiding leaving bruises where they might decrease my value in a sale.' She goes on to describe the—"

"Wellbridge! Hold your tongue!" Rose snapped, causing all eyes to jump to John, whose face was white as fresh-burnt ash. Everyone fell silent, all waiting to see how far Wellbridge had just set John back, in the name of helping ease his mind.

With a full-body shudder, John merely said, "I must learn to hear it spoken, mustn't I? If I am to make amends for it? If it will not harm Miss Swift to hear it, pray, continue Wellbridge. Rose?" He motioned for his wife to take a seat at his side, and she snuggled close to him without delay. Madeline confirmed that she had read it often enough for the shock to have lost its value.

Wellbridge read aloud the entire disturbing, damning incident. The Smithson men had held Angel Bairstowe down, beating and raping, or threatening to rape, her in turns, in punishment for declining Jeremy's marriage proposal. Then, the following morning, Jasper Smithson appeared to talk to her father, after which, she was thrown from the house with no explanation and nothing but the clothes on her back. She was helped by a woman who seemed friendly and said she was a widow. She turned out to be a bawd to whom Jeremy had traded Angel, in exchange for a full fortnight of her 'round-the-clock services—during which he fully intended to impregnate her and leave her and the child to their fates. If he did not, he had promised, he would render her fully compliant for anything the bawd might want her to do in the future.

Jeremy had performed his stated task admirably, carrying out the most disgusting list of deeds Bella could ever imagine, and leaving poor Angel in a brothel, forced to endure pregnancy and childbirth under the most adverse circumstances possible. He was killed not three months later, and when she died shortly after childbirth, she left her baby—Madeline—into the care of Squire Bairstowe, the same man who had thrown Angel to the wolves.

Who proceeded to throw Madeline right after her.

Bella's disgraceful, immoral brother, Jeremy, owed Angel, her daughter, and her granddaughter a debt that couldn't be repaid if he had lived and been tortured for fifty years. That he had been quickly and cleanly murdered in the stews so soon after the attack was far too much mercy for his hellish soul. But John had spent his life tortured, day in and day out, for the past three decades. And his hell wouldn't end until he answered for all his choices before his Creator.

"Madeline, my dear," Bella said, moving to sit beside her new niece and taking Madeline's hand. "I am ashamed I did not know of your existence until now, and I hope very much to rectify the oversight. It would please me very much if you would help me understand how best to be of assistance to you and your daughter."

Chapter III

"Do you think she killed that man?" Wellbridge asked his wife as she removed her jewels that evening before bed, seated before the vanity.

"Her keeper? She was exonerated, which is all that matters. And good riddance."

He hesitated for only a moment before he followed up with, "What do you think he did with the children?"

"I hate to think. I will not rest easy until I've found proof of the fates of those three children."

He turned and caught her eye in the mirror. "What should we do about it?"

Holding the duke's gaze, Bella said, "The man wished to breed handsome young illegitimate boys, on a woman he purchased for the purpose and kept confined to the house for ten years, fifty miles from the nearest neighbor. He bred and traded children for illicit purposes, and will yet trade my niece, even from the grave, given the chance. You, as a putative representative of the Crown, should pretend you have never entertained the question of how he died," Bella said with a stern look over her shoulder. "You need to break that Last Will and Testament if it takes all your political will to do so." She began removing her hairpins and added, "And hope she and Beth will be happy with whatever course she chooses."

He nodded. "My impulses exactly. That, and settle a competency on her, of course. Since you draw the distinction, what is it *you* should do, then, my dear?"

Bella loosened the first of her hairpins, but no more, because Wellbridge crossed the room to remove them for her. As he left the first of several kisses across her shoulders, she answered, "I should teach her to shoot, fence, and wield a knife, and teach Beth when she is a bit older."

Wellbridge laughed. "I pray Madeline does not turn you down flat, as Almyra did last week."

"I pray you put your lips to better use kissing me, Your Grace, for you will never keep me from ensuring a young lady can provide for her own defense, especially a young lady who already so well understands the need."

Chapter IV

Madeline watched Beth playing with Lady Almyra Northope in an open space in the formal gardens, seemingly set aside for picnics or children to play. They ran about, playing some sort of imaginary game, their childish laughter a backdrop for Madeline's racing thoughts.

It had been four days of waiting since the duke and duchess had offered their combined power to set her life aright. Or, as aright as one could for a fallen woman. Four days of being treated like princesses in the Wellbridge London house, surrounded by luxuries such as a village girl could not even imagine. Four days of dress fittings and shopping trips and picnics and musical family evenings with dancing that simply must be taught to Madeline. Four days since she had begun the slow process of feeling safe among these people.

She didn't know what they intended to do with her, a poor relation who had been sold as breeding stock to a madman, with a bastard daughter in tow. Perhaps they would advance her the price of two tickets to America. She and Beth could make a new start in America, make herself a Mrs. forevermore.

And perhaps she might even leave England with all her children.

The duke had engaged Bow Street Runners to find them. The men had come and interrogated her for several hours about anything she might know about Antonin and his sordid arrangements with his perverted friends. She told them everything she knew about that, and everything Antonin had ever told her about their children—the boy who had outgrown Antonin's predilections at around age seven, and the two girls who would never engage his interest, so had presumably been traded away from her.

The duke had said he would challenge Antonin's will before the Chancery Court and petition to have Beth taken under his protection. The duchess would set herself to arranging adequate clothing and shelter for Madeline and Beth—the sort befitting the family of a duke, while, of course, keeping Madeline's sensibilities in mind. Madeline hadn't the wherewithal for anything grand.

Regardless, she and Beth had been fitted for such extensive new wardrobes Madeline could barely breathe to think of the cost. So many dresses for them both, even evening gowns for Madeline, and shoes, hats, gloves, and every sort of underthings. The duchess dressed them from the skin out. Madeline was assigned a lady's maid, which made her nervous as a cat, and Beth shared a governess with the Wellbridges' daughter, Almyra. Madeline had a horse in the house stables, and Beth shared Almyra's pony and cart. Beth had her own room in the nursery, filled with new toys and games the duchess had insisted upon.

Madeline would be provided an income from the duchy, they said, but Madeline suspected she couldn't count on that lasting forever, only as long as she and Beth were a duke and duchess' whim. She would have to develop a backup plan, but for now, it was enough to have a place to lay her head and the promise of the same for the foreseeable future.

She heard a commotion at the garden doors, the butler trying to keep someone out, by the sound of it. Madeline called Beth and Almyra to her and placed an arm around each. She didn't really know this daughter of the duke and duchess, but she would not repay their kindness by leaving their child exposed to danger.

As it happened, it wasn't Almyra they wanted. It was the magistrate, come to take Beth to her legal guardian, by force if required. As the magistrate strode into the garden, the butler trailed behind, his hand waving in the air, insisting, "You must not go further, Sir! You must stop where you are and wait for the duke, Sir."

The magistrate and two other burly men appeared at the opening in the flowers, followed closely by both the butler and the footman who had been standing guard over Madeline and the girls. Almyra and Beth's governess hovered close behind him. Both girls held tighter to Madeline.

"You will do well to give her over easily, Ma'am," the magistrate said. "No need to frighten her." Beth hid her face in her mother's side, burrowing beneath her arm.

"I'm sure this can't be… The duke was to…" The duke hadn't been successful, it was clear. She couldn't hand Beth over to that man. She couldn't. If she were to hang, she could not. She held Beth closer. The magistrate took a step closer, still trying to end things quietly.

"What is this? Who are these men?" The duke barked from the entrance to the clearing in the garden.

The magistrate made a bow. "Your Grace, I am here to enforce the claim of Sir John Astley to the child, Elizabeth Swift. It will be to everyone's advantage if Miss Madeline Swift gives over the child peaceably."

"She will not! And I am incensed you would come here and so frighten my daughter!" The duke roared. "For I have an order from the Chancery Court that supersedes any claim of Sir John's. Was this his last attempt to gain control? After you heard in open court the girl was here with me?"

The magistrate's red face was answer enough. But he still added, "I'll want to see that order from the judge."

"You will remove yourselves to my receiving room, gentlemen, where you will await me. You may be assured you will be allowed to verify my paperwork in short order. First, I must tend to my child and my nieces." The magistrate and his henchmen were corralled, finally, by the butler, who led them into the house. Almyra was enfolded in the duke's embrace, and then her governess's, and led away to the nursery.

Beth would not be peeled from Madeline's side, and Madeline herself was shaking. The duke crossed the clearing to her and placed his hands on her shoulders. "You are safe here, my dear. You will not have to be here forever, but you are safe. Now, stay here with Beth and this young man," he gestured to the footman who had been standing watch. "I will get rid of the vermin who came here to lay hands on our Beth."

LATER THAT EVENING, after the magistrate had gone and Madeline, Beth, and Almyra had been suitably calmed from their ordeal, Rose and John joined the family for supper. Afterward, John called Madeline into the duke's study. He left the door open, and the oil lamp on his desk was turned up to brighten the room. But there was no need for such propriety, for the duchess was already there, seated on a loveseat nearer the fire than the duke's desk. Lord Ostelbrooke offered Madeline the choice of chairs and took a seat next to Her Grace once she was settled.

"I'm sure you wonder why you are here, my dear?" The duchess asked.

"I imagine it could be any of a number of things, so it does not behoove me to speculate."

Lord Ostelbrooke didn't beat around the bush. "We've found a solution to the question of where and how you will be housed."

The duchess smiled and placed a hand on her brother's wrist. "Rather, we have found several solutions, and you must choose the one that best suits you. My brother clearly hopes you will choose one over the others."

Madeline sat back, a bit dizzy. A choice of places where she might live. Offered up by a duchess and a baron, who were her aunt and uncle. It was a bit more than she could easily take in.

The duchess made it even worse with her next words. "We've a cottage in a small village outside Colchester, three rooms up, three down, very like the ones where we all grew up. Or, if you prefer something a bit larger, the duke has two small estates you could choose from, one near Leicester and the other near Bath, with farmland attached, that produce an income."

A cottage in a village or one of two estates with land? It was too much. So, she said as much.

"Your Grace, my Lord, it is all too much. Competencies and manor houses and your unfailing protection for me and my daughter. I cannot allow you to give us an entire house. It is entirely too much."

From the doorway, the duke spoke, "Take the income, as a member of this family. I insist." He slipped into the room and went to the drinks cart for a brandy.

"Take the income," the duchess elaborated, "as recompense for the pain my brothers and father inflicted upon your mother."

"She hasn't yet heard my offer, and I will kindly ask you both to give her all her options before you tell her which to take," Lord Ostelbrooke said. Before the duchess could give her yet another option, he continued, "Madeline, I'd like to offer you a house at Ostelbrooke Farm. We have rather a large menagerie of both animals and children, some of each taken in under one sad circumstance or another. We keep a farm; someone must have told you by now."

"A bit," Madeline admitted. "But I would love to hear more, if you wish to tell me."

"It is far more than a farm," Bella said. "It is a town, in truth."

John shrugged, as he always did when anyone tried to compliment the effort he had put into Ostelbrooke Farm. But he couldn't help enthusing over what had become his life's work.

"There is the manor house, of course, where my family lives, but we have nearly two hundred cottages now, and three thousand acres under cultivation. We have crops, two mills and regular village life—shops, a church, a school, a market, that sort of thing. Everyone pulls together to keep the whole afloat. All the residents are veterans or their widows and children."

"That sounds just lovely," Madeline said, but then offered the most salient of several objections she might make to such an arrangement. "But I have no military men in my family."

"It is no matter. You have been wounded by me, and I have authority when it comes to residency. In addition, you are family, and I would have my family nearby when I can. I assure you; no one will question you, and none will look askance at your past while I have anything to say about it."

The duchess added, with a sly smile, "We will make you a Mrs. yet, my dear."

"My Lord, I am quite overcome at the thoughtful attention you have all given to our living situation."

"A house would have to be built, mind you," Lord Ostelbrooke went on, seemingly oblivious to her underlying bewilderment. "I can't take away a house I've already given to someone else, but we've enough land cleared for another cottage. It is not a manor house, but we can improve upon three up and three down if we are building from the ground up."

"My Lord, I cannot accept a house from you, most especially one custom-built for us."

The duke stood from his leaning position against the mantelpiece. "You will have to accept a house from someone, and an income besides, Madeline, or you will be homeless and destitute and without your child. I'm afraid, as we discussed when I set everything to rights, Beth is now under my protection. She will not be living in squalor. Should you choose to live apart from her to indulge in squalor, that will be your choice."

Madeline felt faint. The duke now had control of her daughter. She hadn't thought through what that meant, beyond removing her from Sir John's clutches. The duke could choose to send Beth away to school or apprentice her to a seamstress or anything, really. He was a duke. He could do anything he wanted with them both, and it was time she came to grips with it. She was lucky what he wanted was to put them up in a house of her choosing.

"I'll not stand for you ending in the workhouse out of misplaced pride," the duke went on. "You may choose any of the options we've presented, or you may propose any similar arrangement, but you will choose something I deem suitable for my ward. I am the duke, and you cannot defy me." The duke raised an eyebrow to show he was serious, but he winked at her to take away the sting.

Madeline had very little choice, but she would take the ones she had. "I should think, Lord Ostelbrooke, living nearby you would give Beth the chance to know her cousins. I believe I shall accept your offer, and we both thank you for it. You are all showing us such kindness, I can hardly credit it."

"No more than is due any member of this family," the duke said, patting Madeline's shoulder.

Chapter V

A few days later, the Ostelbrookes and their five children; the Duke and Duchess of Wellbridge with Lady Almyra, whose brother was back at school; the Misses Swift; and the various caretakers and tutors and servants engaged by the two noble families, left London for the Harvest Festival at Ostelbrooke Farm, where they would celebrate the twice-annual addition of six more families to the township. Each year at sowing and reaping, John undertook a celebration of welcome, to assure the newcomers felt at home from the first.

He provided the cottages rent-free as a lifetime tenancy to people who had been harmed by military service—those who he thought could thrive there—as long as the occupants worked, in some way, in service to the Farm. The new residents had all been invited to celebrate the harvest in their new homes, with new neighbors waiting to welcome them.

At midday, just a week before the celebrations would begin, five crested traveling coaches arrived at the Farm. They were accompanied by six servants' carriages, four baggage wagons, and a slew of attendants and aides. It took a full hour just to get the noble entourage into the house and settled into rooms, with servants unpacking and pressing clothes for dinner.

John, acting as a military commander upon crossing the threshold, quickly took control of the arrangements that had been underway during his absence. Within the next few days, six other families would take up residence in the brand-new cottages John had paid to have built over the summer. Madeline and Beth would take up residence with John and his family while their house was being planned and built.

EVEN AS SHE established herself in the village in the following days, knowing she would be living there shortly, the newly minted Mrs. Madeline Swift (widow of a gamekeeper named Anton, killed on a hunt), was welcomed into the life of the manor house. She assigned herself to help manage the huge crowd of children, assisting among an army of nannies and nursemaids and tutors and governesses. She was reminded of nothing more than the time when she'd had three children under five years old. Before Antonin had an interest in them. Except she hadn't then had staff to help her manage them.

If only they had had the enduring love of a family and father all this time. What would have become of her if she had married Danny all those years ago? If they had run away together? Would she be better off now with happy, healthy children who had never known a moment's hardship? It was hard to say, but in her imaginings, it was always so.

Now, like she had when her children were even smaller than Beth, she pulled endless entertainments out of thin air to keep them all occupied and happy, and encouraged them all to contribute to the effort to make the estate welcoming and cheerful for the new arrivals. She, the nursery staff, and the children gathered pinecones and colored leaves and dying branches and made centerpieces for the tables and hangings for the walls, at least one appearing on nearly every vertical surface of the manor house. She barely let herself imagine she might be making her own children welcome at Ostelbrooke Farm.

When first Rose, then Bella, had explained Madeline needn't

bother herself if she wished to engage in other pursuits, she demurred. "I cannot think of a more delightful pursuit than playing with children all day long, if you will allow it for a time, and I must do my part in the community. Perhaps I can make myself useful in the school after the celebrations are over."

So, of course, they allowed and encouraged her involvement, all the while assuring her she needn't worry about being useful or returning any kindness. It was long past time for Madeline to do exactly as she pleased.

And so it was that Mrs. Swift was at the side of a great group of children—not only those staying at the manor house, but all those from the village, singing songs in the village square as the residents gathered for the harvest festival. Every household brought some food item to share; the manor provided a whole roasted pig, four turkeys, a haunch of venison, and cider enough to leave the whole town sotted.

The children's choir was halfway through *Under the Harvest Moon*, the last of the songs they planned to sing before sending the children for chocolate and roasted apples and chestnuts from the stand Rose had arranged. Buggies and wagons had been depositing partygoers for an hour. The new Mrs. Swift was smiling and laughing, rosy cheeked from the cold, delighted to be sharing such happy moments with her daughter, free of the fear that had been stalking her since her keeper died. Free from the years of terror and shame living as Antonin's unwed wife.

Suddenly, Madeline fell silent. Everything else went on around her. She went white-faced, hand to her throat, lips still, while the impromptu choir kept singing right beside her.

Across the square was the Bow Street Runner the duke had engaged to determine the fate of Madeline's children, and with him, a boy who would be ten now, and two girls, seven and nine. Bella quietly took Beth's hand from Madeline's, and whispered, "Go on. I'll take care of Beth."

At that moment, Madeline sucked in a breath, then shocked the assembled company by crying out her joy at seeing her children again

—alive! The children saw her and broke from their erstwhile caretaker to run to her.

They had all been old enough to know when they had been taken from her. Old enough to remember who she was and what she once represented: safety and love and tenderness they probably hadn't seen since they'd been ripped from her. She imagined she could feel all their hearts beating next to hers as she embraced three wiggling children at once.

It seemed they all had things they wanted to say to her, but were shy and quiet, so she collected Beth from Bella and withdrew from company as a family for a time, removing to the vicarage, with the agreement of the vicar.

Once the greetings had been exhausted and bare sketches of stories told, Madeline insisted that everyone eat their fill, for her children, she thought, were far too thin. So, they made their way back to the festival for food and to meet their new neighbors. There would be a hard road to make her children feel safe again, but they were home with her, and that was a start.

Sometime later, they were seated in the light of the harvest bonfire, a cluster of five with their heads together, making plans for a future none had thought to see, when a man approached, his cap in his hand, twisting it between his fingers.

"Excuse me," he started quietly, clearing his throat. "Excuse me, but are you Miss Madeline Sw…" When he saw her face and she saw his, he gasped and said, "Yes, I can see you are. Maddy Swift. You haven't changed."

"Danny Woodruff. Can it be you, after all these years?"

Daniel Woodruff, the farmer's son who had started Madeline's journey with Antonin by his marriage proposal to Squire Bairstowe. Whom she had met at a township harvest festival, much like this one, more than a decade ago. And, as it happened, a veteran of the Burma War, with a place at Ostelbrooke Farm.

Epilogue

Ostelbrooke Farm, 1836

Maddy's hand shook as she held out the key, so she asked her new husband to share the moment with her, opening the front door of their new home. Danny took her hand in his and together, they slid the key home. The six children all, for once, stood silent at this momentous occasion. Six children in total; four of Maddy's, of course, but Danny had been married and widowed with two children, a boy and a girl. The six of them were like stairsteps, ages seven through eleven–and eleven twice.

As soon as they opened the door fully and invited the awestruck children inside, Danny said, "Everyone knows who they are sharing with, and I'll hear no fighting. In pairs, you can choose any bedroom upstairs besides the one at the end of the corridor."

Alice and Meg, eight and nine, would share, as would Beth, six, and Kate, seven. Paul and Samuel would share a room, though the mischief of two eleven-year-old boys could keep Maddy and Danny awake at night in their room at the end of the corridor, which was twice the size of any of the children's rooms.

There were six bedrooms upstairs, all painted and fresh, ready to have the furniture moved in that would arrive shortly. The duchess insisted they have two extra rooms for guests. John agreed, saying, "You never know at Ostelbrooke when someone new will join your family." Downstairs, a kitchen had been outfitted, and a dining room, parlor, study, and library. Two rooms were outfitted for servants, one in the attic and one off the kitchen, plus a room above the barn for a stableboy. There was no space for a formal garden at Ostelbrooke Farm, aside from the one that had come with the manor house, but behind this house stood a new hothouse adjacent to a stillroom.

The duke and duchess had taken it upon themselves to decorate the new house to some small degree–they ordered paint, curtains, and rugs, and stocked the larder. But the duke had quite pointedly given Danny a sizable sum when they had married, and the duchess an equal sum to Maddy, both with the instruction, "Spend every penny of it on your new house."

John and Rose had involved the whole community, encouraging Maddy and Danny to spend the duke's money on supplies, furniture, foodstuffs from their townspeople, and what couldn't be had in Ostel-brooke was commissioned from London. But none of it was here right now, probably not for another hour or so at least. Maddy expected naught but delivery upon delivery for the next six months.

Before the children could finish choosing their rooms–as loudly and contentiously as possible–a wagon drew up. The Swift family's things from the manor house, where they had been living for more than a half-year, and that was a start. As they moved in each piece of furniture the duchess had pressed upon her, every trunk they had been gifted to hold all the garments the Wellbridges had bought on their behalf, Maddy kept her eye out for one last thing, the final item removed from the wagon and moved into the house. She directed the Wellbridges' borrowed footmen to carry her old workbench into the stillroom without checking the contents. There would be time enough for that once the family was comfortably arranged.

Later that night, all the deliveries had been collected, dinner was finished, prayers were said, and the children were whispering in their rooms. Danny stepped out to the stables to enjoy a pipe, and Maddy took herself to the hothouse and stillroom, empty of everything but plant pots and trowels. There, she lit a fire in the wood stove, then went straight to the workbench and opened the two bottom drawers.

She removed a pile of Antonin's mending, then slid a wooden box from the back of the drawer. Opening it, she touched her mortar and pestle, as familiar as her own hand. She opened the false bottom and set aside the nostrums and herbs that would be the start of a medicine box for her new home. From another drawer, she pulled out her yarn and needlework in a tapestry bag; it had been so long since she had used it, she could barely recall the contents. Then, she took up the few torn garments of Antonin's that had hidden her secrets from the authorities when she was taken for murder. She dropped them into the wood stove and burned them, one by one.

ABOUT THE AUTHOR

Mari Anne Christie (writing as Mariana Gabrielle) writes second chances for scarred souls. Her Sailing Home Series follows the fortunes of Bella, the Duchess of Wellbridge, from her early years as Miss Smithson (*Shipmate*) to her happy-ever-after with the Duke of Wellbridge (*Royal Regard*) and invites others of her family to their own happy endings (*'Tis Her Season*). Her next Regency romance will be John and Rose's love story, in *A Rose Renamed*. For more about Mari, check out her website at www.MariAnneChristie.com, or follow her on Facebook, Goodreads, or Bookbub.

A BARREN VENGEANCE

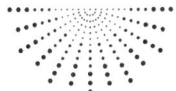

REBECCA D'HARLINGUE

T he ghostlike shape must be a ship approaching in the gray light of misty dawn. I cross my arms and rub them with my hands in an attempt to warm them. I have come here each day for the past week. I have lied to my mother and told her I was helping at the home of a sick friend. Mama is so busy at our print shop that she does not question me closely. Surely today the ship will return.

I am waiting for a ship of the *Vereenigde Oostindische Compagnie*, the mighty East India Company, to dock. I have been waiting for two years. According to the newssheets, the Wapen van Holland was delayed both at the Cape of Good Hope and in Batavia, needing to put up for repairs, but should be coming in at any time now. The VOC keeps track of its ships, as returning captains are expected to give reports on any others they may have encountered while at their destination. Many of the details appear in the newssheets, for trade is the heartbeat of our city.

How appropriate that the name of this East Indiaman ship includes the word "weapon," for the man I await has done murder.

75

Though it is my fervent hope that Marten is on board this ship, I am not at all sure that he will be. I thought about notifying the schout, responsible for enforcing our laws, but I didn't want to appear a fool if I was mistaken in my assumption that Marten would return on the same ship on which he had said he left. Marten may not even have told the truth about the name of the vessel he was taking from Amsterdam.

The schout's men would not have had the patience to wait for one particular ship. Only I, who am burning for vengeance, will stand and wait in the cold for days on end. Besides, it doesn't matter that the schout is not here today. After all, it will be easy enough to summon the authorities later, as an unsuspecting Marten will be residing at my very home. You see, he is my brother.

PERHAPS I SHOULD TELL you a bit about our family, so you can better understand my desire for revenge. Ours had been a reasonably happy family. My father owned a successful printing shop, and my mother often helped with the running of the business. My brother was learning all of the finer points of running the shop, from purchasing the paper and ink, to working the presses, to finding customers for the books and pamphlets we printed.

At my mother's insistence, I also worked in the print shop, though this was less common for girls. Mama's sister had been left a widow at an early age with no means of supporting herself, and Mama was determined that fate would never befall her, nor her daughter. As it happened, Mama had been wise.

I loved my family, and I felt secure in their love. Growing up, Marten and I would sometimes argue, as children are wont to do, but never with any heartfelt animosity. I had told myself our family was one in which harmony reigned. I knew my parents loved me, though Mama made little effort to conceal the fact that Marten was the cherished one and held a special place within her heart, even above her husband. No less did Marten make any effort to conceal that he preferred Mama to Papa, and I was an afterthought compared to her.

Papa looked more lovingly upon me, though not as obviously as Mama did with Marten, and I in turn loved Papa the more. I do not know, though, whether this was from a true feeling, or simply that Papa and I, the two who were not favored by Mama, sought in each other a kind of consolation.

I sometimes wonder whether my mother's doting was the under-lying source of the animosity between Papa and Marten as my brother and I approached adulthood, though I have heard from other girls my age that fathers and sons sometimes seem to compete in a way mothers and daughters do not.

Complicating this was the fact that my father sometimes drank to excess at a banquet or celebration. This is nothing unusual, as many people become drunk at such festivities. Some become merrier, and some even drink so much they pass out. Some, though, and my father was, I admit, counted in this number, become most unpleasant in speech and manner, and it was Marten who bore the brunt of Papa's affronts. As time wore on, my brother bristled ever more sharply, though I begged him to avoid Papa when he was in that state.

It was not on such a night, however, that I heard Papa and Marten arguing in the front room of our house. Neither raised his voice over-much, and Mama and I were each closeted in our own *bedstede*. Mama swears she heard nothing of a quarrel, but then, though she will never admit it, Mama's hearing has become ever less acute these past years. In the end, it does not matter whether they were arguing or no. What is of import is what happened.

I had fallen asleep, trying to shut out the sounds from Papa and Marten, and when I awoke in the morning, I could tell by the light that it was later than my accustomed hour. Mama was usually up first, preparing the morning meal, and when I was awakened by the noise coming from the kitchen, I would go in to help, and shortly thereafter Papa and Marten would join us. This morning, though, there were no sounds. Everyone else seemed still to be abed. This was most unusual, and so I went to and opened the door of Mama and Papa's *bedstede,* not really expecting anyone to be within. I found only my mother, blinking at the sudden light.

"What are you doing, daughter?"

"Mama, where are Papa and Marten? Did they get up and leave early? I see no sign in the kitchen that they have been up and about."

"I don't think your father ever came to bed," Mama said, in an ever louder voice, quickly arising and looking around as though she would find her spouse and son crouching in some corner.

At this, I decided to check in the front room near the door, to see if their coats were gone from the hooks. That is when I saw him.

"Mama!" I screamed.

Entering the room, Mama cried out and thrust herself on the body of my father.

"No! No! Evert, no!"

If the other sounds that came from her were words, I could not discern them. All I could do was stare at my father, a large gash on his head the source of the blood that surrounded him. His eyes were still open, and I remember thinking for a moment he couldn't be dead. Didn't people close their eyes in their last moment? But there was no denying the vacancy I saw, and the lifeless color of his skin.

I stumbled to Mama's side. She was holding Papa's body, but I could not bring myself to touch him, to touch what would surely be cold flesh. And so I settled for putting my hand upon my mother's back, though I do not know whether she marked it.

After some time, my mother leaned heavily on me to rise.

I finally found my voice. "What has happened here, Mama? And where is Marten?"

"Marten? Oh, my sweet Lord, what if he is injured, or worse? We must find him! Judik, we must find him! Search the house!"

Staring at my father, I did not rush out at her command.

"Mama, there is nothing nearby on which Papa could have hit his head as he fell. Surely this is more than an unhappy accident. Someone has attacked him! What if the villain is still hiding in the house? Mama, we should stay together, or leave and seek help."

"No! I will stay here with your Papa, but you must look for

Marten." Pushing down the hurt at Mama's seeming indifference to my safety, I left to search for my brother.

I looked everywhere for Marten, I even climbed the winding stairs to the loft room, though I could not imagine why he might be up there. Perhaps a part of me wanted to make sure, amid my fear, that there was no stranger lying in wait there. Back downstairs, I opened the front door to look for signs of my brother, but then swiftly closed it, lest a lurking murderer force himself upon me.

Finally, as I was making my way back to tell Mama of my futile search, I glanced into Marten's *bedstede* and noticed a folded paper lying on his cover. As though I were afraid of what it might contain, I carried it, still folded, into the front room, where Mama stood in silent vigil over her dead husband. Wordlessly, I handed her the note and read over her shoulder.

> *Mama,*
> *When you see this, I will have sailed with the morning tide on the*
> *VOC ship, the Wapen van Holland. I am sorry.*
> *I love you,*
> *Marten*

It took but a moment to read, then my mother crumpled to the floor, a step from where my father lay. I went to her, my mind whirling, but even in this moment, with so much pressing upon me, I thought with some bitterness that my brother had no word for me. Neither did he mention Papa.

"What can this mean? Why would he leave?" Mama whispered, and it seemed that Marten's disappearance had overtaken her pain over the death of her husband. "What will I do without my son?"

We sat thus for I know not how long, my mother repeating the same questions over and over. Finally, I broke into the litany.

"Mama, we must do something about Papa."

"Do? What can we do? He is gone. Marten is gone. What is there to do?"

"I told you, someone must have done this to Papa. I think we should send for the schout."

"No! We cannot do that! We will let it be known that your father has had a tragic accident. We will say he was so grieved at Marten's departure, that he collapsed and hit his head."

I was surprised at how quickly she had come up with this explanation. Looking back now, I wonder whether Mama, from the first, feared Marten might be lying injured somewhere, as I had assumed, or whether a darker feeling had invaded her. If so, she was quicker than I. Even though I knew of the quarrel, it wasn't until I found the note that I began to suspect my brother of having killed our father.

In the coming days, as we publicly mourned the passing of my father, between the visits of neighbors and friends offering their sympathy, our private conversations repeated the same arguments again and again.

"I think Marten struck Papa and caused him to fall."

"That is impossible!"

"How else did it happen?"

"Did you not think on that day that there might have been an intruder? Perhaps you were right."

"But there was no sign of anyone else having entered the house, and why would anyone kill Papa? It must have been Marten."

"I cannot believe you would even think such a thing about your brother! You must never repeat that nonsense to anyone."

"But why else would Marten leave, Mama? Why else would he say he was sorry?"

"He left because your Papa was giving him no peace! He said he was sorry because he was leaving me."

"What do you mean, Papa gave him no peace?"

"You saw how your Papa plagued him. Finally my Marten could take no more."

"Then how do you know he did not strike out at Papa?"

"Because he would never do that. Your Papa fell. He just fell."

After a few weeks she absolutely forbade me to voice my accusations. I acquiesced, for why bother speaking of something she had set all of her will against accepting? I had lost half my family. I did not want to become estranged from my mother. But I knew she was wrong, and as time passed, my belief in Marten's guilt became ever more entrenched.

AND SO, here I stand in the cold, damp morning, ignoring the comments of the dock workers, and even the strange looks of the waiting burghers. I assume they are investors here to see what their ship has brought in, whether it will return with sufficient profit. How different is my purpose here. And what exactly will I do if Marten is on this ship? I have given this so much thought over the years, and I constantly vacillate between confronting him with my accusations, and trying a more indirect approach. What if he denies it? I will not allow that. I know he is guilty, do I not? My father could not have simply fallen in that way. I have even wondered whether Marten will feign ignorance of our father's death altogether. Will he claim to have left before our father's fall? Might he even say he told Papa good-bye in person, and that is why he did not address him in the note?

This has all gone through my head so many times I have grown weary of its relentless repetition. I recognize that part of my anger toward Marten is not just the murder, but the two years of agonized thoughts and feelings constantly rippling through me. I blame him for the strained relationship that now exists between Mama and me. One would have thought, with Papa's death and Marten's abandonment of us, Mama and I would have grown closer. It is not so. Mama does not forgive me for believing in Marten's guilt.

THE SUN HAS RISEN a bit higher and is burning off the morning fog. A ship has docked and I stop to ask a hurrying burgher if he knows the name of the ship.

"Why, it's the *Wapen van Holland*." Before I can even thank him he has scurried on. I see that there is some movement, and the dock workers are unloading huge crates from the ship. I think about what treasures they hold: spices and tea, dyes and perfumes, textiles, even ingredients for medicines. I don't see other women here. Are there no wives or daughters, mothers or sweethearts who have longed for the return of husband, father, son? If I represent the sole longing for the return of a long-gone sailor, it is sad indeed, as I am motivated by the smoldering embers of rage, embers that can quickly burst into active flame.

Finally I see some of the crew begin to disembark, and as one after another appears, I realize they are not the hardy men, strengthened by work and adventure I had envisioned. It is strange that the few who are a bit older do seem more robust than their younger companions. Perhaps they had positions that did not require as much of them, or perhaps they are the kind of men who thrive amidst adversity.

Most of those who pass by seem little more than shambling suggestions of broken men. I see no trace of joy in them. They are too weary, too worn for that. The best of them simply seem resigned. They will get off the ship, for that is the next thing they have been told to do.

I think I see him, but my anger does not flare, for this man is a sorry sight. But no, as he approaches I perceive that it is not my brother, and I feel a kind of fear. Fear is not an emotion I have associated with this moment. The fear is not of my brother, but for him. I have heard many do not survive the voyage to and from Batavia. What if that has been Marten's fate?

My anxiety must come from a love that still lingers, but it is mingled with another agitation. What if I never get to confront Marten for what he did? What if I never get to rain down on him the words of condemnation I have practiced a thousand times? What if I am never able to get him to confess to Mama that, yes, her darling son is a murderer? What if I can never threaten to tell the schout, who, even now, will care about a patricide?

Then I catch sight of him. And I am stunned. Even the scarecrows of men who have preceded him off the ship have not prepared me for seeing my brother in such a lamentable state. He walks at an excruciatingly slow pace, and I can see each step costs him dearly. Though his skin is red and rough from the sun, I detect, even from here, that underneath there is an unhealthy pallor. He struggles to carry a bag that I recognize as having come from our home, but it is clear there is but little heft to it. Are these all his worldly goods? He has not come home triumphant.

He almost walks past me, but I call out, "Marten!" He seems to recoil, and even turning his head seems to him a torture, and he stumbles toward me.

"Judik," he says, but I know this only from the movement of his lips, for it is no more than a whisper. "You have come."

"Yes, I have come."

"How is Mama?" I feel the familiar stab of jealousy. It is I, not Mama, who has come to meet him. But then, I have not come from the goodness of my heart.

"What has happened to you?" I cannot keep from asking.

His response is a surprisingly strong, bitter laugh. "Happened to me? I have survived a voyage with the VOC, though many times I did not think I would. Many times I did not want to."

In my countless visions of the moment of confrontation, I had never pictured where we would be. I had wanted to excoriate him before we were at home, where Mama would defend him. But now I see there is no help for it. I will have to take him home. I even take his bag to ease for him the burden of walking.

We do not talk. I do not think he would have breath for it. I take his arm as we walk up the few stairs to the door. When we enter the house I call out, "Mama!" but I see that her marketing basket is not in its usual place. She will be getting food, but only for her and me, since I had not told her that Marten might return today. I did not want to give her false hope. And I did not want to give her hope.

I lead Marten back to the kitchen, as he looks at everything as though it is strange to him. I put bread, cheese, and beer on the table in front of him, but he shakes his head no, not looking up at me.

"We have to talk," he says, and at least now his voice sounds more like himself.

Despite my longing to do just this, I want him to be at least a bit strengthened before I confront him. "Eat first. We can talk after."

"No, I need to tell you before Mama gets home."

The look I give him does not invite further comment. I make a show of getting myself something to eat and drink, and I sit down across from him.

"Why? Why must you tell me before Mama gets home? Because you don't want her to know what you did, or you want to try your excuses on me first?" This might be harsher than I mean to be at this moment, but it is so much less than what I had planned only hours before.

"Because my guilt has been destroying my soul since the day I left."

At first I am shocked into silence at this admission, but then I recover. "So, you did murder Papa?" I say, and the sinking feeling tells me that, despite what I had told myself all this time, my heart still hoped I might be wrong.

Marten recoils at my words, then answers softly, "Not murdered, Judik."

"You are denying it, then?" I say as I rise from my seat, the better to tower over him. "So why did you leave the way you did?"

"Not murdered, Judik. Killed."

"What are you saying, Marten? What do you mean, 'Not murdered. Killed.'?"

"So all this time you have thought that I murdered Papa?"

"I heard you arguing with Papa that night. Papa was not so clumsy as to simply fall, and there was nothing close by on which he could have hit his head in such a manner."

Marten looks at me, then turns away as he says, "You have given this much thought." After a pause he asks, "What does Mama think?"

"What do you imagine? Of course she denies you could possibly have done anything wrong." I know there is a look of disgust on my face. It is more than for the murder, it is for Mama's denial of it, and

Marten's hope to count on that. Even he, though, must wonder how she could unquestioningly believe in his innocence.

"How did she explain the fact that I left, and my note?"

"She made no attempt to explain it. All she did was insist you could not have done anything wrong. After a while she forbade me from speaking of it, and I complied. I could see she did not want to consider your guilt, and I was hurting her. She was all I had left."

I see he has not eaten much, but he now pauses to take a bite of cheese. "I am sorry, Judik."

I pound my fist upon the table and the beer splashes from the mugs. "Sorry for what?" I shout. "You cannot think it is so easy to erase your guilt."

"No, no, I don't think that. I just mean that I am sorry to have put you through that."

I study his face to measure his sincerity, then I plead with him. "What happened that night, Marten? Please."

Marten lowers his eyes as though contemplating how he will explain. "Papa and I were arguing again, and do you want to know something, Judik? I no longer even remember what it was about. Oh, it isn't that I've forgotten that night. No. Everything that happened afterward is seared into my mind. Into my heart. There is not a day goes by I do not relive it." He pauses a moment, as though the obligatory daily remembrance is plaguing him even now.

"Marten..."

"I pushed him, Judik. I pushed him and he hit his head on the corner of the table. You know the one that stood next to the wall with his ledgers on it? I see it is not there now." Then he shakes himself to resume his story. "I quickly pulled his body away from the table, as though I could erase the injury by moving him from the offending object. There was so much blood, Judik, so much. I was afraid. I collapsed onto the bench and stared at him. I don't know how long. It was as though I were in a trance. Oh, Judik, if I had done something at once, if I had called for help, maybe he could have been saved. But I didn't. I sat there, and when I dared go near the body again, he was gone." Tears are streaming down my brother's face, and at first I am incensed.

"Stop your tears! You don't have the right to grieve for him! Or is it only your fear of the consequences that make you weep?"

"I am trying to make you understand! I do grieve, and I have suffered so much! If I could change what I did that night, do you not think I would? I would do anything, give anything, to have him live again. I would give my life. But my death will not bring him back." He breaks into sobs, and against my own will, I feel sorry for him. I feel sorry for my brother.

"What is it that you want from me, Marten? Forgiveness? My complicity in hiding the truth from Mama? In letting her continue to believe you are blameless?"

"No!" he howls, and the vehemence in his voice unnerves me.

I do not respond for some moments, then I quietly ask, "Why did you leave, Marten? If it was truly an accident, if you did not mean for Papa to die, you could have explained that to us. It was your abandonment of us that led me to believe your act was deliberate. Oh, Marten, why did you not trust us?"

"Can you honestly say, with certainty, you would have stood by me, would not have called for the schout? Can you, Judik?"

I study his face, and I know I cannot.

"I ran from the house when I realized what I had done. I knew of a place down by the docks where a crimper would hold the men he had tricked into signing up for a VOC ship. I went there, and I begged him to take me on. Why would he not? The soul seller would get his money for one more recruit. It just happened that the ship was to leave the next day. I came back, packed my things, and left the note. Oh, Judik, at least I told you what had become of me. Was that, at least, not better than leaving you to wonder?"

"Telling someone of an evil deed you are doing does not mitigate the guilt."

He nods. "You are right, of course. I confess, when I left, I hoped to escape punishment, but what I went through on that ship was daily torment. My self-recrimination only left me when I was too hungry, or too exhausted, or too sick to think of anything but obeying orders. There were many times like that, but even food or rest could bring me no relief, for then my accusing thoughts returned."

I studied my brother, and realized I no longer saw a path forward for what I should do, for what I wanted to exact from him. "What will you do now?"

"That depends on what you do. I tell myself I would embrace a just punishment, but I know it is not so. I am a coward. I do not ask for your forgiveness, only for your tolerance. And your silence."

I look at my brother, a shattered body harboring a shattered mind. I do not think he could withstand any kind of punishment. I do not know if he can ever recover, or whether his body and self-recriminations will destroy him.

"Oh, Marten..." I begin, but then we hear our mother coming in the door. She enters the kitchen, stares, then drops her basket to the floor, not noticing the food that falls from it, for she is running to her son. They embrace, both sobbing, Marten saying nothing. All I hear is my mother's repeated, "My son! My son! Thank God! Thank God!"

She does not seem to notice the sorry state he is in. I suspect she does not want to see. She brings him more food, though he has not eaten what is before him. She does not question him at all, but just repeats her pleasure that he is home. She even begins to talk about how much we have missed his help in the print shop, and how the business will flourish now that he is home. Marten does not respond with more than grunts, as astonished as I at our mother's willful blindness.

Finally, my mother looks over at me and says, "Judik, do you have nothing to say? Your brother is home! Marten is home!"

I take in these two: my mother and my brother, who have never held me first in their affections. My mother, set upon an early path to old age by her widowhood and her son's abandonment. My brother, tortured by his actions and beaten down by the cruelties of life at sea. They are all I have.

I walk toward Marten, and though it is but a few steps it seems a long journey. I lay my hand on his shoulder, and he flinches. My fingers feel his bones, even through his clothes. Does this frail man deserve more punishment than he has already visited upon himself? Can I be the one to call down the wrath of the authorities? Would my father wish me to further rip apart the family he loved?

I look into my brother's pleading eyes, and I gently enfold his emaciated body in my arms.

"Yes, Mama. I know he is home."

ABOUT THE AUTHOR

Rebecca D'Harlingue writes about women in the seventeenth century forging a new path. Her novels, *The Lines Between Us* and *The Map Colorist* have each won numerous awards, including the Eric Hoffer Book Award, the IPPY award, and the Independent Press Award. Four of her short stories have been published in anthologies. Rebecca has an MA in Spanish Language and Literature, and an MBA in health services administration. After leaving her job in health care, she taught English as a Second Language to adults from all over the world. You can find out more about Rebecca and her books at rebecca dharlingue.com.

CALL OF THE TIGRESS

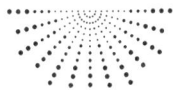

VANITHA SANKARAN

Note: This story contains discussion of young parent death, war death

THE MALABAR DISTRICT, BRITISH-OCCUPIED INDIA,
JUNE, 1939

Before Independence, before World War II and the eviction of the loathsome British Raj, the forests of India were allowed to grow free. The animals of India were allowed to grow free. The people of India... well, that was a sore story.

Abhita carried her daughter into the heart of the Parambikulam forest, where the morning mist swirled around towering trees and the leaves whispered secrets to the wind. Protected by the grace of the gods themselves, man scarcely touched this land, but it was a haven to animals and birds, reptiles and fish. Here, langurs and macaques swung from tree to tree, shrieking in play and war alike; pythons and pit vipers sunned alongside skinks and geckos while a tortoise ambled by; storks and eagles battled for the best fish dinner; and nearby, leopards and boars drank from the clearest waters.

Then there was the tigress. Once, the tigress had been the

protector of their town. Once, she still cared. She hadn't been seen in years, but the people cleaved to her nonetheless.

Hiking past the marshy grasslands and bamboo breaks into the montane-mixed lands of evergreens that gave way to sandalwoods, teaks, and peepals, Abhita carried four-year-old Savitri in a sling over her chest and pointed out the gifts the gods have given them.

"See that tree over there?" She pointed at a tall canopy tree with a hairy trunk. "That's the *anjili* tree. Most people love its fruit." She gave Savitri a spiny yellow fruit pod. "It's delicious, and we'll collect some on the way back, but what I want you to know is this tree gives the best wood for building. If ever we need to build a home here, that tree will be our shelter."

Savitri giggled, as she often did, but said nothing, also as she often did. Abhita caressed the chubby cheeks of her only child and tried not to let her worry show. Her daughter had once been like every other child, bright and bubbly and full of chatter. She had been her father's shadow, trailing behind him with the same sturdy walk, the same tactile nature. Even her face made the same reactions as her father's: dimples for happy laughter, sulky pouts when she was discontent, and a frown resulting in the worst tempers. She had helped him pick fruit and fish for their meals and accompanied him on his evening rounds as he checked on their neighbors and friends. She'd even sat on his shoulders as he walked into his office in town where he served as a desk clerk at the police station in the employ of The Raj.

Then, a Second World War broke out, and the viceroy of India, a tall British man with a cynical twist of his lips and a perpetually arched eyebrow, declared India's support. Many in the Indian-led Congress had quit in protest even as their Muslim countrymen pledged their lives to the cause.

Her husband had been sent to Madras to rebel protesters rallying for Indian control of India's future.

"I must do this, must secure our future. For all of us, but especially for Savitri." He dropped a kiss on the curly black locks of their daughter's head. "I won't be gone long. Two weeks, perhaps three."

He'd never returned home. The day she'd gotten the news, Savitri stopped speaking.

"How about a story for your *amma*, now?" She tickled her daughter's face, but Savitri only gurgled a happy burble back. She wasn't an unhappy child and in all other matters, she behaved as usual—walking, running, stealing sugar from the kitchen. She just never spoke.

They finally reached the small woodside clearing Abhita used for her dance practice. She couldn't often come out here, much less with Savitri. Most of her days were taken up with spinning and weaving cotton. Since the loss of her husband, Abhita's twin brother, Nithin, served as the man of their meager house. He, too, was employed by the British Raj as a police officer, the position given to him as recompense for the loss of Abhita's husband.

It was strange, the calculations the British made on what constituted fairness.

Abhita unhooked the sling around her shoulder and lowered her daughter to the ground. The older Savitri grew, the more Abhita saw her husband in their little girl, not just in her stockiness and her stubbornness, but in the elegant sweep of her eyebrows, the way she wanted to touch everything. But there was some of Abhita in her, too, in the brightness of her big eyes, the long taper in her fingers and hands. The surety of her steps.

Abhita was a *theyyam* dancer, one who communed with the spirit of this forest. It was a duty that came from a long line in their family. She had learned from her late mother, who had learned from her own mother, and so on. This was Savitri's birthright. It was also her responsibility to their land.

"Watch me, baby," she told her daughter now. Savitri was ever an attentive child and stopped her study of some ants in the dirt to watch.

Abhita stretched, the cool soil beneath her toes and the energy of the forest coursing through her. The air was rich with the scents of jasmine and cardamom, and the birds sang in celebration of this new day. She moved with the rhythm of centuries-old chants, her arms sweeping through the air like branches swaying in the breeze. Each step and gesture was a dialogue with the divine, invoking the tigress deity that watched over this forest.

Savitri pulled herself to her feet and mimicked her mother's graceful movements.

"Follow my hands, Savitri," she said gently, her voice as soft as the rustle of leaves. "Let them flow like the river." Her heart swelled with love as she watched her daughter try to follow, tiny hands imitating the fluidity of her mother's movements.

Savitri stumbled, her feet tangling on the uneven ground, but Abhita laughed with a warm smile. "Keep trying, little one. The tigress sees your spirit."

The forest was their sanctuary, where the ancestral dances breathed life into the air, where the boundaries between the human and the divine blurred. The tigress deity's spirit intertwined with the rhythm of the dance, moving through Abhita and into the forest. Here, she felt connected to her ancestors and to the land that sustained them. Here, she felt safe.

The trees in their grove rustled, and Abhita stilled, her senses heightened. Her twin brother, Nithin, pushed past the foliage. A hands-width taller than her, skinny but ropy with muscles, he was as lithe as any dancer she'd seen, though his interest had always lain with the martial arts of their people, the *kalaripayattu*. Normally, his presence brought a lightness to the grove, his exhausting drills matching the beat of her dance rhythms. But today, his face was grim, worry muddying his sharp features.

"Brother, have you come to dance with us?" She greeted him with a tentative smile.

He tracked her presence, then searched for Savitri. Seeing her smile with open arms, he picked her up and faced Abhita. "No, not today," he said, his voice heavy. "I bring news from the city."

News from Kozhikode was rarely a good thing. Plus, she sensed the unease in her twin's voice, a heaviness she couldn't ignore. "What is it?" she asked, steadying her voice for Savitri's sake.

"The British..." He took a breath, then dropped his face into his niece's curls. "They've decided to demolish the forest, Abhita. They need space to build new homes for the soldiers."

Her heart stilled, and the air seemed to grow colder. "No," she breathed, the word barely escaping her lips. Her eyes scanned the forest, orange paint slashed across trees that had stood for centuries, the home of their ancestors and the sanctuary of their tigress deity. "This is our home. How can they—"

"I don't know," he interrupted, his face lined with frustration. "I don't know what we can do. They've already marked the trees."

Her gaze hardened, and she took her daughter from his arms. "We cannot let them take this from us."

He shook his head, his eyes searching hers. "We are outnumbered. They have soldiers, guns... Remember what happened when your husband—"

She cut him off, her smile still focused on her daughter. "We have our spirit, we have our strength." She looked up at him with pleading eyes. "And we have the tigress."

Her twin's shoulders sagged, but he took a step forward. "I will stand with you, Abhita. But we need more than dance to stop them."

She turned towards the forest, her hands reaching out to the trees as if they could give her answers. "Then we'll find another way. We will protect our home."

Sending Savitri back to town with her brother, she focused again on her dance rhythms. It had been months since she'd felt the mother tigress in these forests, years since she'd been able to summon the deity. Whatever had rendered her daughter mute had done the same to Abhita, albeit in a different way.

"Please help us protect this land," she whispered to the tigress deity that had chosen her family centuries ago. "Please help us protect your home."

She bent her knees into a deep stance and began her dance anew.

NITHIN CARRIED his niece on his shoulders as he rode his rusted bicycle back to town. The chain needed oiling and the bell needed fixing, and never mind about the worn-out brake pads, but there was never any time to tend to all that needed repairing in their lives. The burden of his khaki uniform, loaded with the chevrons that marked him as Head Constable, pressed harder on his shoulders than Savitri's meager weight. It rankled that even a small town such as Parambikulam was well-staffed with police in the employ of the ever-greedy Raj.

Frankly, he'd never wanted a job within the police corps their British overlords controlled. He'd chosen a different path back when he'd turned eight and started training in their local martial arts tradition, the *kalaripayattu*. Many aspiring *theyyam* dancers had trained alongside him—the movements between the two disciplines were the same, the weapons brandished were the same, even many of the dances were based on stories of the great *kalari* warriors.

But when the day came for his mother to choose her successor as dancer to their tigress protector, she'd taken only his twin. Every day from dawn to dusk, she swept Abhita into the forest to strengthen the connection between their family and their tigress.

"I wanted to dance like your mother," he told Savitri, surprised as this buried desire fell past his lips. "But our mother tigress courts only girls." From adolescence through cronehood.

"I'm sorry," his mother had said when he'd begged to go with her long ago. "Our protector has no use for boys or men. You will have to find another way."

And so he had, training to be part of the town guard, protecting the temple, the homes, and the people, settling disputes without involving The Raj.

Then, his sister had married, and her new husband forced her away from their family to another town in another state as he sought better fortunes. Their parents had withered with Abhita's departure, for who would nourish the soul of the tigress, who would heed her call now that their daughter was gone?

Certainly not him, though he had tried courting the tigress with his fight moves, his dance moves, even his prayers.

When news of Savitri's birth reached them, the village rejoiced. The succession to the tigress line was intact, if far away. Though his parents soon perished in a flash flood while delivering a batch of cloth to a British merchant who'd insisted on receiving the goods despite the dangerous weather conditions, they had died with hope. When the tigress failed to appear at the cremation, though, Nithin had shuttered any hopes of his own. He would have to protect their home in his own way.

Then Abhita's husband was killed in the line of duty in a faraway place, and The Raj offered him a job in recompense. He scarcely had a choice, not if he meant to feed and shelter his widowed sister and her child. The very day they arrived, Abhita took her daughter into the forest. They didn't return until morning, Abhita downcast, her baby asleep against her breast.

"She is gone. The tigress is gone." A single tear ran down the side of her nose. "She does not forgive me."

Ironing his khaki uniform for the cursed job he had inherited, Nithin only nodded. It was better she understood the tigress would not save them, neither their family nor their town, from the ravages of the British Raj and the greedy whims of a faraway king with his eye on all the natural treasures of their land.

"Mmm, mmm, mm," Savitri gurgled now as he parked his bicycle in the racks behind his office and carried her inside.

His best friend and fellow policeman, Biju, met him at the front door and took Savitri, who was already reaching out to him. Beyond the threshold, a bevy of junior assistants shuttled folders back and forth as if they were actually entrusted with some meaningful task. Overhead, ceiling fans mottled with dust and cobwebs rattled in slow motion as they pushed against the heavy humid air. In the narrow corridor between the two long sections of paper-strewn desks, a lone woman cleaned the floor on her hands and knees using an old rag and a red plastic bucket full of dirty water.

"Inspector is in a mood." Biju tickled Savitri under her chin until she laughed, then whispered his real message to Nithin. "You told your sister?"

He leaned against the metal bars of the nearest open window. "I don't know what she can do."

Biju was a fellow *kalari* fighter, one who used his lithe body and flexibility as ably as he ferreted their employer's secrets. He was the one who had uncovered the British plans for demolishing their forest to make space for their swelling ranks. Biju's plan of using their *kalari* fighters to join the resistance was fraught with risks, especially given how few of their men remained in town.

A few years ago, when he was still on his own, he would have seized the opportunity to wag his tail in the face of these accursed colonizers without question. But now he had a family to care for. He might not be a married man, but he had the same duties as a brother and uncle. Biju had no way of understanding.

Damn the British for starting this fight on his doorstep. Damn the gods for letting it go this way.

"We have a plan. Just be sure you are assigned to the attack force." Biji straightened as the *chai* seller wheeled his bicycle to the verandah and unhooked a tea urn from his handlebars. "Hey, *ya*, what do you mean showing your face here? After that swill you served the Head Inspector?" He took off with Savitri, barking orders all the way.

Nithin took a minute to pull on his persona of a docile and dumb employee and walked into the hot and harried police station. It wasn't hard to blend in with the other men his age, eager to look productive without truly doing anything. This close to the morning tea break, the place was abuzz with activity, not just with peons carrying dossiers but with junior constables announcing what needed to be filed by whom and in what cabinet, and even more junior assistants clacking at typewriters like their fingers were firing rifle shots. The smell of cheap *bidis* was rank in the hot air, smoke from the shredded tobacco hand rolled in a *tendu* leaf and tied off with cheap string, an addiction Nithin hated acquiring. When he could spare a few rupees, he savored the cultured taste of smoking Mohanlal Hargovinddas-branded *bidis*. The kind his employers smoked without thought. The kind they didn't realize funded Gandhi's movement of self-reliance.

Breathing in the smoke despite himself, he moved through the chaos, his face a mask of neutrality as he gave his individual constables a quick but approving nod. The Chief Inspector had taken over his office, so he knocked.

"Enter," came the curt response.

Nithin stepped inside, saluting smartly. The room was dimly lit and hot, the only light coming from a small window near the ceiling. Shutters were bolted shut over the main windows, making the room seem like a small oven. The ceiling fan in this office was no better than the rest, circling lazily without impact. The air was thick with the scented odor of foreign tobacco and over-brewed tea and stifling with accents of the chief's overly sweet cologne.

"Ah, Head Constable. Good timing," Chief Inspector James Adam Addington said, looking up from a stack of reports he'd strewn across Nithin's immaculate desk. A steady stream of blue smoke drifted from the cigarette in his thick fingers. "I have new orders for you."

"Yes, sir," Nithin replied, still at attention.

Addington tossed a folder across the desk. "The operation to clear the Parambikulam forest will begin in one week. The demolition party will arrive in two days under the command of Sergeant Josephs. Be sure he and his men have adequate lodging here."

Nithin's heart sank. The sergeant was well known to his men as a bully and a staunch loyalist of The Raj. With Josephs in charge, their forest stood little chance of survival. Letting his worry show openly in his furrowed brow and deep frown, he perused the details of the demolition plan—it was far more extensive than he had originally thought. Housing was only one small part of a larger scheme to build canals and produce crops in this lush land. The very thought made him nauseous. "Sir, I must confess I have concerns about this operation."

Addington leaned back, golden eyes curious. "Oh?"

He closed the dossier and met the inspector's gaze. "The forests around this area are sacred to the local people. They hold rituals among the trees and have built temples to the gods in the woods. Destroying this land will cause significant unrest."

The stout Englishman stroked his reddish mustache with one hand, his vague smile gone. "We are here to enforce the law, not to cater to superstitions. The development project is vital for our plans, and it will not be interrupted. Do you understand?"

"Yes, sir." Nithin nodded, though his stomach churned. "But still, we must prepare for resistance."

Addington stubbed his cigarette out on a corner of Nithin's desk and waved the worry away. He brushed his manicured nails against his uniform and held his hand up to the light. "I am certain Sergeant Josephs can handle the local rabble, but you have a good thought. I'll tell Josephs to double his men."

"No!" That was the last thing he wanted.

The inspector lowered his hand. "Constable?"

"Sir, I saw in the plans this area is meant for significant development—canals and crops." Who were they counting on to do such hard labor? Certainly not Britishers. "If we can keep the peace and explain why we must deforest, perhaps we won't lose the local workforce. After all, it will take many men many years to see this work done."

The inspector's smile reappeared. "Good thinking, Constable. I am pleased to see your allegiance indeed lies with The Raj. Your village should be singing your praises."

Despite himself, he stiffened at the implication. "Understood, sir."

"I will tell Josephs he will lead the demolition, but you will handle any local resistance. Be sure to take as many of your men as you need. Dismissed."

Outside his office, he let his relief sag with his shoulders. Step one of the rebellion was complete. He would be leading the resistance after all.

BACK IN THE VILLAGE, in the courtyard of their small temple to the goddess Durga, Abhita gathered the elders and the strongest among the villagers. Nearly eighty people sat cross-legged on the stone ground, bursting with anxious whispers. Worship of the deity, often shown riding a tiger, was strong in these parts, a fact that unsettled the Britishers. They avoided the temple by a wide berth, turning their faces from its open doors lest they catch sight of the powerful goddess of protection, strength, and war.

Abhita wasted no time sharing the news. "My brother, Nithin, has just learned the British are planning to clear a good portion of our forest. They say it is to make way for new homes, but we have the homes we need. I don't know their true plan, but it is clear we cannot allow this."

The villagers murmured among themselves, their fear palpable. A field worker, dark and strong with a scythe at his waist, stood. "The Britishers will not find us so easy to take."

Many of the younger men raised their voices in approval.

"Sit down, Jagan," admonished an elderly woman with a thinning silver braid and a dark red *sari*. "If boys like you and my son take on the likes of the police, you'll only get beaten and thrown in jail. And then where will we all be?"

"But how can we fight them?" asked one of the town's buffalo herders. "They have guns, and we have only our hands and our traditions."

"We have more than that," Abhita said, her mind tumbling over itself with plans made and discarded in a moment. "We have our spirit, our strength, and the tigress deity that watches over us."

"That is all well in theory," the elderly woman said, waggling her head. "But how long has it been since the tigress has appeared, Abhita?"

She heard the real question behind the woman's words: how long has it been since you've been able to summon the tigress, Abhita?

It had been months since she'd felt the tigress, years since she'd glimpsed the divine animal. Since before her husband's death. Since before Savitri had even been born. It had not been her choice to leave home—she'd argued against it to no avail—but perhaps the tigress cared not for their traditions, the expectations a husband put on his wife.

"The world is changing, *paatti*," she said, addressing the woman as she would her own grandmother. "Even in our small village, we feel it. And we must change too. These British policemen torment us at the behest of one man. A distant man, a distant king, but one with power. One woman, one village dancer, cannot hope to draw the same power. But if all of us call the tigress to our side, maybe she will hear our plea and join our cause."

A warm wind rustled through the palms and teaks around them, somehow approving.

"What do any of us know about the *theyyam*?" a young mother asked. She had an infant in her arms, and two children not much older clinging to her legs. "You have spent your entire life learning the dance, your mother and grandmother before you. This is in your blood, and yet even you cannot call her forth."

A murmur of assent rose around the courtyard.

But Abhita would not be dissuaded. "Do the old stories not tell us it isn't the size of the offering but the intent behind it that pleases the gods most? A king could build a palace for a god and still, it would pale in value beside the offering of mere grains of rice that is all a mendicant could afford. I have been too long from our goddess, that is true. But when she sees all of us together, when she sees I have brought you to her, she will heed our call."

Not many were convinced. But the elderly woman in the back nodded her approval. "I will do this."

The young mother didn't add her voice, but two other mothers near her did. "We will do this, too."

"So will I." Nithin strode into the temple, his police uniform discarded for the simple cotton *mundu* wrapped around his waist with a matching white cloth draped over his chest. He deposited Savitri with Abhita, then addressed the small crowd.

"The British plan to turn our forest into a commerce center." He explained how their district wasn't growing as much rice as they used to. "We are being told to plant more crops and create more waterways to transport our goods. It is, they say, for the public good."

Abhita traded a look with her twin as his words sunk in. She dipped her face into her daughter's hair and smelled the comforting scents of coconut oil and jasmine. The British had done this with other parts of India, used the idea of the public good to build grandiose buildings that seemed as foreign to their land as these white men commanding them.

"What if it *is* good for us?" the field worker with the scythe asked. The men around him nodded their interest.

"Is it?" Nithin asked in response. "Certainly, they will look to us to build the canals and plant the rice, to harvest and maintain, to arrange for shipments and pack the cargo. And they will pay us. But do we not work enough already? Do we want to work more?"

This caused another round of conversation.

Nithin pressed on. "And when we cannot keep up with their plans, do we want our village to grow? Do we want to become a town, a city? Who will they bring in? More workers like us, or ones they educate to behave like them? Worse, those who bend their heads and their wills to foreign interests?"

The murmurs grew heated.

Abhita kissed her daughter's cheek, then placed her on the ground between herself and her twin. "A person should have the chance to dictate her life. So should a village, a community, a people. The question isn't whether we want this vision the Britishers have dreamed up. It is whether we want to dream for ourselves."

A few voices cheered her words, with many others applauding. Still, a few looked undecided.

The buffalo herder stood again. "It is a good sentiment. Only, my original question remains. How are we to stand against men with guns?"

Nithin broke into a bright grin. "I am so glad you asked. Because I have a plan."

THE NEXT DAY, Nithin left his office and walked toward the forest, his steps purposeful, his mind racing with plans. The sun dipped low on the horizon, casting long shadows that danced like ghosts among the trees. He had hand-picked the team he would lead on the day of the demolition, ensuring those sympathetic to the British cause were front and center. This, he figured, would show his superiors that he had done his best, even as he orchestrated a resistance from within.

At a clearing not too far from the village's edge, a few dozen men waited for his arrival. These were his trusted allies, fellow police officers, and friends from his *kalaripayattu* training. Their faces were serious, their resolve clear.

"Brothers," Nithin began, his voice low but firm, "we are the first line of defense. Our task is to hold the British soldiers at bay, to protect our people behind us. They will see our faces and think we are here to do their bidding. But we know the truth. Our hearts beat for this land, and we will not let them take it."

The men nodded, their eyes filled with determination. His best friend, Biju, stepped forward. "We have trained for this, Nithin. Show us the way."

Nithin spent the next hour leading them through a series of *kalari* moves, each motion precise, each step calculated.

"*Meipayattu!*" he called out, then launched into a sequence of body conditioning exercises designed to enhance flexibility and strength.

In front of him, his men flowed through their movements with grace and power, executing high leg raises and deep lunges that mimicked the fluidity of animal movements.

"*Kaithada!*" he called next, pairing off his men so they could practice intricate hand-to-hand combat techniques. Arms and legs, hands and feet, these were their most basic weapons.

For hours, the men practiced swift strikes and controlled parries, their bodies moving in a blur of motion. The sound of flesh meeting flesh echoed through the clearing as they moved on into weaponry practice using thick staffs made from the very woods around them.

Finally, Nithin demonstrated a series of offensive and defensive maneuvers with a weapon—staffs and staves, sticks and poles. He twirled his own staff with practiced ease before bringing it down in powerful, sweeping arcs. The men mirrored his actions, their staves whistling through the air with each precise strike and block.

After three straight days of six-hour practices, Biju pleaded for a stop. "We have this, Nithin. We know our art. What we need to understand is your plan."

A wolfish smile spread across Nithin's face. "I was only waiting for you to ask."

Under the light of a nearly full moon, he led them to a clearing less than half an hour's walk away. Here, his twin had been teaching the other villagers some basic *theyyam* movements. Her group was still singing the *thottam*, the invocation of the deity chanted in a melody that, with the chorus of the other villagers, blended a harmonious plea to the divine.

"Watch," Nithin told his men. "Pay attention to how their hands and feet move. It's not so different from what we do."

"Why weren't we practicing this with them?" Biju asked after a few minutes, eyes fixed on the way Abhita stepped from one foot to the next.

"We needed to come together as our own team. Come, follow me." He took a position in front of his men, the steps of his sister's dance as familiar as his fighting drills.

Abhita moved from the initial invocation to the *meipayattu*, similar to her brother's *kalari* exercises, but with a distinct rhythm that embodied the spirit of the *theyyam*.

"Start with the basic dance steps," she instructed, demonstrating using her feet to tap out a rhythmic pattern on the ground. The villagers followed, their movements tentative at first, but gaining confidence with each step.

Nithin's men kept the rhythm on the side, easily adapting to Abhita's faster rhythm.

Next, they moved on to the *mudras*, symbolic hand gestures that represented various aspects of the divine. "These *mudras* can be your primary attack mode," she explained. "You can be a snake biting a face or a bird plucking an eye with your hands.

As she explained other basic movements to her audience, Nithin emphasized how similar the *mudras* were to the strikes and blocks in *kalari*.

From there, Abhita led them through the powerful stances that formed the foundation of *theyyam*. "Plant your feet as firmly as you need to, knees bent as low as you need to go so you can't be toppled over."

Nithin was pleased to see his men in stance even before Abhita detailed her instructions.

As her villagers struggled to adjust to this low and hard foundation, Abhita moved among them with a small pot of turmeric paste, its rich yellow hue glowing in the dim light. She stopped by each person, drawing stripes across their foreheads and cheeks.

"This turmeric grows in the depths of these forests," she explained softly, her voice carrying a blend of reverence and determination. "Generations ago, an ancestor of mine planted this crop, and we have tended it within our family ever since. Turmeric contains a unique essence that intertwines with the soil of this place. By wearing this paste, we affirm our bond with this land. We claim it as our own."

Nithin saw the effect of her ritual right away: The villagers straightened, feeling a renewed sense of connection and purpose as the cool paste touched their skin. The turmeric, with its deep roots in the forest soil, symbolized their own deep roots in their ancestral land. This simple yet profound ritual united them in their cause, reinforcing their determination to protect their home.

She passed the pot to him with no more than a grave look. But when she spoke again, she called to his men, too, telling them all to join her in a circle.

"We will use our dance, our *theyyam*, to call upon the tigress deity. She has protected us for generations, and she will do so again. But you, too, will be our protectors, for how can we ask the tigress to shelter what we won't defend?"

She moved through the dance with a newfound resolve, her arms sweeping through the air, her feet beating a slow and strong rhythm that echoed through the forest. The *theyyam* was a dance of patience, starting early in a low beat and lasting for hours before the actual rapid steps called the tigress to bear. Only a quarter of the villagers, alongside all of Nithin's men, made it through the full four hours.

Savitri was one of them, as stubborn as Abhita, even for her young age.

As the sun rose, casting an orange glow over the clearing, Nithin and Abhita spent one long moment of indulgence in being honest with each other.

"This will not be easy," Nithin said, his voice heavy with worry. "We are outnumbered and surrounded."

Abhita nodded, her gaze fixed on the horizon. "I know. But we have no choice. This land, these trees, this forest is our home. We must protect it."

Taking her hand, Nithin squeezed tightly. "I have done all I can to prepare. I have recruited those who will stand with us, those who understand the importance of what we are fighting for. But I fear it is not enough."

"It will be enough. We will make it enough." Abhita's eyes blazed. "The tigress deity will hear our call and she will keep these British devils at bay."

But he only sighed, the weight of the coming day pressing down on him. "And if she does not? What then?"

She looked into the depths of the forest, where the shadows of the night gave way to a new dawn. "Then we will fight with everything we have. We will stand until we can stand no more."

THE DAY OF RECKONING ARRIVED. Nithin stood at the edge of the clearing, his heart pounding as he scanned the horizon. The sun climbed higher, casting long shadows that danced like specters among the trees. The air was thick with anticipation, the forest holding its breath.

Sergeant Josephs and his team arrived, their presence disrupting the morning's serenity. Josephs, a burly man with a perpetual sneer etched on his face, strode forward with an air of superiority. His men, a mixture of Englishmen and locals but all staunch loyalists to the Raj, followed closely, their laughter harsh and grating.

"Well, well, Head Constable," Josephs said, his voice dripping with disdain. "Quite the gathering you've arranged here. Ready to clear out these savages and their sacred trees?"

Nithin clenched his jaw but forced his words into calm. "We are ready to proceed as ordered, Sergeant."

Joseph smirked, glancing at his men. "You hear that, lads? Our dutiful constable is ready to play his part. Let's hope he doesn't get cold feet." His men chuckled.

Nithin's blood boiled, but he kept his expression neutral. He turned to his team, those he had strategically chosen for their loyalty to the British. "Follow Sergeant Josephs to the starting point. I will join you shortly."

As Josephs and his men moved deeper into the forest, a *kalari* war cry pierced the air. Nithin's heart lifted at the signal. His team, his real team, was ready.

He moved swiftly, meeting Biju and the others at a predetermined spot. "Remember, our goal is to protect the villagers and the forest. We draw the soldiers in, but we do not engage directly unless necessary."

Biju nodded, jaw set in determination. "Understood, Nithin."

Dressed in dark brown and black, the *kalari* fighters moved like shadows, their movements fluid and elusive. They appeared and disappeared among the trees, drawing Josephs and his men further into the forest. The British soldiers, frustrated and disoriented, followed the fleeting figures deeper into the heart of the forest.

It was then that they stumbled upon the troupe of fifty villagers dancing the *theyyam*. The sight was mesmerizing: vibrant costumes; painted faces; and movements that blended grace with raw power. The villagers danced in unison, their feet pounding the earth, their arms weaving intricate patterns in the air.

Josephs scowled at the sight. "What nonsense is this? Disperse them!"

But Nithin's *kalari* fighters were ready. They engaged Josephs' men with precision, keeping them occupied and away from the *theyyam* dancers. The air was filled with the sounds of battle: the clash of sticks; the grunts of exertion; and the booming drum beat.

Abhita led the dance, her movements a blur of color and energy. Between breaths she felt the tigress watching, could sense her listening, a presence just beyond the veil of reality. But the deity remained elusive, her spirit hovering at the edge of perception.

Josephs, caught in the chaos, shouted insults and commands, his frustration mounting. "You think this primitive dance will save you? You're all nothing but savages!"

The words struck a chord in Abhita. Her movements became more fervent, her steps more forceful. The villagers, inspired by her intensity, matched her pace, their collective energy rising.

Savitri, her eyes wide with determination, joined her mother in the dance. Her small body moved with surprising grace, her face alight with a fervor that belied her years. She danced with a purpose, her movements echoing those of her mother.

As the dance reached its climax, the air grew thick with a palpable energy. Abhita felt the presence of the tigress drawing closer, her spirit intertwining with the rhythm of the dance.

"Mmm-ma," Savitri gurgled, the closest to words she had come to since her father had been killed.

Tears filled Abhita's eyes, but she only used them to fuel her dance. "SHE draws near!" She yelled the words between breaths. "SHE hears us!"

Josephs, seeing the growing intensity, shouted, "Look at them! Pathetic! If this is your defense, it's a wonder this country lasted as long as it has."

Abhita's heart blazed with resolve, and her movements became a whirlwind of power. The villagers, sensing the shift, matched her intensity. The forest seemed to pulse with their energy, the very ground beneath them trembling.

Savitri, caught in the fervor, let out a cry—a sound that echoed with the spirit of the tigress. Her small hands moved with grace, her feet tapping out a rhythm that resonated through the clearing.

And then, as if summoned by their collective will, the tigress leapt forward. She emerged from the shadows, majestic and awe-inspiring and larger-than-life. She was a coil unsprung, a fearsome force that landed on the ground with a fluid, predatory grace. Her lithe body was cloaked in silence and warning, muscles rippling beneath her striped coat.

The villagers gasped, their movements faltering for a moment as the divine presence made itself known. En masse, they fell to their knees and bent their heads in prayer.

"Fools," Josephs yelled. "Carry on!"

But his men held back. The tigress continued moving forward, whiskers twitching, eyes glowing with an otherworldly light. Pausing, she growled, a low, resonant rumble that evoked a shiver among the men still standing. Her golden eyes regarded each and every man; none dared stare back. Not even Josephs.

Finally, eventually, irrevocably, her gaze found Abhita, found Savitri. Tail flicking in a slow, deliberate rhythm, the tigress's imposing presence softened. She padded toward the girl on velvety paws, her fearsome demeanor giving way to a rare gentleness, an inexplicable bond forming in the quiet of the forest clearing. She nuzzled the girl's hand, a gesture of acceptance and protection.

Savitri, her face radiant, leaned into the touch of the tigress and began the dance anew. One by one, beginning with her mother and her uncle, the rest of the townspeople followed her lead. The tigress growled in approval and paced back and forth in front of them, keeping the rhythm.

The sight was enough to shake even the most hardened of Josephs' men. They hesitated, their resolve wavering in the face of the divine.

Josephs, however, was unrelenting. "Do not be fooled by their tricks! Press on!"

But it was too late. The presence of the tigress had tipped the balance. Emboldened by the deity's appearance, the villagers danced with renewed vigor. The *kalari* fighters, inspired by the display, redoubled their efforts, driving the British soldiers away from their forest.

Nithin, seeing the shift, shouted, "Hold the line! Protect the dancers!"

The forest echoed with the sounds of resistance, the clash of cultures and wills. This time, though, the strength of Parambikulam was true. Before this land had held people and culture, it had held the forest and the animals. The tribes that had settled here thousands of years ago had built their lives in harmony with the land. The villagers who'd come to fight for that harmony understood the same. They fought for their lives, fought for their homes; they fought for the sanctity of the forest they loved and the tigress who protected them once more.

Against such resolve, the British soldiers had no quarter. Outmatched and outmaneuvered, their morale shattered. Only Josephs could be heard as they retreated.

"You useless fools!"

As the last of the invaders fled, the villagers collapsed to the ground, exhausted but triumphant. Abhita and Nithin stood at the center, their hearts filled with pride and relief. Savitri, the tigress by her side, looked up at her mother with shining eyes.

"The tigress heard our call," Abhita whispered, her voice filled with emotion. She dropped to her knees and held her arms out, hoping.

The tigress nuzzled Savitri's cheek, then glided forward until her head pressed against Abhita's chest.

"Oh!" Abhita wrapped her arms around the animal's head and buried her face in the tigress' fur as she had done as a child. Tears streamed down her face, but patient as the deity was, she pulled back after a few moments and licked Abhita's face clean.

Abhita turned her shiny eyes to her twin. "We did it."

Nithin nodded, his eyes reflecting the flickering firelight of the setting sun. "Yes, we did. This time. But they will come back."

Abhita didn't answer immediately. The villagers gathered around them, their faces alight with hope and determination. The forest, their sacred home, stood as a testament to their strength and resilience, a symbol of hope for generations to come. Her eyes were focused on Savitri, who had thrown her arms around the tigress and was marking her with their turmeric paste now.

"They may come back, but we will never leave," Abhita finally said. "This land is part of us. We will fight for it, dance for it, and live for it."

Nithin watched his niece with the tigress, a sense of peace settling over him. "I think we understand that now. And we'll be ready."

Abhita turned to the villagers, raising her voice so all could hear. "This forest is our legacy, our home. Together, we called upon the tigress. Together, we will stand against any threat. Let this day be a reminder of our strength and our unity."

The villagers cheered, their spirits lifted by the victory and the presence of the divine tigress. The bond between them and their land had been affirmed, stronger than ever before.

As the celebrations began, Nithin and Abhita shared a look of mutual understanding and resolve. The path ahead would not be easy, but they would walk it together, guided by the spirit of their ancestors and the fierce protector of their forest.

Together they could face any future, so long as their tigress walked alongside them.

HISTORICAL NOTE

The art of *theyyam*, also known as *theyattam* in the more formal setting, is a unique blend of dance, costumes, music, and rhythm that derives from ancient tribal traditions and the Dravidian customs unique to south India. This performance is a sacred ritual that focuses on the dancer assuming the role of their chosen deity in order to be a vessel so devotees assembled could seek blessings, protection, and guidance from said deity.

There are reportedly over 450 different *theyyam* performances that honor the gods and goddesses, spirits, myths, and legends. In this story, I keep the *theyyam* dancer and her deity apart for plot purposes.

The next step for Abhita and Savitri will be to reconcile with the tigress so they can evoke her spirit through their bodies. If they can make it happen.

ABOUT THE AUTHOR

Vanitha Sankaran writes fiction based on history, legend, and mythology. Her literary historical novel, *Watermark: A Novel of the Middle Ages*, traces the introduction of paper in southern France at a time when heresy was aflame. By day, she works in medical strategy and by night, she capers through collections of folklore. For more about Vanitha, please see her website at www.vanithasankaran.com, follow her on Facebook, Instagram, or BlueSky.

BEG, BORROW, TOMORROW

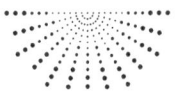

ANNE M. BEGGS

SISTERS OF SAINT GOBNAIT'S CONVENT, IRELAND,
AD 1234

Maire woke to the sound of bells calling her and her convent sisters to morning prayer.

"Muireann, wake up. We are late. The bells are ringing," Maire said, shoving the sleeping form next to her. "Where are the servants?"

Was she to do everything herself? At four and twenty, she had many pressing responsibilities. Waking on time was not one of them.

Saint Gobnait's was a convent built by and for the nobility. It was not as grand as the Royal Abbey of Las Huelgas, and no queens of any royal courts had yet taken retirement here, but these sisters lived a comfortable life as their station prescribed in this small, orderly convent with the best reputation—a place where the nobility could safely deposit their inconvenient women. She was grateful not to be of the poor laborers and serfs, those who might find redemption with the Clarisses, followers of Poor Clares, vowing to live in poverty, obedience and chastity.

Now that she was awake, she heard urgent voices and crying. What now? Why the disturbance in this quiet convent devoted to beauty, peace, and prayers? Was nothing sacred? She looked about the bedchamber. She and Muireann were the only ones still sleeping. Bother, had no one the decency to wake them in a timely manner?

"What is happening?" Maire asked as two servants rushed into the chamber.

"Sorrow, so much sorrow. Oh, the convent is in uproar. The abbess is wringing her hands with grief and worry," Orla, one of the servants, said. What peasant family would choose to name their daughter *golden princess*, even if she was that pretty? Maire always meant to ask, and then forgot. Most likely she was named after the lady of the manor. Maire's nickname had been *lucóg*, mouse, for her brown, thin hair, and her adorable little face. Maire hated it, and gladness upon her none at the convent knew it.

"What sorrow?" Muireann asked, rubbing her eyes. Muireann was portly. She enjoyed good food but didn't know when to quit. Maire enjoyed good food too, but felt overindulgence was not showing proper gratitude for God's abundance. What beauty and peace was there in overeating? Nothing peaceful about a bedmate burping and farting all night. But Muireann was a good sport and generous when Maire was in a financial bind. As she was today.

Maire had convinced most of her sisters to contribute to a glorious triptych for the altar. Oh, the convent had never had such an ornament. What a tribute to God, the Virgin, and their Savior Jesus Christ. Her skin tingled with the thought of its magnificence, and she let the sensation spread to her core, igniting sparks within her. Two payments had been made, all the funds from her sisters applied, except the money she owed. The sparks diminished. She'd spent the money at the market after Easter. All the sisters were buying wool and linen for new garments. She could not resist the stunning silver cross pendant with jewels that were from Outremer. Oh, to venerate the Virgin and her Son's sacrifice for them all. This excellent piece of work must be given to the abbess, for Maire had much gratitude for her and the great opportunity to live in Saint Gobnait's. Even then, Maire borrowed more money for the extraordinary slippers she was sliding her feet into just now. Oh, lovely things they were, gold thread and pearl beads that radiated God's creation from nature. How could she not revere this treasure?

A glimmer of the first flush of pleasure she had felt returned. But oh, her father's extra funds had not yet arrived. The third payment was due tomorrow. She took the slippers off. She may need them, but oh how sad to loan them out. And to Ossnait, that obnoxious sister. Nothing was ever good enough for her.

All of the sisters at Saint Gobnait's were as servants to Ossnait, fawning at her feet as if she were holding court. Even the abbess overlooked Ossnait's resistance to pray and abide by the rules. Sister Ossnait did have money, so much money. Once again Maire would also feign great reverence, acknowledging Ossnait's good graces, and beg for more funds, offering these slippers. But God had wanted her to have them, in His honor.

Ossnait had been ill, complaining about her courses and all manner of discomfort, as she always did. Maire would escort her to the garden, where the summer flowers were most stunning, a tribute to Maire's skill and God's glory. Surely, Ossnait would extend more credit for past owed money, as well as a loan for the triptych. Truly. If not, she would offer the slippers, at least as a hostage per Irish custom.

She glanced at Muireann. Muireann would lend her more, on the promise of repayment as soon as her father sent more money. She had sent the letter ages ago.

How did this date creep up on her anyway, she thought as Orla helped her dress? *I am so busy. Too busy to remember dates and money.*

"What happened?" Muireann asked again, drawing Maire from her plans.

"Sister Ossnait died last night," Orla said.

Maire froze. Died? Last night? But–

"Seems something ruptured. A fever hit, and she felt much pain, then she just quit breathing according to the attending sisters," Orla said, bowing her head as she waited for Maire to cooperate with dressing into the somber dark tunic worn for mourning or the highest holy day, or a bishop's arrival. Orla expressed no emotions for this horrifying news.

"Well, the young shrew has met her maker," Muireann said, also dressing with the other servant's assistance.

Both servants tried to suppress their chuckles. Ossnait had been difficult, but her money made it easier to overlook.

"For shame, Muireann, Sister Ossnait has passed. We shouldn't speak so of the dead," Maire said, calculating.

"Most of us said it behind her back while she lived, why not now? Has she become saintlier in death?" Muireann retorted to more chuckles.

Maire was deep in thought now. *Ossnait. How could you? The convent needed you. I needed you.*

"I would think you would be the most relieved, Maire. You owed her plenty."

"Do not speak it," Maire scolded. "Do not." Did anyone else besides her, Muireann and Ossnait know how much money she owed? She prayed not. Crossing herself, Maire started reciting prayers for Ossnait's soul and her family. Grievous indeed. Of course, she prayed no one knew her indebtedness, greater this day without Ossnait's loan. Where would the money come from? She prayed her father's funds would arrive this day. *This day God, we count on Your mercy.*

IN THE CHAPEL the abbess stood before them, as upright and solid as the protective convent walls, her face stern and scowling more than usual. It always amazed Maire that a woman who dedicated her life to the convent, particularly this grand place, was always so upset and angry. This was not some leper colony where God's unfortunates went to suffer their fates. Just thinking of tending lepers, to their needs and stench, their wounds and clothes, made her queasy. This convent was dedicated to praising God's miraculous accomplishments, where beauty and peace were acknowledged as His highest calling. A place where she and her sisters could pray for all the souls in need, uninterrupted by squalor and sickness, war, and treachery. Jesus the Savior came to teach them to love one another and here they did, or at least they tried.

"As you all know, we have lost our beloved Sister Ossnait," the abbess said, as if any needed reminding after all the prayers, singing, and lamentations they had already conducted. Caught up in the grief and mourning, Maire was already planning a funeral, the trappings, and new clothes they would need. Sister Ossnait need not die in vain; something lovely should be made of her death. She must be made prettier in death. Isn't that what God would want? Maire felt the familiar flush beautiful things aroused in her. Her cheeks felt rosier and her heart beat with God's good wishes for Ossnait's funeral finery.

Blessed Saint Gobnait's, where the sisters had some freedom in dress. No one cared that some of the women wore the finest linen or silk chemises under the severe tunics and scapulars, with jewelry also hidden under coif, bandeau, wimple, and guimpe. Maire enjoyed the feel of the head gear, it seemed queenly to her, still all the fashion. They were allowed to vote on the colors of holiday and seasonal tunics, scapulars, and veils, making those occasions feel festive and exciting, like the banquets they'd left behind—some by choice, most by their family's need to be rid of them.

Not Maire, she chose this life for herself, free from husband and maternity. If they all wore the same color garments, the abbess made no complaints. Maire didn't see it as vain, but as honoring the colors God Himself had created.

Hearing Ossnait's name spoken brought her back to her plans. "She was but thirty, young and in her prime, with so much more to give," the abbess said.

"So much more to give," someone said to snickers, for they all knew the abbess meant her family's endowment to the convent. Blessed funds to help sustain them all.

"It is true that Sister Ossnait's family paid handsomely for her residence here, and her loss is the convent's loss. I will, of course, write letters of condolence. Letters showing our grief and loss. Until that time, we are in mourning and not to speak of Sister Ossnait's death to anyone outside these convent walls. No one! My letters must be the first news."

"She doesn't want to lose the funds from the family," Muireann whispered in Maire's ear. "Trying to find a way to milk the allowance, I would wager."

"Shush, now, that is a terrible thing to say, true as it may be," Maire said, already thinking how she would love to help the abbess write those letters.

Breaking fast, Maire listened with half an ear to all the conversations and murmurings about Sister Ossnait's death. How was she to fund the triptych? What bad timing for this premature death. But Maire formed a plan.

Getting up with head bowed, Maire approached the abbess at her table with the other esteemed, elder sisters.

"Abbess, blessing upon you and our convent in this time of mourning and need," Maire said.

The abbess bobbed her head. Was that the only acknowledgment of Maire's condolence? Maire inhaled and continued.

"I offer to assist you with the arrangements for Sister Ossnait's funeral." Oh, yes, a funeral like no other. Let her be remembered in serenity and beauty, Maire thought, the images forming of flowers, lamentations, and smiles. Let them smile, showing acceptance of God's will and their perseverance to duty. She remembered the lavish ceremonies Saint Gobnait's had performed over the years, not only for the convent, but for the nobility and visiting church members. The stories of grandeur from Las Hueglas and other convents rang in her ears, of those sisters performing equal duties of a noble wife, managing their convents as the estates of God. The balance in their society: power and protection of the nobility, prayer and salvation of the Church, and the labor of the workers. God's plan, all supporting each other.

"And those sad letters. I can write," Maire offered. "Let me help you. When the time is right."

The abbess gazed at her, rubbing her stiff, gnarled fingers. Could such wretched hands create letters of beauty? God was mysterious. God was wise. Beauty could be forthcoming from something unattractive.

"That would be helpful. May you have goodness. I accept your offer, sister. With blessing," the abbess said with a shadow of a smile, mayhap the best she could offer under the weight of this painful day. This loss of revenue Maire understood all too well. What would any of them do without Sister Ossnait's endowment? Yet, one less debt for Maire, she prayed again that no one knew.

"Gladness upon me to help," Maire said, nodding and returning to her seat.

Oh, glory upon her. Her mind raced to the details of both endeavors. Of course, they would need funds for the funeral. Many of the sisters would want new attire. Something fresh, symbolizing new life, as they bid farewell to Sister Ossnait as they, the Blessed Sisters of Saint Gobnait's, lived on in God's glorious light. Maire went weak in the knees, closing her eyes, feeling the luxury of a new silk chemise upon her flesh, she swooned. Glory be, she prayed.

Maire could already hear the keys clicking in the locks of the stout wooden chests under each sisters' bed. Every sister counted her coins and marble or savored the jewelry each had stored away. Maire had a chest filled with her sister Anu's letters, most unfinished, waiting for her to read them thoroughly. Another day.

"Sisters," Maire said to the small, second assembly of convent sisters. "As you know, I have joyously offered to manage Sister Ossnait's funeral."

"So you have, and better you than me," Sister Émer said. She was one of the young widows sent to Saint Gobnait's against her will. She would have preferred a secular life with a new chance for husband and children. Maire always thought her blessed, though Sister Émer didn't realize it yet. Widowhood was so sad, but the risk of bearing children was hazardous.

"Let the shrew be buried with the humility she never practiced in life," another said.

"That is fitting," another agreed.

"We are sisters in God's service, and our covenant is to honor God, our Savior Jesus, and our Lady the Virgin Mary. Ours is the way of serenity, forgiveness, and prayer. We are to find and revere beauty in all God has given us. How better to find beauty in Sister Ossnait's death than to send her off in a show of rebirth, fresh, new clothing, and adornments with joy in our hearts that she too, may be reborn in Christ's light," Maire said in her most inspiring voice.

"New clothes! And how are you, in particular, to pay for them?"

"Mayhap those who can, would donate to the funeral fund," Maire said.

"Mayhap you should pay me what you owe, then I could be reborn," Émer said.

"True, you owe me for the Easter celebration. All that sacrifice of Lent, only to lend you my good fortune," another said.

"Did the other sisters agree to this? Or are you just moving on to new victims?" Émer said.

"Sisters, what skeptics. Of course they agreed. Each made generous promises and offers of funds." This was partially true. They did promise to consider matching funds if the other sisters agreed. That was generous. Maire assured those sisters that this group she was with now would happily donate to cover the cost of food and beverages. Didn't Sister Flidais's family have a vineyard? Why should they not donate more wine for our suffering in Sister Ossnait's death? Oh, piety upon us in our grieving.

"You don't want to seem cheap, do you? And it would be vulgar to compare our offerings. Isn't that what the servants and workers do? Jabber, gossip, and lie about who gets paid what and when." It was important that the sisters not question or compare. It was to her advantage, and the convent's, that each sister donated honestly and from the purity of her heart. The more they believed and the more they donated, the better they would all feel when this cheerful ceremony took place. And how good the wine would be. Maire licked her lips in anticipation. "Sisters, we are not so low. Each of you and your families will know of your charity and goodness before God." This was true. Maire was helping them all honor their sacred vows of serenity and beauty in God's service. She crossed herself and brushed a tear away.

"I suppose," Émer said, "if the others have."

"My family may have some fine ale. If we sisters don't consume it, we might trade it," another said.

"That's the spirit," Maire said, feeling the bounty and seeing the banquet they would hold, all in their new splendor. Oh, where was her father's messenger with those funds?

"The triptych is coming tomorrow. What a lovely thing to adorn the altar for this funeral," Muireann said.

Maire's stomach clenched. The triptych.

"Maire, are you well?" Muireann asked.

"You do look pale," Émer said.

The triptych. The final payment was due tomorrow. Her morning had started with this deadline, dead as Ossnait, and her hope for another loan. Oh foolish, careless mind.

"The triptych! A shame its first appearance is the shrew's funeral," Émer said.

"Her name was Sister Ossnait, and she paid for most of it," Muireann said, offering a smile at Maire.

She should have paid for the remainder, until Maire's father sent the promised funds. Well, the requested funds. She had sent that request a month ago. Plenty of time for a gift of additional funds for this worthy gift to the convent.

"We do need a collection," one of the sisters said.

"Ridiculous. There is no time. The funeral should take place tomorrow or the next day. Let us celebrate, and plan for a ceremony of renewal in a few weeks, a month, when we have time to get new garments, and plan accordingly," said Émer.

A postponement, of course. She had to speak with the abbess.

"You are correct, Sister Émer, what a grand suggestion. A month. That should be plenty of time." Maire clutched her hand to her heart for this reprieve, already disappointed the new garments would have to wait. Bother this final payment for the triptych—of course she couldn't wait to see it and pay homage to God, the Savior, and Virgin Mary, a glory to behold, but that final payment. Her father really should have sent the money sooner. How could she juggle all this? Serenity, she counseled. And the beauty that would come.

"Muireann, would you be so very kind and write down the contributions for me. I know you all will be as generous as the rest. We are sisters of mercy, sisters of gratitude," Maire said. "I must speak with the abbess immediately."

"DEAREST, HIGHEST ABBESS," Maire said, nearly groveling at her feet, "continued blessing upon you in this dire hour. The funeral arrangements are underway, and each sister has come forward to pay tribute to our fallen Sister Ossnait." This was partially true. She would make the arrangements for the actual funeral soon, the next thing on her list, for tomorrow, or the day after. Responsibility upon her.

"May you have goodness," the abbess said, "fast work, sister. I am impressed."

"A thousand blessings upon you, I would relieve your burden, and I will be available after the service, in two days, mayhap," Maire said, giving herself another day to find serenity. "To help you with any letter writing you need done. I am a handy scribe, abbess."

"Again, may you have goodness, I will excuse you to your duties," the abbess said.

Maire didn't rise to leave.

"And?" the abbess said, glancing at Maire with a cocked eye of suspicion.

"Sorrow upon me to burden you with a minor detail associated with Sister Ossnait's passing. A small thing really," Maire said, truly a small thing in the scope of the convent. "A minor inconvenience due to the slow delivery of letters and funds."

"What? What are you saying? What inconvenience of funds? And what has it to do with Sister Ossnait? Her accounting is clean and paid."

"Ossnait was a good sister, responsible and efficient, as was, is, her family," Maire said, stating the positive. "There is a final payment due for the triptych. Tomorrow. Ossnait was going to pay this for me, while I awaited my father's tardy payment of funds. Which is due any day, upon my word." This truly was her father's fault, he was negligent in funding her, rather, funding the convent.

"Upon your word! Again, you have spent more than you have. Again, you have become a debtor, against the commandants. The convent doesn't have that amount. This was your idea, your contribution. Now you have the audacity to ask the convent for money? It is your function to bring in your living with your endowment, to bring in funds to support our work in service to God."

"True, abbess, true, but—" Maire scrambled. "My father's contribution is merely late. It will come." It must, she thought, crossing herself. "Abbess, by your will, we do not want to renege on the craftsmen. The convent should not be seen as not paying its debts."

"This is your debt, Sister Maire! Not the convent's!"

"True, true, but only for a few days. Sister Ossnait was going to cover the payment for me, at no burden to the convent. Surely, you understand the bad timing in this. I would never come to you for such a trifle. It is just bad timing."

"Trifle! Bad timing! You promised to have all the funds. You were responsible. Where is the money you promised months ago? You claimed all was collected."

She had the money then. Well, she would have had the money then, had her father's letters come on time. Had her sister Anu's prayer money not been cut by half. Bad timing, that! And the Easter celebration. Lent had been so trying this year, so much sacrifice. They all needed to imbibe and show their gratitude to God for his spring bounty, didn't they? Their lovely new garments were so soft upon the skin, radiant in God's creation. The silver cross the abbess wore even now caused Maire to glow.

"Only eight gold coins on the morrow. I shall pay it all back. Just as I would have to Sister Ossnait. Until then, let us not show bad faith to the craftsmen who have labored on this triptych. Let us rejoice in the beauty of their work, and the glory it shows in our reverence. Did not Jesus preach against the love of money? We are not to hoard it, but to spread the wealth."

"Maire! You go too far. You spend wealth that is not yours and claim to do it in God's and the Savior's name. You shall pray all the harder and go without food this day. How am I to recoup your losses? Foolish, frivolous girl, be gone from my sight."

"Abbess?" she asked, not leaving. "Your necklace. It is easily worth seven coins," she said, believing it a relic." Might we contribute that—"

The abbess's angry face became more rigid with hurt.

The abbess removed the cross necklace and slammed it on her desk.

"Maire, to give a gift—" The abbess said, her voice deep, "—then expect it returned is low and unworthy of even you."

Maire backed out of the chamber, head bowed, as the abbess's complaints and curses continued. But the payment would be made. All would be well, and surely this moment would be forgotten when the golden triptych was in place. Said item would redeem her. Serenity and beauty. The necklace could be bought back when her father's payment arrived. Shame and disappointment upon her for hurting the abbess. This was temporary. A quick remedy was at hand in a few days.

In the hallway outside the abbess's chamber, Maire tripped on a cat.

"I know you, you are Eclipse, Sister Oss—" It was Ossnait's beloved little feline. A black cat with white on her face, chest and all four paws. "Sorrow upon me, she is gone. The chamber must be so empty. We already have a cat residing in our chamber, or I would invite you to join me."

The cat rubbed against her legs, purring.

"I will do what I can," she said.

Maire joined Muireann in their chamber, and following her example, Maire picked up her distaff and spindle. What a day this was. Mayhap the rhythm of spinning would ease her mind.

"Sister Maire," The abbess said, stepping in the chamber, some comportment restored. "You have a letter from your sister."

"May you have goodness," Maire said, accepting the letter. Praying her sister had sent her more indulgence and prayer money.

The letter:

As you may recall in my past letters, my husband Lord Branán has been very ill. He is older than our father and seems to suffer the effects of old age more keenly. My youngest daughter and your namesake, Maire, has suffered a lingering illness and the surgeon has come frequently at great expense and with little success. You may recall from previous letters, unanswered by you, dearest little sister, that we are struggling, and I send what I can. Yours and your sisters' prayers are no more effective than the surgeon, but I hope this small sum will still earn continued supplications and indulgences.

Maire looked at the pittance of money enclosed and dropped the letter on her bed, the remainder unread. Disappointed, she evaluated her situation. *What do you expect, marrying and bearing children?* she asked her sister in her mind. *You chose that risk, the unbearable consequences. Blessed are your daughters to still have you alive.*

"That is enough to pay me back for the money I lent you for your new slippers," Muireann said, reaching for the coins.

"I–" Maire protested as the money was wrenched from her hand. "The convent needs that money."

"Your debts are huge, Maire, and all I see you do is beg for more money to indulge yourself further."

"How dare you," Maire said, rising in self-righteous indignity. "All I do is for our beloved convent and the glory of God."

"I don't see God wearing those new slippers."

"I wouldn't dishonor God with bare feet."

"While the Magdalene washed Jesus' bare feet with her hair."

"Are you suggesting we do that? Debase ourselves in a mockery of the saint's noble sacrifice? You hypocrite."

"Hypocrite, is it? I am not suggesting it. Nor do I claim false piety and exaggerated glory in spending extravagant amounts of convent funds on myself. I stay within my endowment. My family gives generously, and I live a grateful life within those means."

"False piety? We are sisters, true sisters, we share a bed. How can you be so cruel?"

"I am your sister, and I will tell you the truth. You must pay your debts to me, the sisters, and the convent. It would be cruel to let you keep sinning."

"Sinning?" Maire felt her eyes bulging, and surely her cheeks flared red as Hell's embers. Sinning, her? Eclipse hissed. At her or Muireann? "Compulsion upon me to share my good fortune with others. I want us all to thrive—"

"Borrowing money from someone to buy them a gift is not sharing your good fortune; it is squandering theirs."

"But—"

"It is wrong, you must desist. Go help the abbess with the letters you promised," Muireann said, "I too have work, spinning and prayers."

But, Maire thought, her argument unfinished as Muireann turned away from her. *I have such good ideas, I see things so creatively, for others and myself, all in the name of God.* That internal rush she got when planning, creating, anticipating, had to be the Holy Spirit within her. *It's not my fault my father, my blessed father, is so tardy with his messengers.*

MAIRE SAT at the table in the scriptorium of the convent, staring at the stacks of parchment. The abbess was still contemplating when to notify Ossnait's family. Maire thought it wrong to wait, but she was in bad grace with the abbess, and she kept her opinion to herself. So many letters to write. It was an excellent idea to again invite the wealthy families of all Ireland to consider the convent as a home for their unmarriageable women, whether they be young, elderly, or in between. Maire had begged to come here at thirteen with no regrets. She knew she would never marry or have children. Never. The brutality of the birth-chair was not for her. Saint Gobnait's was her calling.

The inkwell was full of black, boring ink, when she would prefer colorful paints, and she was continually sharpening the shortening goose quill to write.

My Dearest—

Whomever, each letter started,

I am writing to you from the Sisters of Saint Gobnait's Convent, an order of the most devout and pious, dedicated to the veneration of the Virgin Mary, the teachings of her son, our Savior, Jesus Christ, and most earnestly to all God's creation and wonderment. Ours is a quiet life of continual prayer, contemplation, and sanctity in our secure abbey, away from the pain and fear of the secular world. A place where your own daughter, sister, widow, aunt, cousin may come to live in safety and devotion. All our combined prayers give your name and family added favor in Our Lord's sight.

Ending with a generous space for the abbess to sign and stamp it.

These letters were stark and plain. Oh, how much better she could convey the message of serenity and beauty if only she had the proper tools: some paints, and brushes, not just a stale old quill. She could embellish the margins with intriguing scenes of their life. Mayhap not scenes, for that she would need a tutor. Bother. Yet, why not? What would a tutor cost? There must be a sister here capable of teaching her, at least helping her. Together they could do it. She only needed the proper tools and supplies to entice her sister to help. Oh, the letters they would create. The girls and ladies they would attract to Saint Gobnait's. So many funds and endowments would be forthcoming.

MAIRE WAS one of the last to scoot into the long, mournful, dreary afternoon mass, grieving over the loss of Sister Ossnait. *Whose idea was this sad theme,* she thought. *Weren't we celebrating Sister Ossnait's life? At least I organized the prayers and recitations for the funeral tomorrow, after we break fast.* The abbess droned on about how privileged they were to be here, how the sisters led a life of luxury in daily prayers and contemplations on God's wonders while others suffered in a myriad of ghastly ways.

A life of privilege? Were not she and the sisters born into the nobility? Had God not shown them supreme favor in most, but not all things? It was God's will they spend the hours of the days in gratitude for all the goodness that God created. Who better to contemplate the glory and give thanks? They were joyous brides of Christ in service to create and maintain serenity and beauty.

Of course, if others, like the saints, chose to serve lepers, let them. They would surely reap God's reward in Paradise. Orphans and widows, again, let those with a calling aid them. Again, was it not God's will? Were there not others who found their calling in those horrendous places? Bless them, she prayed for them, and would add more prayers for them. Yes, more prayers. God is listening. *I will pray more. I pray my father's messenger and the funds arrive. This triptych will show our devotion to God and the holy family. We are so grateful, and so in awe.*

"Amen," the abbess said.

"Amen," Maire said, thinking how inconvenient to end the mass now—she wasn't done with her prayers. She and her sisters shuffled to the dining hall.

Two servants met the abbess in the dining hall, concern on their weary faces. Maire was quick to rush to her side to hear the news. Was it her father's messenger?

"The craftsmen. Four of them. With the triptych," one of the servants said.

"Four? Is it that large?" the abbess said.

"They said it needed proper handling and assembly."

"Of course they arrived just in time to eat. We must eat, and it would be rude to make them wait, hungry as they must be. Expensive inconvenience," the abbess said with a huff.

"We set up tables in the courtyard, abbess, we will give sustenance there."

"And give them Sister Maire's wine portion, she has cost the convent enough this day, without the added cost in food for four hungry men."

Maire had not considered that inconvenience or expense. She must remember this detail next time. Curse her father's lazy messenger who had still not arrived. He would receive no such benefit.

The dining hall was aflutter with the news of the triptych. Oh, sacred day. Sacred treasure upon their very own altar. Maire wished she had a new garment for this momentous occasion. A cat rubbed her legs, and she looked down to see Eclipse's yellow eyes looking up at her. Maire quickly looked about the room, before breaking off a tiny morsel of the cheese to pass down to the black and white cat.

"Sister Maire," one of the senior sisters said in a scolding tone. "If you feed the cats they won't hunt. That is their function."

Maire dipped her head in feigned remorse. It was a small portion, and the cat was so lonely. A miniscule act of generosity, especially for Sister Ossnait's cat.

ALL THE SISTERS crowded into the chapel as the four men assembled the triptych, explaining in detail how to handle it, move it, clean it, and care for the magnificent piece of religious art. As the originator of the project, Maire was among the abbess and senior sisters to get this lesson in maintenance. It was not a trifle to be left to rot. It required labor to keep it glowing.

The clouds moved in, and the customary rain followed. But the golden paint on the triptych glowed all the brighter in the dim light.

Three wooden panels, with simple paintings, depicting the Annunciation, The Birth of Jesus, and the Crucifixion. Oh, how the sisters had argued over the images to depict. Maire persuaded them it should venerate the Virgin Mary as much as possible, being a humble woman as they were. Maire lost out to the last image being of Christ Resurrected and walking among his followers in the purest sunlight. Rather a grisly, not serene, crucifixion was chosen. Even now Maire wept with the visage. So much suffering and agony, when the resurrection was their redemption. He died that they might live in Heaven. To walk in God's and the Savior's light.

"It does glow. More so in the rain," the abbess said, "inspiring us all of God's glory."

It seemed all the sisters burst into tears, kyries, and hallelujahs at that moment.

But Maire thought how shabby the altar linens looked. They must create a grander cover for the altar to honor the triptych. Yes, the finest linen, no, silk, and the most exquisite thread for the work. And beads, jewels. A familiar tingle started in her core, igniting the sparks of joy spreading to her chest down to her toes. She must write to her father once again. She and her sisters could sew this piece all the while saying prayers for the lepers, orphans, sick and infirmed. And the pilgrims in Outremer. So many need prayers. Lapis Azul, dare she dream of it? Yes, it venerated the Virgin and all they stood for. *This convent needs me*, she thought. *Needs my vision and commitment to serenity and beauty.*

WHILE SISTER SIBÉAL was busy writing letters, Maire visited her other sisters. Again, Maire reflected on the abbess's neglect in asking her to write to Sister Ossnait's parents.

From chamber to chamber she went, met with the same skepticism and, surprisingly, rejection.

Her sisters refused to part with even the smallest uncarved piece of marble.

"Not another thing until you pay me back for the last two loans, Maire."

"You still owe me from Twelfth Night, Maire."

"The abbess said the convent had to pay your portion of the triptych. You must pay those funds back first."

"Slippers for you. New garments for Sister Ossnait's service. How about that ring you could not live without?"

"Write the letters, let your words serve God and the convent, not frivolous spending."

"Maire, how could you?'

"You still owe me."

"You still owe me."

"You still owe me."

Sullenly, Maire returned to the scriptorium. What stingy sisters she had. Her debts would be paid, as soon as her father's messenger arrived. Just this last time, and she would stop.

"Pleasure upon me to see you, Maire," Sibéal said, "my hands ache so, I have written eleven more letters. My soul and fingers long for assistance."

"It goes slowly, but all will be well. I am here now and I will write too," Maire said, putting on a smile, and taking her seat.

HER BODY PLAGUED her with discomforts and worry. Oh, sister Anu, you who knew so well a mother's love. God favored you with her love and a quiet home. You tried, surely, but you were a child and could not replace the love I never knew, because Mother died.

Mass started with another dreary session of wealth and poverty, sacrificing in God's service. But, of course, all they did here was in God's service. Wealth was to be invested in the soul through virtuous deeds. Wasn't that what she was doing? Of course, serenity and beauty in all things. Oh, blessed mass of renewal and validation. She clasped her hands together and looked up in joy.

"Abbess, there is a man to see you and Sister Maire," a servant said.

"Is it my father's messenger?" Maire asked, hope rising again.

"It is not, sister, it is your brother's messenger."

"My brother?" Maire said.

Oh, joyous moment, her brother's messenger. He must have come with news and funds. More prayers for my beloved brother, Maire thought. Mayhap her brother has welcomed a new baby. A niece or nephew, and the baby must have a gift from his beloved Aunt Maire.

The man stood in the courtyard inside the convent walls, looking dismal on this sunny morning.

"I have letters and a message to impart, but no funds," the messenger said. "I suggest we talk somewhere private, abbess. This is a very serious matter."

They retreated to the abbess's office.

"I have two letters. One from Sister Maire's brother and one from her father. I also have instructions." He handed the first letter to the abbess. She looked it over quickly, her face drained of color.

Then she read it aloud.

Abbess,

My father Lord U'Cléirigh has been relieved of his duties, leaving me the sad occasion to manage our estate. Great sorrow upon me and my family.

He has squandered all his funds on overwhelming debt and indulgences. We will be unable to continue paying for Maire to live at Saint Gobnait's.

This is no reflection of our high regard for the convent. We are grateful for the years that Maire was able to take comfort and sanctuary there. But no more payments will be forthcoming.

Despite the severe misfortune, there is great light. Lord Conan of the U'Neill's has generously offered to take Maire as his beloved wife and erase our debt against him and pay off much of the rest, assuming our estate as his own. This is a magnanimous offer. We rejoice in the merging of our families.

I will retrieve Maire in two weeks. I pray she can stay at the convent until then. This is a dire time, and the soonest I may come.

Lord U'Cléirigh, the Younger

"This is unfortunate news. For your family and ours," the abbess said.

Maire's hands shook so badly, she could not read her father's letter. Somewhere in the words it must instruct her not to listen to her brother. There was a huge misunderstanding. She would not marry. Father had promised.

"Maire, would you like me to read that to you?" the abbess asked.

Maire shook her head; she would not share her father's private letter.

"Lord U'Cléirigh, the younger, asked me to beg your forgiveness, as he does in his letter. He tried in vain to intercede, but Lord U'Cléirigh, the Elder, kept too many secrets and spent money as if there were no end to his wealth or estate. He gave money to his friends, made bad loans, and—" the messenger left the rest hanging. "Your brother has taken responsibility for the estate as it is and is making every effort to keep your father from prison."

"He bids me tell you to do your part," he said to Maire.

"This is dire news indeed. May you have goodness for bringing it to us in all haste. Sister Maire and I have much to contemplate. Do you need anything from us, sir?" the abbess asked the messenger. "Do you have arrangements to spend the night in town?"

"First, I pray that Maiden Maire can stay here the two weeks, and not travel back with me. I am sleeping in stables or rough on the return."

Her brother could not even afford a room for his hired messenger. How poor were they? And did he call her Maiden Maire? A shriek was building within her, threatening to burst through her chest.

"I see. That is rough. Sister Maire may live and work here for the next two weeks, but that is all I can promise."

Sister Maire! Of course, she would live here. Forever. The abbess would find a way.

"I will be at the livery, in the stable, if you have any questions or letters to return with me, someone can find me there until I leave in the morning."

The abbess excused him.

"Sister Maire, this is horrific news. Gratitude upon us all that no one has died, your family is healthy. But this reversal in fortune. Unfortunate. Unexpected. Disappointing."

Maire knew she should say something. There were so many words in her head. Was she speaking? She could not, because she didn't know what to say. Useless words clouded her mind. Poor. Married. Disappointment—more like betrayal.

"You and your father suffer the same affliction. Debt and sorrow upon us all. Two weeks is not enough time to work off your debts to the convent, but we will get out of you what we can."

Two weeks to find a way out of this problem.

"Maire, you are to reside in the servants' quarters. Your labors start now. Everything in your chamber, including those slippers, are forfeit, confiscated, until I can calculate. Have you anything to say?"

She had much to say, but she was mute with disbelief. She needed to go to bed and think.

"Orla," the abbess called out.

When Orla entered, she was instructed to take Maire to the servants' quarters first, find her a place to sleep, and then send her to the kitchens and have the head cook put her to work.

Orla looked as shocked as Maire felt. Work in the kitchen? When would she wake from this nightmare?

"Wait, first, by your will, let me write to my sister. Let me implore her to intercede," Maire wailed at the abbess.

"Write to your sister. Even your brother. I will have them sent to the messenger," the abbess said.

"My lady sister, Anu, is a kind woman, and has supported me here."

What a letter I will send her, Maire thought as she stalked to the scriptorium. So much betrayal by all of them. I shall never marry. Not take a husband, not risk pregnancy and death. Eclipse nearly tripped her and she cursed the retreating feline.

WORK SHE DID. What filth and hard labor. When the cook realized she knew nothing of food preparation, Maire had to clean the ashes, gather wood and peat, then help stir the soup for the evening meal. Numb from the reversal of status, Maire moved through the day. Though famished, the thought of eating made her retch.

"You have done nothing but make more work for us all. Your misfortune is our punishment, Sister Maire. Still, you must eat. Sit and get this in you," the head cook said.

Maire looked at the hard bread before her, rat-chewed from the night before.

"You soak it in the watered ale," the cook said. "Then you can swallow it."

Maire stared at the woman.

"You are no longer an esteemed sister in the convent. You are not the first one to have her benefactor dry up or disappear. It happens to many sooner or later," the head cook said.

"You are lucky, in two weeks you will marry and once again live a life of privilege," another maid said.

"I will never marry. I will work off my debts here," Maire said.

"The abbess extends you great courtesy, sister. See you honor her," another said.

Honor the abbess? For sending her to the kitchen? The vegetable gardens! Her skills and talents were wasted in both places. The abbess, and God, must be testing her. She would soon return to her chamber with Muireann. Her work in the scriptorium with Sister Sibéal. Oh, how they complained about those long hours writing. What a luxury those hours seemed now. How long would it take for her fingers to be free of the filth of the kitchen and the dirt of the vegetable garden? The flower garden was never so messy, was it? It was. She played in the dirt, planting the seeds or cuttings, yet that dirt washed away – no, it lingered as a reminder of her service to serenity in the moment and the beauty to come. The dirt of the vegetables should serve as a reminder. *I am listening. I am humble.*

Ten days later

"Maire," Orla said, with a nod, "you received a letter."

"Who is it from?" Maire asked knowing Orla couldn't read.

"The abbess said it was from your sister."

Anu, finally, oh gracious sister, true sister, Maire thought as she grabbed the letter from Orla's hand. The seal was broken. The abbess had read it. Curse her. Maire was sure the letter of outrage and insult she had sent back with her brother's messenger would have brought her sister, if not her family to their senses. Beloved, practical Anu.

Maire, you selfish child. How dare you refuse to marry Lord Conan of the U'Neill's? How dare you refuse anything your Lord Father or brother would ask.

They didn't ask, Maire thought, outraged. *They demanded.*

We are destitute. Father's records reveal outrageous amounts of funds

sent to you well beyond the monthly allowance, while we struggled with
mounting debts, taxes, servants' demands.

It is your turn to serve this family and your Lord Father, who has
foolishly and extravagantly supported you in a life none of us enjoy.

In all these seven long years, you have never written back to me
inquiring of my husband's failing health or my beloved daughters. When
you do write, it is to ask for money or refuse your obligation.

Selfish child. I have burdens you cannot imagine.

I will see you at your wedding.

Anu

Maire hardly knew what to make of this. To be so dismissed by her sister. A sister who benefited from a loving mother and a home of serenity and beauty. Selfish child. Burdens. Ones Anu chose willingly. *I will not marry, I will not have children.* Anu was there for her beloved daughters. Maire's mother died in her childbirth. Kind as the nurses were, she had no one to call mother. No child deserved that. She would never risk that fate.

A strange noise caught their attention, and both women turned to see Eclipse scoot by, her normal sing-song disrupted by a mouse in her mouth. She is getting fat, Maire noted, feeding this little cat was no detriment to her hunting.

"More bad news? Orla asked.

Maire glared at her. "Didn't the abbess tell you what it said?"

"Of course not. But your expression. I would offer condolences and prayers for your family."

"May you have goodness," Maire said, of course a servant would honor a family as hers. "The news is not what I hoped, but no one has died."

Maire followed the cat to the scriptorium. She would write Anu a letter of contrition, and her brother. Was the cat purring? Melodious little creature. Her hands could barely write the words, *I will be ready, Brother.*

MAIRE'S KNEES hurt so much, she burst into tears just thinking about another day bent and cleaning. But sweep and scrub she must. At least in the kitchen and vegetable garden she was safe from the view of her convent sisters. Not one of them came to her aid. Not one offered her succor or space in their bed until the time she could unravel her financial disaster. It seemed all they remembered was the money she owed them. Loans she always meant to pay back. Blast her wasteful father.

Financial disaster. Her life in shambles. Scorn, ridicule, and isolation. Could married life be worse than this? She would not have to bend to low work like this. She would dine at a table with her family.

When was her brother coming? Four days. Four more days, and this could be over. Secular life must be better than life as a servant, a slave to the convent with no hope for a better situation. *Be done with this*, she told herself. You will make a serene and beautiful life with your—she could barely think the word in her mind—husband. How did it come to this? Don't think of him, think of the peace and glory you can both find in God's service.

God...how could you? You must have a better plan for me. I have reconciled. I will marry and leave this life of servitude. Four days. I will be ready.

THE DAY CAME bright and sunny, a glorious July day. A day to rejoice in God's favor before the altar and the triptych, the flower garden or even the laborious scriptorium. Oh, bother, not today, for never again would she be part of this life. Today her brother was coming and good riddance to this convent and the sisters of hypocrisy. She would be Sister Maire no longer. Again, she fought back those bitter tears, thinking of her new life as a proper lady of an estate. Lady U'Neill.

Maire stood to stretch her aching back, her mind drifting to what this day would hold— *She would save her family after all. The prodigal daughter.*

"Get back to work, you," the cook barked. "That only prolongs your suffering."

Sweeping out the hearth, Maire's mind returned to her future. *We will rejoice in this homecoming.* A hot trencher placed before her. Her beloved nieces at her knee, *Auntie Maire*, they would sing, throwing their arms around her. And new garments. Fresh, clean chemises in the finest linen, and surcoats and tunics. Would these be waiting for her, or would she order them herself? If only she still had her slippers. On the contrary, leave that painful memory behind. She was almost feverish with the feel of a clean linen chemise upon her scrubbed flesh. The glimmers of her religious rapture welled within her while considering beautiful things, once for her and the convent.

All this she thought of as the day wore on.

"You'll work until your Lord Brother comes for you. Heaven knows you have created more for the rest of us than you contribute. Good riddance, I say," said one of the kitchen servants, and not for the first time.

"Keep at it. And may you gain some humility and kindness for your servants when you are a high and fine lady again," Orla said, giving a polite nod.

Beloved Virgin, Maire thought, *protect me from a cruel*—again the word caught. *Blessed Virgin, Mother of us all, by your will, grant me a gentle husband. If I am called to your service thus, he surely must be a good, kindly man. In this I am most scared.*

The sun passed slowly on this summer day. A day of new beginnings that seemed to take forever. Where was her Lord Brother? Why the delay? Was he not to spare her all this continued humiliation as a mere laborer when she was of the nobility, like the Virgin Mary, the Queen of Galilee? Curse her tardy brother. Was everyone in her family so deficient in time management? She stopped. Like herself, mayhap, didn't she also miscalculate, forget the day? She had to admit, she did. A family trait.

As the sisters said their evening prayers, Maire prayed with them, though she still bent to her work. Prayers were prayers, and this ritual had become part of her being. Was this the time her Lord Brother would come? To hear the prayer song, it was a beautiful time of day, when she stole a moment to gaze about. *Brother, oh brother, I am listening for the hoofbeats.*

The sun set, as much as it did in July, and for once Maire was not wishing for the luxury of even her servant's pallet, she should be sleeping in a bed in an inn. Well on her way from this drudgery.

"Maire," the abbess said, joining her in the courtyard. "Your brother is not coming today. Sleep and see what tomorrow brings."

HE DID NOT COME. He did not come. And again, he did not come.

On the fourth day of him not coming, the abbess summoned Maire to her office.

"We must accept he may not come. I extended him much courtesy to keep you here at the convent, rather than turn you out. But we must consider the future," the abbess said.

"What future? He will come, and until then I will persevere," Maire said. She had already suffered indignities for this foolish episode, and it made her mad at her father yet again. To be so careless with his money and forget his promise to her: That she live here forever free from the horror of marriage and childbirth. This was to compensate for having no mother.

"Until that time, I must consider what is best for the convent. You still have unpaid debts to the convent as well as to your sisters here. Everyone complains to me of your inability to put in a full day's work, and all must work the harder to clean up after you. You continue to be a burden."

Were the insults and persecution ceaseless? How dare they complain that she didn't work hard enough. A waste of her talents and skills before God. She crossed herself as inappropriate words crossed her mind. *I will be peaceful and find beauty.*

"I am better fit to serve the convent in the scriptorium, Abbess."

ONE WEEK LATER, a letter arrived for Maire from her sister, Anu. Again, Maire found herself in the abbess's office with no privacy to read the contents.

> *Dear Maire,*
>
> *So much has happened I am still breathless.*
>
> *My Lord Husband died from his long-suffered malady. A relief for him, his last days were fraught with financial worry and grief. God has welcomed him as sure as I take breath. Our time of mourning was too brief, almost not all.*
>
> *My daughters and I needed the protection and guidance of a grand lord, and Lord Conan U'Neill was only too happy to accept us as his willing and loving family. We hid your true feelings from him and told him your convictions to the convent were incontrovertible for you to consider marriage. This he accepted. Understand, Maire, we do not have the funds to support you at Saint Gobnait's. You must fund your own way, as you insisted yourself.*
>
> *We were married one week ago, keeping Brother Lóch here for the service.*
>
> *You are free to continue your chosen life as a sister of Gobnait's or whatever convent you choose. Your family obligations to us are at an end, as are ours to you.*
>
> *I will endeavor to send indulgence and prayer funds as I can. I am still your blood sister and will keep you in my prayers as I hope you will us.*
>
> *Lady Anu U'Neill*

Maire read the letter again. Her own letter of contrition, agreeing to marry, arrived too late if at all. Lord U'Neill. Her family obligations were at an end as were theirs— did that really mean Lord U'Neill would not continue with her annual endowment? Or send the money she still owed as Father had promised?

She must write another letter explaining her misunderstanding, her true convictions as Anu said. Oh, a beautiful, hand-painted letter to convince the beneficent Lord U'Neill what an honor that his own sister-in-law was one of the esteemed Sisters of Saint Gobnait's and the power of their combined prayers would continue to ensure the good health and fortunes of him and his cherished family. She had to get back to the scriptorium.

"We both know what the letter says," the abbess said. "You are a poor girl with no family resources. You had a chance at marriage and refused. Your brother-in-law has no legal responsibility for you. As we both understand from your brother's and father's earlier letters, he has taken much of your father's debt. He refused to assume yours as soundly as you refused him. What am I to do with you?"

"With me? Abbess, I have many skills worthy of the Sisters of Saint Gobnait. By your will, let me return to the scriptorium. The letters I would write. First to my new and illustrious brother-in-law. Already the words and letters form in my mind. A letter of beauty and piety."

"You never learn, frivolous girl. You are a child of God, but I have been too lenient. You and your father, both. A plague upon us."

"By your will, let me write letters. Even if by candlelight after my long day of labor. I love Saint Gobnait's. I know this is God's place for me. You have seen my handwriting, I can contribute."

"By candlelight. Bah, a waste of candles, and with your carelessness you will burn the convent down."

Maire hung her head, hoping she looked penitent.

"You do have a good hand when you work, and Sister Sibéal needs assistance. Clean up a bit and meet us there. We must get a letter to Sister Ossnait's family. I have let the weeks sail by. Shame upon me. Sorrow upon us losing her endowment as well as yours. Sorrow."

"May you have goodness, Abbess."

Joy upon her to be back in the scriptorium. This she could do, and without all the complaints of the others. She picked up the quill and it felt foreign as if her fingers had forgotten how to hold it after her long labors. This sacred tool, power in her hand, she could read and write. A gift she never appreciated until this moment. *May you have goodness, abbess, saints, the Virgin, Saviour, and God.* She started writing to Sister Ossnait's parents.

Dear Lord and Lady FitzHugh,

I requested the honor of writing to you, though it is with the greatest sorrow that I do.

Your beloved daughter, Ossnait, was chosen too soon by God to ascend to Him in Heaven. We all suffer great sorrow in her loss. She was a true treasure among the sisters, one of God's brightest lights of beauty and peace, the reason we are here. To honor beauty and maintain serenity as pleases the Virgin, her son, our Savior, and our Lord God."

Maire went on in brief description to tell them of Ossnait's short, sudden illness. Proving to all how God longed for her in Heaven. It did not seem necessary to sadden them further by telling them how she complained all the time about this and that, ailments and aches, and grievous anger upon her.

"Maire," the abbess said from the doorway, "You may finish tomorrow. Blow out the candles and come with me. It is time for bed."

INSPIRATION STILL WITH HER, and eager to prove to the abbess she belonged in the convent, Maire rushed to the scriptorium at first light. Her greatest work to date.

There on the table was her letter. But it was not as she left it. The quill was not to be seen. There was a dead mouse by the tipped inkwell, and across her elegantly written letter were cat prints. Her letter, her masterpiece.

"Eclipse, what have you done? Oh, foul fiend, how could you?"

Maire started to cry. So many weeks she had fought the weakness, as if the tears rained defeat. In trying not to be wasteful, she had been careless. Could she salvage the letter, the valuable parchment? She wiped her eyes with her apron and looked for the quill. It was under the table, well chewed. "Eclipse!"

Quill in hand Maire returned to the letter.

Sorrow upon me that Sister Ossnait's cat has walked across this letter to you. Parchment is so dear, ink too, and I am but an indebted sinner to have been so careless, when I had wished to send you warmth in your beloved daughter's memory.

It seems this cat is my only friend at the convent. Not only did she walk across this letter of bereavement, but she left a mouse, that this poor sister might have sustenance after all. Oh, selfish girl, mayhap the cat has left her gift in memory of your lost daughter and not me at all.

Humility upon me.

Sister Ossnait was once considered a shrew by some. She must have suffered greatly in her soul to show this to the world. What turmoil, what pain distressed her? But here she could be viewed in beauty. Her contributions eased the suffering of many among us, while I caused grievous pain. I wanted to share as Sister Ossnait did. I thought if I were more like Sister Ossnait I could fill the void in my heart left by my mother's death. A mother I never knew. We do not know what others suffer, especially if we do not ask.

I squandered my chances and remained the mouse my family thought me. I will try harder to follow in the true light of God's plans for me.

Sister Ossnait of the FitzHugh's brought beauty to Saint Gobnait's. Her kindness and generosity extended to her beloved cat, who in her absence has become my constant companion, her purrs and hisses mayhap guiding my steps more than I understand.

Our hearts are broken as surely as yours are. Our grief is immense, but we honor the light and goodness Ossnait provided for the short time she walked among us as a sister of Saint Gobnait's.

Maire had kept writing as if her hand were possessed. When she finished, she looked at her words. What had she written? Had she truly written she was a sinner, when she meant sister? What careless handwriting. The words had flowed, not at all what she thought she would write. No one liked Ossnait. Yet, the cat's presence erased her harsh memories, and replaced them with longing and remorse. Did the cat know things about Ossnait that she did not? Had a saint come in the form of a feline to show her a better way? Nonsense. Maire would be cast out by the time the letter reached them. What bitter shame she felt in that revelation. *What is wrong with me?* she asked, still trying to make beauty here.

Once the ink was dry, she folded and melted the sealing wax. *What fate this?* she wondered. There was a cat whisker by the metal stamp. She placed it on the melted wax and sealed it in. "Let this be from both of us, Eclipse."

EACH DAY BROUGHT MORE WORK, more weariness, and so much ugliness. She felt useless and unfit. Her nights were haunted with nightmares of being lost in town. Lost in the woods. Being pursued. Unwelcome. Naked and dirty, so dirty before God that she tried to hide as Adam and Eve had.

Each night when she fell back on her hard pallet, with the thin woolen blanket, she was grateful the abbess had not cast her out yet. More so on the nights when Eclipse and her new kittens curled up with her. She found enchantment with the cat's purring. Eclipse and her mixed kittens were small beauties, one black, one gray tabby and one black and white, but without her mother's distinct marking as a sister's uniform. *You should be hunting and earning your keep,* Maire thought, stroking the beautiful mother cat. Tomorrow. There was always tomorrow.

A MESSENGER ARRIVED WITH A LETTER.

Maire had long given up hope on correspondence from her family. She prayed daily for them, even without the expectation of indulgences and funds. In her days of longing and remorse, she finally made time to read her sister Anu's letters.

Correspondence of the illnesses, deprivations, and concern for her. Was she hungry? Did the abbess take all her endowment and leave her and the sisters unattended? They heard rumors of terrible convents. Brothels. Father reassured Anu it was not so. And always sorrow that Maire had not known their mother. It was hard on them all to lose Mother. But hardest on poor baby Maire, who had barely known her mother's touch, her serenity and beauty.

Why hadn't she read these letters as they came? Now she savored and relished each one. Anu had fretted and worried over her as a mother would. With all the suffering in Anu's life, she kept Maire in her thoughts. Dear, kind Anu. Maire felt small and petty, the mouse. Not understanding her family's problems, she had been a selfish child. Was she still? Making more work for others? Letter writing took much time now, as the abbess dictated letters for her to write, leaving her to do many of her cleaning chores by the summer light of night.

How had Anu known the deepest longing in her soul? Seeking serenity and beauty, mayhap seeking what she thought a true mother's touch would be like.

MAIRE AND SIBÉAL were hunched over the scriptorium table, Eclipse hunting while the kittens played at their feet. Hissing and jumping, they were an adorable distraction from the scriptures they were copying. It was such sacred and tedious work.

"Sister Maire," Orla called. Maire relished anew when Orla or the others forgot and called her by sister. What joy she took in the sound and meaning.

"The abbess needs to see you."

Maire stood and stretched, before rushing to the abbess's office.

As Maire entered, Eclipse came out from under the desk and greeted her. A well-dressed man and woman sat on chairs.

"By your will, sister," the abbess said, and Maire thought she was going to ask her to remove the cat. Eclipse jumped up on the windowsill. The abbess shook her head and Maire looked over her shoulder, mouthed, "Eclipse, go feed your kittens." Maire walked to the desk and the stern abbess glared at her further.

"This is Sister Maire," the abbess said.

So, she was Sister Maire for this couple. She stared at them in their fine travel attire. The man stood. He seemed her father's age, though she hadn't seen her father in seven years. He had brown hair and beard, and both showed much gray. His green and gray surcoat was made of sturdy wool for travel, and his unbleached tunic had small, detailed seams and stitches speaking to his wealth. A war sword hung from his belt, along with a large dagger, his traveling pouch at his side, and a letter in his hand. His wife, for she could be no other, Maire thought, was clad similarly to him, garments finely made but subtle— a travel surcoat and chemise and a riding wimple with a veil pulled up. Her lined eyes were red, and even now she dabbed at them with a hand cloth.

"Sister Maire, this is Lord and Lady Fitzhugh from Leinster, Sister Ossnait's parents. They have come all this way to meet with you."

Ossnait's parents.

Lord FitzHugh bowed to her.

"Sister, pleasure upon us to finally meet you. By your will take a seat and let us speak," FitzHugh said, sitting.

Maire took a stool by the desk. Was that her letter he held? What now? She quickly glared at Eclipse. *See what you've done?* Eclipse lifted her leg and licked herself.

"Sorrow upon us to hear of our daughter Ossnait's passing. So young. So much life yet to give."

The wife was weeping yet smiling through her tears. What manner of grief was this? Maire wondered, worry upon her they found great fault with her letter. Sweat formed under her arms.

"Your letter," he held it up. "Your kind words of Ossnait brought us great comfort in this dark time."

Would she witness a lord cry? Pray not.

He read: "One of God's brightest lights of beauty and peace, the reason we are here. To honor beauty and maintain serenity as pleases the Virgin, her son, our Savior and our Lord God." His wife fought her tears. "You go on to praise her and her deeds, that God needed her in Heaven." He sniffed back his own grief.

The abbess glared from FitzHugh to Maire.

"Our daughter was a difficult child, grown into an obnoxious young woman. Marriage was not forthcoming, nor could we manage her in our home any longer with the disruption and chaos as she berated her siblings and the servants with a viper's tongue."

She was all that, Maire remembered, not at all fitting with Saint Gobnait's mission.

"To know she found redemption; found God's light here under your guidance, Abbess, and her sisters," he nodded to Maire. "What more could a parent hope for: a lost child found, reborn."

"And the cat," Lady FitzHigh said through her sniffles, "I love cats. Ossnait did too. They were her one love and weakness. This letter, her cat, your understanding." She took the letter from her husband's hand and held it up for the abbess to see. "This speaks to me as if Ossnait sent the letter herself. My precious child redeemed. You," she glanced at Maire, "or a saint, or God himself sent a whisker in the sealing wax. I tell you this is a miracle."

"Sister Maire, you called yourself a sinner and doubted your worth to be here, yet I see no sin in this letter. And truly, if my daughter, if Ossnait could find salvation, you are in the best hands with the abbess and your sisters here."

Had he read sinner rather than sister too?

"Is her cat still here?" Lady FitzHugh asked.

Fighting her own tears, Maire pointed to Eclipse.

"Sister Maire has taken great care of the cat since Ossnait left us. Prodigious care," the abbess said, changing her allegiance to the cat so quickly it made Maire's head spin. Hadn't they all told her to stop spoiling the cat?

"Her name is Eclipse, black and white. She has three kittens now, in the scriptorium with Sister Sibéal," Maire said. "She should be there now feeding them, yet here she is."

The abbess and the FitzHugh's all looked at the cat still licking herself on the windowsill.

"Before God and the saints, I tell you that cat has never come into my office before. Never. What mystery this?" the abbess said, still staring.

"Eclipse, Ossnait?" Lady Fitzhugh called to the cat, as if the cat may well be her daughter's spirit. The cat ignored her and continued cleaning.

"Cats do what cats do," Lord FitzHugh said, returning his attention to the meeting.

"As I say we have gratitude that our daughter found her way and had as big an impact on you as you did on her. This is a sacred place. A worthy place."

"May you have goodness, my lord, a thousand blessings upon you and your house," the abbess said, head dipped nearly to the desk's flat surface.

"We would like to keep Ossnait's memory shining bright despite her short life. If you are willing and amenable, we would like to propose a humble endowment for Saint Gobnait's in the name of Sister Ossnait. Might we discuss this? And in her lifetime as a sister of Saint Gobnait's, it would be meaningful for us if Saint Ma—" He paused and chuckled with his slip, "I started to say saint, but I meant Sister Maire was to administer it. To keep the light shining for others."

"That is most generous, my lord, most thoughtful. Saint Gobnait's would be honored, in Ossnait's and FitzHugh's name," the abbess said with a saintly smile of beatification.

"What do you say, Sister Maire?" he asked.

"I would love nothing more, my lord. Honor upon me." But Maire was not truly a sister anymore. Dare she say it? "The abbess and I have much to discuss, my lord. This is not a decision I should make without consulting with her," Maire said. Eclipse was rubbing against her legs; the purring filled the small office.

"I think Eclipse has spoken," Lady Fitzhugh said, smiling. "Ossnait demands that Sister Maire administer her memory."

Time for truth, time for reckoning.

"This cat has guided my hand and my soul, mayhap it is the work of Ossnait, a saint, or God. I am unworthy of answering. It is also true, sin upon me. My wasteful ways lost me the privilege of being a sister of Saint Gobnait's. I begged for money, borrowed funds beyond my or my family's means. I had—" She stopped. Her visions, her dreams were excessive. Her sister, Anu, and her friends here had warned her, counseled her otherwise. No more excuses. "I labor in the kitchen and garden for our food. My reward is to work in the scriptorium."

"I don't understand," Lord FitzHugh said, looking from her to the abbess.

"Her father can no longer pay her endowment," the abbess said. "And I have allowed her to continue living and working here."

"My Lord Father was no better at managing his estate than I. Blessing upon me not to be cast out. I love it here," Maire said. "I have nowhere else to go. And the cat needs me," she said, reaching down to stroke the rubbing, purring cat.

"We must talk then," Lord FitzHugh said as his stern expression moved from Maire to the abbess and then to his wife.

Sister Maire. How sweet the sound, she thought, holding the purring Eclipse in her lap, the three kittens playing on the floor. Maire had requested and was granted a pallet set up outside the chapel. As a sister of Saint Gobnait's once again, she no longer need sleep with the servants, she could return to her chamber, mayhap her bed with Muireann. But not this night. Maire needed quiet to contemplate her future.

"I have been granted a reprieve and redemption," she whispered, both to the cat and God. "Lord FitzHugh decreed that I must administer his daughter's memorial endowment. We discussed a feast day, and—" It was so much, and a further spark. "I must pray for guidance." Eclipse rubbed her hand as if in question, *what spark*, or just demanding her full attention on the gentle strokes and chin scratches.

"I recounted all the debts I could remember, and that drew greater memories from me. Debt and deceit, all in a wrongful desire to serve God. Yet Lord Fitzhugh demanded to repay it all, saying he needed forgiveness and redemption. Confusing that, what did he have to atone for?

"Eclipse, I tell you my hands shook. I felt awash with relief, and the budding flush upon my skin at the thought of the glory I could create with those funds." The false glory, misdirected service.

"Heavenly Father, holiest Virgin, weakness upon me. I desire to be strong in Your service," she said, starting her prayer in earnest. Did she really need to ask anything? She thought of her dear Anu, and the gracious letters full of heartache and struggles. Her brother's hard-fought battle to save their father from prison weighed on her. All three of them had lost a wife and mother. Mayhap it was harder for her siblings to have lost a mother they knew and loved. Maire had not gone unloved, she had nurses, siblings, and a father. Further, they had all stood by her, granting her more than she deserved. She had been a selfish child to assume she had suffered the greatest loss.

"Redemption upon me in repaying my debts. I will work to prove I can resist temptation. You have provided much, Heavenly Father, and I will honor Sister Ossnait's memory and the generosity of the Fitzhughs, but I cannot yet be trusted with the funds. I must learn how. I will listen to the abbess and my sisters. I will mark the days with care and honor the labor of all around me."

Maire was trembling again. Was this a new awakening?

"May you have goodness," she whispered in thanks to God. No more begging, no more borrowing. Tomorrow would come without deceit on her mind.

SISTER MAIRE BID a tearful farewell to the FitzHughs as well as two of Eclipse's kittens. Neither she nor Eclipse need ever worry about leaving Saint Gobnait's.

"They will be back in six months, sister," the abbess said. "You will have a full report for them on the progress with Sister Ossnait's memorial, and they will tell of the kittens."

"A miraculous turn of events, isn't it? Unless it is sacrilegious to use the word," Maire said as they turned to leave, Maire to the vegetable garden, the abbess to her office.

"I would never have expected it," said the abbess. "That a letter

bespoiled by a cat would have such a profound effect. That a cat
— Honestly, sister, it is hard to believe. The little fiend—"

"The Fitzhughs are dear people. What a kind and noble family.
Blessing upon me to have them sponsor me as part of the endowment
of their daughter."

"Strength and redemption upon you for refusing to take responsibility of the funds upon yourself," the abbess said. "Or their generous
offer to pay off your debts to the convent and sisters."

"I need to prove it to myself and before all of you I can live within
my humble means. I must continue my labors in the garden and
kitchen at a servant's wages to pay those debts, no longer hiding from
my shame, my deceit. My work in the scriptorium is more precious
than ever," she said, still feeling the potential within her, the rightness
of her place in the convent to make beauty and serenity with her own
hands. The spark was igniting. "Then, together we will all make Sister
Ossnait's name shine, just as God desires."

HISTORICAL NOTES:

In the Middle Ages, convents were a rich and powerful part of the
economy. They weren't even built unless a wealthy patron, like a king,
duke, or count, donated land and built structures. As they grew,
convents acquired properties that were worked by tenant farmers and
conducted trade that made them even more wealthy. Noble girls who
entered the convent paid a dowry to do so. They lived in single cells
that were well furnished, received personalized meals, and followed
few rules. Girls from humble origins, however, were given manual
labor. The abbess ruled over it all like a feudal lord.

ABOUT THE AUTHOR

Anne M. Beggs is an award-winning author of historical fiction and has published articles on mounted archery and horsemanship. Her debut novel, Archer's Grace, Book One in her Dahlquin series, starts this family saga when a young noblewoman in medieval Ireland is set on a quest to save her family and ancestral home. Additionally, three short stories appear in Paper Lantern Writer's anthologies, including the award-winning *Unlocked*. Still married to her high school sweetheart, they live on and manage a horse boarding ranch, Equisance, in Watsonville, California. Anne is a member of the Historical Novel Society and the Paper Lantern Writers. For more about her writing, horses, mounted archery and more, see AnneMBeggs.com.

AN EYE FOR AN EYE

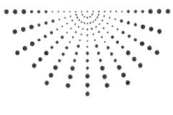

C.V. LEE

Note: This short story is based on a real villain and deeply unsettling true events, including infanticide.

FEBRUARY 1555, ISLE OF JERSEY

Reverend Richard Averty hummed as he ambled up the path toward home. He paused at the curve to rest beneath the elm tree and gaze out at St. Berlade's Bay. The sun dipped below the horizon and streaks of orange and purple peeked through the thick cloud cover, accompanied by the thunderous crash of winter waves against the shore. Such unfathomable beauty. One of the many blessings from God.

Despite the wave of heresy disguised as reform that had swept across Europe over the previous forty years, Richard remained steadfast in the true faith. His devotion had earned him a position of proctor in the Ecclesiastical Court. When Queen Mary ascended the throne a little more than a year previously, she had committed to the eradication of the Protestant movement from England. Richard was sensible to the honor of being chosen to further this same God-given mission on Jersey.

He would have stayed longer to marvel at the glorious majesty of God's creation, but the cold had seeped through his many layers of clothing. He hastened along the path to his humble cottage.

The aroma of stew greeted him as it bubbled on the stone hearth and mingled with the scent of fresh cut rushes. A trencher, chalice, and pitcher of ale waited on the table.

Marie Bellèe, a buxom young woman with light brown hair whom he employed as a servant, looked up as she stirred the pot. Her smile quickened his pulse. "I trust you had a profitable day, Reverend."

He hung his cloak on a peg beside the door. "Indeed. Every day spent in the Lord's work is a profitable day." He stepped to the fire to soak in the warmth and dispel the chill from his bones.

Marie fetched a bowl and ladled out a portion of stew and placed it on the table with a curtsy. "Supper is served, Reverend."

His eyes locked with hers, then dipped lower. Her blue cotehardie strained across her ample bosom. A smile tugged at the corner of his mouth and he licked his lips. Her breasts looked like plump pomegranates ready to be plucked. "It can wait. I prefer to take my pleasure before I sup."

Marie glided toward the bedchamber. She glanced over her shoulder, a sultry look in her eyes. What a marvel that this beautiful, sensual creature had been sent to serve in his home. So many talents, not only in the kitchen and housekeeping but also the way she warmed his bed and satisfied his baser needs. Another of God's gracious blessings. He followed, eager to taste her sweetness.

The chamber had been straightened, and the bed turned down. A fire crackled on the hearth, and Marie's hair and skin glowed like an angel in the firelight as she stood beside the bed. He would lie with her, and afterward, they would sup together, then sit before the hearth and talk, while the flames chased away the harsh winter cold.

Richard eased up behind her, unlaced her cotehardie, and pushed down the sleeve of her kirtle. He brushed her hair aside and placed a line of kisses along her shoulder. She turned in his arms and let the kirtle drop to the floor as she unbuttoned his cassock.

With nothing left between them, they fell onto the bed, impatient to explore new heights of passion. After, he wrapped his arms around her and she snuggled up beside him. He sighed contentedly. *A bit of heaven on earth.*

She ran a finger down his breastbone. "Your ardor today is unmatched, Reverend. Pray tell, what has brought this about."

Pride swelled his breast. "I removed the benefices of two priests who refused to forsake their wives and children."

Marie's eyes widened. "With no means of support, how will they survive?"

He kissed her crown. How he loved her innocence, her complete lack of comprehension about the wrath of God. "'Tis not my concern. They freely chose to feed the desires of their flesh and took wives. The punishment is just. They cannot expect to continue to minister after the betrayal of their vows."

"But what of us, Richard? Have we not done the same but outside the bonds of matrimony?" Her voice was so hushed, he strained to catch her words.

"You and I are different. Ours is a holy union sanctioned by the God of Heaven."

She sat up, drew in her knees, and wrapped her hands around her legs. "How can you be so sure?"

"Must I remind you again, 'twas revealed to me by an angel." He grabbed her hand and gathered her to him. "Lie down. I wish to show the Lord again how much I cherish this wonderful gift He has bestowed upon me."

"Then you will be pleased to know you are doubly blessed." She smiled shyly. "I am with child."

Richard rolled away, his stomach queasy, too stunned to speak. Always fastidious, he pondered why this possibility had never crossed his mind.

Marie pulled the woolen blanket up to cover her naked body. "Is something wrong?"

"When is the babe expected?"

"Around Trinity Sunday."

Richard rose from the bed, crossed to the wardrobe, and removed a plain brown habit, and quickly donned it. "You best go."

"But you have not eaten." Her voice hinted of dismay.

"I am not hungry." He moved to the fire and settled into a chair. He did not watch Marie dress the way he often did. The rushes crunched, and he knew she was taking her leave. "Does anyone else know about the child?"

"The midwife. She confirmed my condition."

"Does she know I am the father?"

"No." From the conviction in her voice, he reckoned she spoke the truth.

"Promise you will tell no one," he said in a stern voice. "If you do, I shall deny it as a vicious slander, and will be forced to send you away."

Her voice trembled, and he hoped this was not a prelude to tears. "Are you ashamed of me?"

"As a member of the clergy, it is complicated. 'Tis best if I acknowledge the child in God's time."

"I understand," she whispered.

"You may go."

She quit the chamber, crossed the common room, and the outer door clicked shut.

Once she had gone, Richard quit the chamber. At the table, he filled the chalice with ale, which he quickly drained and poured himself another. He stared at the bowl of stew, now cold, and his stomach churned at the thought of food. How had he not anticipated such an entanglement might arise? Had he presumed God would close her womb?

He dropped his head into his hands. Fornication. Sexual immorality. Did not the scriptures warn against such? Doomed to the fires of Hell he was. 'Repent! Repent!' screamed in his head. But how could he when he felt no remorse?

Richard rose and paced the room. He paused now and then to stare out the window at the darkening sky. For nigh an hour, he circled round and round the cottage, his soul in anguish. He stepped outside to breathe in the night air. Above him, the stars twinkled; a bit of light in the gloom as glimmers of long-forgotten conversations struggled to surface in his consciousness.

He recalled many rumors about other men of God before him, bishops, cardinals, even popes, who had kept mistresses. And what of the whispers about Pope Julius III? 'Twas no secret that the man only granted ecclesiastical livings to those whom he had buggered. Was that not a graver sin than bedding a servant? His mind wrestled to reconcile the conflict between the pope's divine vocation and his unholy sin, eager to make some sense of it. If God was truth and righteousness, how could such a contradiction exist within the Vicar of Christ?

Of course, the answer had been there all along. The key to the puzzle. As a new priest, he had been instructed that the vow of celibacy meant he could never marry, a vow he swore to uphold when he took his ordination. Yet, no mention had been made of restraint in easing the yearning in his loins. He need not give up Marie; she had been given for his learning. *If God had not wished me to experience these spiritual heights, He would have made me a eunuch.*

Warmth seeped through his body, and his guilt fell away. What grace God had bestowed on him. Oh, blessed, merciful God, who had entrusted him with a greater understanding of the mysteries of Heaven. Indeed, this blessing meant he could count himself among the chosen few of the clergy for whom God had granted this exception.

Having justified himself, he re-entered the cottage, removed his robe, and climbed into the bed where he and Marie had shared sublime unity only hours earlier. His conscience clear, he slept peacefully, and dreamed of his child sitting upon his knee and listening with rapt attention as he received instruction in the Word of the Lord.

May 22, Wednesday before Pentecost

THE SUN STOOD DIRECTLY OVERHEAD as Richard plodded down the path toward home. The morning had been hectic. He stopped beneath the elm tree, wiped the sweat from his brow, and stared out at the water that sparkled in the sunlight. Gulls circled and shrieked overhead.

Richard contemplated the obstacles to stamping out the heresy that had invaded his homeland. Today, he could only take satisfaction in having pronounced judgment over an errant priest, caught naked in the arms of his wife. Regrettably, the only penance the man would know was exile. What became of the priest, he did not care, so long as it took the man far away from his family.

Such a tragedy that every attempt to have these heretics burned at the stake had been obstructed by Governor Hugh Paulet and Bailiff Helier de Carteret, both unapologetic reformists who stood staunchly in opposition to Queen Mary's decrees. The governor's opposition was particularly troubling, given his brother was the Dean of Jersey. The pitting of brother against brother was just one of the tragic consequences of this unholy reformist movement.

In his modest opinion, the governor and the bailiff were tools of the Devil. Their reformation was more about the justification of mayhem and greed than religious renewal, manifested by the destruction of sacred church property and the seizure of its wealth. Why Queen Mary had not removed them from their offices remained a mystery. Until such time, his noble work for God would be hampered.

He turned his mind to happier thoughts; Whitsuntide was but a few days hence. Such a blessing to spend the day making merry with his friend, Sir John Paulet, Dean of Jersey. He licked his lips in anticipation of the wonderful food and the abundant supply of wine amongst good company and sport. His stomach rumbled, and he resumed his journey along the path toward home, hungry for the midday meal.

But his once quick step had slowed to a trudge in recent months. Since Marie had revealed herself with child, he had watched her girth thicken. Initially, his heart had swelled with pride knowing his seed grew inside her. But of late, his thoughts wandered to the laity. How vicious would the gossips be once they learned he had a child? And with the recent changes in Rome—

The cottage door stood ajar and moans sounded from within. He quickened his step and pushed open the door. The table was already set with a trencher, a chalice, bread, and a pitcher of ale. But instead of tending to the meal, Marie stood, bent forward. One hand rested on the table, the other on her belly, her feet in a pool of water. "What happened?"

She looked at him with fear in her eyes. "The babe is coming."

His heart felt heavy, his mouth sour. "So soon?"

Marie moaned and stiffened. He hastened to her side, placed a hand about her waist, and led her to the chamber and helped her into the bed.

She clung to his hand. "Please do not be angry about dinner."

"Certainly not." Richard squeezed her hand. "Rest here while I fetch the midwife."

She tensed and groaned as another contraction seized her body. "Thank you, Richard," she said breathlessly. "Pray our babe arrives hale and hearty."

He nodded, then hurried from the cottage and down the path toward the village. Once the cottage was out of sight, he stopped beneath the elm tree and closed his eyes and tried to slow his rapid breathing. He needed more time.

He dropped to the ground and sat with his knees bent, hands over his face. What had he done? What he had once considered a blessing now felt like a curse.

Curious how a death a thousand miles away could give rise to a chain of events that created havoc in his life. All had been well under Pope Julius, but halfway through Lent, news arrived of his death. His successor, Pope Marcellus II, was called home but twenty-two days later.

Bad tidings followed when Cardinal Gian Petro Carafa became Pope Paul IV. As bishop and ambassador to England, Carafa had made his mark when he preached abstinence from sensual pleasures and the shunning of material possessions as the proper path to salvation. Now as pope, the man had the power to impose his views on the entire clergy.

Richard wiped his sweaty palms on his habit. Soon, his sin would be exposed. What would happen when word reached the Ecclesiastical Court that he had fathered a bastard child? Would he be relieved of his position? Or worse. Carafa had embraced violence to stamp out the reformist movement, even persuaded Pope Paul III to institute a Roman Inquisition. The man's famous words echoed in his head. "Even if my own father were a heretic, I would gather the wood to burn him." What chance did he, Richard, have against one so zealous?

Perchance an hour or two passed while Richard agonized over his impending humiliation. To lose the approbation of his peers and perhaps his post as proctor of the Ecclesiastical Court was more than he could bear. This would not be suffering for righteousness' sake.

The sun dropped lower in the sky, and he realized he had left Marie alone for far too long. He scrambled up, brushed the dirt from his habit, and hurried back to the cottage. He heard Marie scream; her time must be close. He hastened inside and barred the door.

Marie lay on the bed, her eyes wild, tears streaming down her cheeks. "Water," she panted.

Richard removed a cup from the shelf, filled it with water from the bucket, and entered the chamber. He lifted Marie's head and brought the cup to her lips.

She took several sips, then asked, "Where is the midwife?"

"She was called to attend another birth. She will come when she can." He lowered her head onto the bolster and placed the cup beside the bed, his conscience untroubled by his deceit.

Marie's eyes darted from side-to-side. "But the babe is nearly here!"

"Do not be afraid." Richard arranged his face in what he thought was a concerned look. "I am here."

"What do you know of delivering a child?" she moaned and curled over her belly.

He stroked her hair. "Eve did not have a midwife. You can guide me through this."

"Get hot water." Marie went rigid as another contraction gripped her body. When Richard quit the room, she gasped out, "And clean towels."

In the common room, Richard searched for towels and poured water from the bucket into the empty kettle that hung over the hearth. He added a knife to cut the cord. What he really needed was a drink. He needed courage for what he knew he must do. He filled the chalice and settled into a chair and sipped slowly, then poured another.

"Richard!" Marie screamed, her voice filled with panic. "Where are you? The head is cresting."

He grabbed a towel and a knife and rushed into the room, where he found Marie attempting to rise from the bed. He dropped the items and pushed her down.

Her breathing was fast and heavy. "The birthing—is easier—if a woman stands. Bring me a chair."

He retrieved a chair from the hearth, then stepped back toward the fire. She grabbed the back; her legs spread wide as she bore down; her face twisted in anguish. He turned away and stared into the flames.

"This is no time for propriety," Marie cried. "You must catch the babe or he will fall onto the rushes."

Richard grabbed the towel and knife, knelt down, and unfolded the towel just as the infant made its appearance into the world. The babe hollered when laid on the bed. Richard seized the knife and sawed through the cord and fumbled to tie it off, wishing the constant howls would stop. *This would be so much easier if it would stop flailing its tiny arms and legs.*

"Boy or girl?" Marie asked.

He drew in a deep breath and let it out slowly. "Boy," he said gruffly.

Marie smiled. "Oh, Richard. We have a son."

How did she look so beautiful with her damp hair plastered against her head, her kirtle streaked with blood? And how could she express so much joy after the pain she had just endured?

He wrapped the towel around the infant. "I will baptize him." He picked up the babe and carried it from the room without a backward glance.

"I wish him to be named Robert," Marie said, her voice raspy.

He could not look at Marie, not right now. It had come to this because he had made a mockery of his priestly vows, a sin for which he must atone.

The babe yelped when Richard set it on the table. He fetched the bucket, then removed the babe from the towel and immersed it in the water. "I baptize thee in the name of the Father, the Son, and the Holy Ghost." He lifted the babe, dripping wet and face red with outrage, and laid it back on the towel.

He took a deep breath and wrapped his hand around its throat and squeezed until the crying stopped. Little legs kicked against his arm. Richard squeezed harder and did not release his grip until the kicking ceased.

Rushes crunched. Richard glanced over his shoulder. Marie stood openmouthed in the chamber doorway.

Her scream pierced his ears. "What have you done?" She rushed to the table, grabbed the babe, and dropped to the floor. She held him close and pounded his back as tears flowed down her cheeks. "Wake up, Robert. Wake up!"

Richard turned his back, unwilling to comfort her or express any compassion for her grief. *I have done the right thing.* He crossed himself and lifted his hands. "It is finished. Lord, have mercy on my soul."

A fist pummeled his back. "You killed him."

He turned, and her fist struck his cheek. Lifting his hands to protect his face, he barked, "Calm yourself, woman."

Her blows continued even as she clutched the babe in one arm. He grabbed her, forcing her backward into the chamber and shoving her onto the bed.

"Murderer," she spat and kicked at him with her legs.

"'Twas not murder, but mercy." He knelt before her and caught her free hand. "In time, you will come to understand."

"You are a monster." She struggled to release her hand from his grip.

"As a bastard, he would be an outcast, easily tempted into a life of sin. I have ensured our son will live forever in paradise. Is that not what you would wish for him?"

"Yes, but—" She gasped for breath. "You promised to acknowledge him. Under your protection, he would have been safe."

"That was before."

Her mouth gaped, her eyes wide. "What do you mean?"

Richard swallowed hard. This would be difficult for Marie to hear, but some things needed to be said. "The new pope frowns upon any hint of immorality."

"Why would I care what the pope thinks?" She pushed Richard away and rose from the bed. "I shall summon the constable. You will pay for what you have done."

Richard drew himself up to full height. "Remember who you are. You are a mere servant whom I can dismiss."

Her eyes widened. "You threaten to cast me from your house? If you do, I shall tell all that you murdered our child."

"And when I deny it, who will people believe? The priest? Or the fallen woman?" He smirked. "And who would employ such a person?"

Her face crumpled, and her shoulders shook.

Perchance he took too much pleasure in tormenting her. The search for another comely maidservant eager to warm his bed might prove difficult. "There, there. 'Tis but a lovers' quarrel. I did not mean it." He pulled a kerchief from the pocket of his habit and wiped her tears. "Do you love me?"

She hesitated, a sharp look in her eye.

He stroked her cheek. "Answer the question."

"Yes, I love you," Marie whispered.

"And you will prove your love?"

"Whatever you ask. Just do not send me away."

"You must not breathe a word of this to anyone."

Her eyes met his. "On my oath, but pray allow me to mourn my baby."

He leaned in and kissed her cheek. "That is why I love you. Any godly mother would grieve the loss of her child. Now hand the babe to me so I may bury him."

She held the infant tighter. "Tell me you mourn for Robert."

Richard put on his most sorrowful face. "Indeed, I do." The deception must have worked, for she relinquished it to him.

She shivered and wrapped her arms around her body. "So cold."

He searched the wardrobe for a clean blanket and tucked it around her.

"Where will you take him? I cannot bear not knowing where my son is laid."

"I will bury him here in the cottage where he will always be with us."

Whilst Marie rested, Richard laid the babe beside the hearth, tiptoed from the house, and strode to the cottage of a nearby neighbor to borrow a shovel. When he returned, he removed the stones from the hearth and began to dig.

The ground beneath was hard and the work arduous. His back ached, his hands blistered from gripping the shovel. Praise God he had not been fated to this kind of work. Unfortunately, the current problem was not something for which he could seek help. This was a chore he must do alone. When the work was complete, no one would ever be the wiser. His future within the Church would be secure.

Seven days hence

RICHARD APPROACHED THE COTTAGE, apprehensive about the forthcoming encounter with Marie. A sennight had passed since her child had gone to dwell with Jesus. Marie still seemed distracted and distant; an awkwardness abounded which was not conducive to a godly spirit. Thus, his home was no longer the sanctuary it once was. He surmised all would return to normal once their lovemaking resumed. If her time of purification proved difficult for him, how much more difficult it must be for her, given the woman's insatiable desire for sensual pleasures.

Uncertain of his reception, he took a deep breath and pushed open the door. Nothing was as it should be. No aroma of stew; only a flagon and a chalice were set out on the table. Marie sat there, head buried in her hands. She looked up, her eyes swollen from crying. She scrambled up from her seat and nearly knocked over the chair, then prostrated before him. "Reverend Richard, please forgive me. I have wronged you terribly."

He knelt beside her and placed a hand on her head. "Take comfort, my child. I comprehend your distress. We both have suffered a dreadful loss. Of course, I forgive you." Richard rose and helped Marie to her feet, placed a hand on her back, and led her back to the chair.

She resisted. "You misunderstand. You must leave directly."

"And go where? Come, sit." He settled her back into the chair. He filled the chalice with wine and held it to her lips. "This will calm you."

She pushed the chalice away. "Please, listen to me. The soldiers may already be on their way. You must flee at once."

A knot formed in Richard's stomach, and he set the chalice down a bit too forcefully. A bit of red wine splashed on the floor. "What have you done?"

"By my troth, I did not mean to tell." Tears streamed down Marie's cheeks.

His muscles trembled, his voice angry. "Who did you tell?"

"The midwife. She came this morning, for she knew my time was at hand." Marie sniffed and wiped her nose on her sleeve. "I said her services were no longer needed. She asked to examine the babe, and —" Marie sobbed, "The story just poured out."

Richard slapped her face. "You stupid, stupid woman. Tell me she agreed to keep your confidence."

"After much pleading, yes. That is when we heard a noise outside the window. The neighbor had come for his shovel and overheard our conversation. I implored him to never speak of the matter, that he had misunderstood, but he hastened away to fetch the constable. So you see, you must leave forthwith before it is too late."

"Silly woman." He glared at Marie. "Do you not understand? You have signed your own death warrant."

Her eyes widened. "You lie! I have done nothing wrong."

"You will be seen as an accomplice," Richard replied.

She grasped his arm. "Then take me with you."

Richard jerked away. "My chance to escape is better if I travel alone."

He spun on his heel and entered the bedchamber. He removed his black cassock, donned a simple brown habit tied with a cord, then added a pectoral cross around his neck and looped his black rosary securely through the cord. This was his best chance to pass unrecognized into Saint Helier. Thankfully, it was summer and many trade ships sailed from the harbor every day. It should be simple to board a ship bound for France.

He picked up his Roman Missal, pocketed the coins stored in the wardrobe, and stuffed his few worldly possessions into a satchel. In the common room, he grabbed bread and cheese. He took care to avoid looking at Marie, who wept bitterly near the hearth, his heart untouched by her plight. She had only herself to blame for her troubles. Had she not come into his home and played the Jezebel, none of this would have happened.

Richard hastened out the door toward the copse of trees behind the cottage, away from the main road. *I can take sanctuary in the Coutances Cathedral in France. I shall be safe under the protection of Bishop de Barqueville.*

Mayhap all this was part of God's master plan. In the magnificent cathedral, he would live in luxury, something he could never aspire to on Jersey. Under the bishop's guidance, he would gain a deeper connection with God while he prayed in awe-inspiring chapels and dined sumptuously.

Scarcely had he entered the wood when soldiers on horseback approached the cottage. *God has surely smiled upon me, for He has provided me an escape.* Hounds barked, and his heart pounded.

Richard drew the hood of his habit low over his face and tramped through the trees. When he emerged on the other side, he spotted a group of monks. He pressed his palms to his eyes and looked again. The monks were still there. By some stroke of good fortune, they were making a pilgrimage to the Hermitage, the tiny house built high on the rock near the port, where St. Helier had lived many centuries ago. Dressed as he was, Richard would blend with the brotherhood. He raised his arms in praise. *So many ways that God provides.*

Sun glinted off the bald pates of the monks who plodded along the sandy shore toward St. Aubin's Bay. Inclined as they were to refrain from conversation, no one questioned Richard's presence. Twice, soldiers passed and asked for any information on the whereabouts of one, Richard Averty, a priest. Each time, they shook their heads and continued on.

Sweat trickled down Richard's back, and he longed for a drink. Occasionally, he waded through the waters along the shore to confuse the hounds should they pick up his trail. The waves swirled about his feet and ankles, and he imagined Jesus himself washed his feet. A baptism of sorts that absolved him of sin.

When the procession of monks entered the port town of St. Helier, the number of soldiers who milled about increased. Richard resisted the urge to run, for it would only draw unwelcome attention. He must employ great caution, for if a monk approached a seaman in town or lurked about the port, it might raise suspicion. His best chance for escape would be to board the next ship ready to sail. He could arrange for passage to Coutances from any destination.

Their arrival coincided with low tide. Richard paused beneath an alder tree, knelt down, and pretended to adjust his sandal. The monks continued their pilgrimage, plodding across the damp sands toward the hermitage. When he glanced up, there was not a soldier in sight. He hastened along the line of ships and found one where the seamen were raising the sails. His heart leapt when he spotted a rope ladder hung down the seaward side. He clambered up and hoisted himself over the rail.

Everyone on deck appeared too busy to take notice of him. *Perhaps a priest onboard is not uncommon.* Even so, he must use caution. He scanned the deck and spied the hatch a short distance from the mainmast and sidled closer. He peered around before opening it, then lowered himself into the hold and closed the hatch slowly and quietly behind him.

It took a few minutes for his eyes to adjust to the dim light, then he felt his way along the crates and barrels to the farthest reaches of the hold. There, he hunkered down to wait for the ship to lift anchor and get underway. He crossed himself, grateful for all the miracles that had allowed him to avoid capture.

He relaxed, although not completely. That time would come once the ship was safely out to sea. He clutched his cross and prayed to Saint Christopher to keep him safe during the voyage. He pondered how long the journey might be. Three days and three nights perchance? The same number of days that his Savior had laid in the tomb. When he emerged from the hold, it would be like a resurrection, he a new man far from his earthly home, a pilgrim and stranger on the earth.

Footsteps clomped about the deck for what seemed like hours. Could these men not work faster? Loud voices sounded above and Richard strained to catch the words, but could not make them out.

Hinges squeaked. The hatch opened and light filtered into the hold. Four men lowered themselves down, one held a lantern. Richard's heart hammered as the men checked each crate and barrel. Hopefully, their search would end soon. What would they think if they came upon him? A priest hidden in a hold would provoke questions.

The hunt continued, methodical and thorough. They neared, and Richard tried to squeeze into the narrow space between the last crate and the hull. It was too tight, and the crate scraped loudly against the floor. His breath caught.

"Did you hear that?" one man asked.

"I heard it," replied another. "'Tis a rat."

They all laughed. "That is exactly what Richard Averty is, a rat," the first man said. "That means he must be here. Keep searching. Several seamen testified they spotted a clergyman on deck."

Richard's armpits dampened, and his heart raced. He had miscalculated; he ought to have stayed with the monks. Better to have braved Hell's Gate, as the islanders called the rapid flood tide around the hermitage, than place his fate in the hands of apostates.

The men inched nearer, and Richard clasped his hands together and mouthed, "God save your humble servant."

The beam of light reached the crate where he hid, and within moments, it was full on his face. Richard shielded his eyes from the lamp's brightness.

"Found him," shouted the man as he shoved the crate aside. "Come out Richard Averty. There is no escape now."

Slowly, Richard lowered his hand and noted the sword at the man's side. Soldiers. He stood and, as befit a humble man of God, meekly surrendered. Another soldier placed manacles around his wrists. The two soldiers grasped Richard's arms and led him over to the hatch, far more roughly than warranted. Richard smiled. *Just like the soldiers who arrested Jesus in the Garden of Gethsemane.*

The two soldiers climbed out of the hull first and pulled Richard up onto the deck. A few minutes later, the remaining two soldiers emerged. Once they disembarked from the ship, they clamped shackles around Richard's ankles and pushed off his hood, revealing his face to the gathering crowd. Richard lifted his chin. He would not allow these men to shame him. Soon, the good folks of Jersey would understand this was persecution for his unwavering faith in the true church.

The attorney general, William de Carteret, stepped forward. "Reverend Richard Averty, you are under arrest for murder."

"This is an outrage." Richard glared at the five men who surrounded him. "I demand you fetch Dean John Paulet."

William inclined his head. "One of you fetch the dean. The rest will take the fugitive to the dungeon at Mont Orgueil, where he will await trial."

A soldier hastened down the road toward St. Helier's Church

while the others prodded Richard along the path which led to the castle. The crowd grew as they progressed, and the heckling never ceased. The cold fetters dug into his feet and ankles. *But a small taste of what our Lord Jesus Christ endured. I am blessed to be counted worthy to suffer for his sake.*

Saturday, June 27, 1555

THE CART RUMBLED down Longueville Road from Mont Orgueil into the town of St. Helier, jostling Richard from side to side. The sun warmed his skin, a blessed change from the drafty dungeon where he had been confined for the past many days. He had lost count, discouraged by the dean's inability to obtain his release; another sign that the reformist had insufficient respect for God and his true church.

Ahead, a mob congregated in the square. At least the dean had convinced the warden to allow him to wear a white surplice so all present would be reminded he was a man of God. The cart jolted to a halt in front of the Royal Court, and two warders dragged Richard from the bed and guided him through the crowd to a row of pillories. Marie and the midwife occupied two, the midwife with her hair cut short while Marie's had been completely shorn. Richard nodded his approval. *Appropriate for a harlot.*

The soldiers lifted the upper beam and removed Richard's manacles and the white surplice, then shoved his head and hands into place. The beam dropped, and the key scraped as it turned in the lock. Murmurs rose from the crowd and soon turned into shouts of "Murderer! Let him hang!" *Just like the crowd who shouted 'crucify him' when Our Lord Jesus Christ stood before Pilate.*

From the position of the sun, Richard determined two hours of daylight remained. Already his back ached from the awkward position. Soon the breeze off the water would pick up. Richard had always been sensitive to the cold. Hopefully, the torture by his captors would not include an entire night in the pillory. His stomach clenched and his legs quivered as he recalled no one saved Jesus from the cross.

Richard glanced at Marie; her face reflected comprehension of her sin and shame. Conversely, the midwife's expression was rigid, as if set in stone.

Two men pushed their way through the crowd until they stood beside the attorney general. Richard recognized Governor Hugh Paulet, a sturdy man in his mid-fifties, his hair and beard still dark brown with hints of gray.

When Bailiff Helier de Carteret stepped up beside the governor, Richard's heart sank. At nigh four-score years, Helier had served as Jersey's bailiff for almost two-score of those; longer than many men lived. A proud reformist and a new father, he was unlikely to show much compassion. Richard's position as a proctor should have afforded him special privileges, but somehow, Helier had thwarted proper justice.

The crowd milled about; the air buzzed with murmured conversation, peppered with renewed shouts of "murderer." Occasionally, a stone or piece of rotten fruit was hurled in his direction. Everyone seemed to be anxiously awaiting someone or something; perchance the dean's arrival and his release. There was a flurry of activity when the twelve jurats filed out of the Royal Court to stand before the crowd.

Helier stepped forward. "Let the trial begin."

"Point of order," Richard shouted. "It is unlawful to try a member of the clergy in a secular court."

The attorney general ignored his protest. "Governor, Bailiff, Jurats of the Royal Court, and citizens of Jersey," William began. "We are gathered to hear the case against Richard Averty, charged with the murder of the infant, Robert Bellèe. Marie Bellèe, mother of said infant, and Thomasena Clement, midwife, are charged as accomplices for concealing the crime."

William moved to stand before Marie. "Marie Bellèe, were you delivered of a live baby boy on the Wednesday before Pentecost?"

"Yes." Her voice trembled, and Richard felt nothing but disdain for her weakness.

"And who attended the birth?" William asked.

"Only Reverend Averty," Marie whispered.

"Only a priest? Explain how this came about."

"I have been in Reverend Averty's employ for several years. My travail began whilst I prepared his midday meal. The reverend returned home and discovered me in distress. After he assisted me to his bedchamber, he left to fetch the midwife. He returned alone as she was attending another birth."

Thomasena spoke out. "'Tis all a lie. I was at home. Reverend Averty never came."

William turned his attention to Richard. "Is that true? Did you not fetch the midwife?"

Richard met the attorney general's eyes. "I did not."

"Pray tell, why not?"

"Marie is unwed. I sought to spare her from any gossip that might ensue."

"That is very noble, Reverend. And so you delivered her babe yourself?"

"Yes, and baptized it before it died."

"Marie, you witnessed Richard Averty murder your child," said William. "Why did you not send for the constable?"

A tear slid down Marie's cheek. "I was distraught at the loss of my child." She sobbed between her words. "Reverend Averty said no one would believe my story and threatened to dismiss me if I told a soul."

William moved on to question the midwife. "Thomasena, you stated Marie confided in you that Richard Averty murdered the newborn infant. What hindered you from reporting this crime?"

"There was no time. When the neighbor overheard Marie's confession, he went straightaway to the constable."

William strode back to stand before Richard. "Marie claims you strangled the child. What say you?"

"The babe was a bastard, born in sin and would suffer contempt his entire life. His death was an act of mercy."

"Do you confess you buried the child beneath your hearth?"

"'Twas only right to give him a proper burial."

"The place of the grave suggests you understood the nature of your crime, an attempt to hide the evidence," William replied.

Richard cocked his head and smirked. "Your supposition is in error. I only desired to keep Marie's sin from being exposed. I did not wish for her to become the subject of ridicule."

"How dare you?" Marie hissed. "You speak of my sin whilst you ignore your own."

Fortunately for Richard, her head and hands were locked in a pillory, for she glared at him as if she would happily thrust a dagger through his heart.

In clear tones, she announced, "As God is my witness, Reverend Richard Averty is the babe's father."

The crowd gasped, and William glared at Richard. "You murdered your own son?"

"I did what My Lord instructed." Richard curled his hands into fists, his voice edged with anger. *Where is Dean Paulet? A man of God should not have to endure such abuse.*

Helier stepped forward. "As a man of the cloth, you cannot possibly believe that God would ask you to disobey His precepts. Or perhaps you have forgotten the commandment 'thou shalt not murder.'"

The crowd chanted, "Guilty. Hang him. Hang him."

Helier addressed the attorney general. "I see no need to continue this trial. The defendant does not deny his guilt. Let us take a vote of the jurats."

Each of the twelve jurats stepped forward and voiced a verdict of guilty.

"The Royal Court has spoken," Helier said. "On this day, the 27th of June, in the year of our Lord 1555, Richard Averty, you have been found guilty of murder. You shall hang at sunset, your body left on the gibbet till it rots."

Richard gasped and his stomach wrenched, unable to move with his head and hands clamped tight in the pillory.

Helier addressed the warders. "Release the women."

Four warders stepped forward and opened the two pillories. Marie collapsed to the ground, her body wracked with sobs. Thomasena knelt to comfort her, then helped her up. Marie, head bowed, leaned against Thomasena as they hastened away from the jeering mob.

Fear gripped Richard's heart at the sight of the bloodthirsty crowd. A movement caught his attention, and he could scarce believe his eyes. A man dressed in a white robe weaved his way toward him. *An angel come to rescue me.* Tears pricked Richard's eyes.

Dressed in a white surplice, the dean stepped out from the mob. "Governor Paulet, Bailiff de Carteret. This is a grave injustice. Richard Averty must be awarded the Benefit of Clergy."

"I fear you are too late," replied Governor Paulet. "He has been tried, convicted by his own words, and sentenced to death."

"This sets a dangerous precedent," the dean replied. "For centuries, the Ecclesiastical Court has judged members of the clergy. We cannot allow a secular court to rule in matters involving sacred men of God. Release him immediately so he may be tried in the Bishop's Court."

"Ecclesiastical Courts rule in matters spiritual and religious," Helier replied. "His crime is neither."

The dean drew himself up to his full stature. "Bailiff de Carteret, I know you to be a God-fearing man. I plead with you to uphold the traditions of the Church. I promise to try the case quickly and rule justly."

Helier turned toward the jurats. "The Mosaic law is often quoted, 'an eye for an eye, a tooth for a tooth.' It also states 'he that killeth any man shall surely be put to death.' Nevertheless, the Ecclesiastical Court has a long history of never handing down such a sentence. Jurats of the Royal Court, what say you? Should this man be released and tried in the Bishop's Court?"

The twelve jurats huddled to discuss the matter. Within minutes, the first jurat stepped away from the group. "We have considered the request made by Dean John Paulet and determined the crime is too heinous. The defendant, Richard Averty, will not be turned over to the Ecclesiastical Court."

The dean faced the governor. "I pray you, do not allow the Royal Court to undermine my sacred authority. Brother, we are flesh and blood. Already you have inflicted grave harm by your flagrant opposition to the Church."

"I have no authority in judicial matters," Governor Paulet replied. "You must make your appeal to Bailiff de Carteret."

Helier waved a hand in dismissal. "Do not waste your breath. Throughout my years as bailiff, this is one of the worst crimes presented before the Royal Court. The babe did nothing wrong except be born alive. The sentence stands."

"Then grant me this one petition," the dean said. "Allow Reverend Richard Averty to wear the surplice so that he might go to the foot of the scaffold adorned in the ornaments of the Church."

"Granted," Helier replied.

A warder unlocked the pillory. When the top beam was removed, Richard stumbled but caught himself. The dean stepped forward and helped Richard into the white robe. "Alas," Richard said, determined to hold back his tears, "you promised to save my life."

"Hush," the dean whispered back. "I will bring them to repentance."

"Sadly, that will be too late for me."

Dean Paulet buttoned up Richard's surplice. *A white garment! 'Tis what the saints wear when they stand before the throne of God. The dean has declared my innocence.*

Fetters were once again clamped around Richard's wrists and ankles. The crowd parted, and a warder appeared, led by two black hounds pulling a wooden hurdle. Two warders forced Richard onto it and attached the chains of his shackles to the frame.

Helier held up his hand, and the crowd quieted. "Drag him to Gallows Hill," he shouted.

A cheer arose from the crowd as the dogs started off. The hurdle bumped along the path which led up the hill to the scaffold. The crowd followed, their glee evident at the chance to witness another hanging. How long it lasted, Richard could not say, only that the distance was long and his body bruised from being dragged across the bumpy ground. *Vestiges of the walk of Our Lord Jesus Christ to Calvary. I, too, shall die a martyr.*

They arrived at Gallows Hill just as the sun set. A warder released Richard from the hurdle and walked him to the scaffold, where the warder ripped the white surplice from his body. Richard shook uncontrollably as they helped him ascend the three steps up to the platform of the scaffold where the executioner awaited. Someone had placed a small crate beneath the crossbeam and the noose, and beside it hung a gibbet. *I am not ready to die. But as Our Savior spoke in the Garden of Gethsemane, let thy will be done.*

Both warders helped Richard up onto the crate. The executioner slipped the noose around his neck. *Yea, though I walk through the valley of the shadow of death—.*

The executioner kicked the crate away, and the noose tightened around Richard's throat. He struggled to breathe, and his body twitched and jerked. With each move, the rope tightened. *Oh, God, into thy hands I commend my spirit.*

Everything went black, darker than anything he had ever witnessed. He heard the flap of wings. *'Tis the angels come to take my soul to heaven.* From the darkness, a fearsome creature emerged with huge black wings, a bird's head, and lion's claws. Richard's mouth opened in a silent scream. It was cold, so cold. He plummeted downward, accompanied by the demon. A glow pierced the darkness. The cold turned to warmth, then unbearable heat. God Almighty rendered His righteous judgment.

ABOUT THE AUTHOR

C.V. Lee pens compelling tales about forgotten heroes and heroines of the past. Her series, The de Carteret Chronicles: Legacy of Rebels, features inspirational lesser-known historical figures whose actions shaped history. Blending fact, fiction, and folklore, her novels bring to life the courage and resilience of those who dared to make a difference.

For more information about C.V. Lee, visit her website at cvlee.com, or follow her on Facebook and Instagram.

AND THE RIGHTEOUS PREVAIL

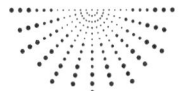

LINDA ULLESEIT

On January 11, 1875, so many people packed the plaza in front of the Brooklyn City Courthouse that a casual observer might have thought the tourists, organ grinders, and sandwich vendors in the crowd heralded the coming of a circus. The ticket scalpers, lawyers, reporters, and concerned parishioners, though, told a more sensational tale. Today the greatest scandal in the world would culminate in the civil trial *Theodore Tilton v. Henry Ward Beecher.*

A carriage approached the front of the courthouse along a narrow lane protected by a police cordon. Moses and Chloe Beach sat with their friend and preacher, Henry Ward Beecher, and his wife, Eunice. Chloe brushed at the skirt of her dress, dark to mark the sober occasion but burgundy rather than black. Nobody would die here today. She refused to appear as if she was mourning. After all, she tried to tell herself, this trial had nothing to do with her. She was here to support her preacher.

Eunice wore a plain black silk dress with understated jewelry. A severe bun of white hair, combined with her stern visage, gave her an air of dignity. Eunice had been staunchly supportive of her husband through the entire ordeal as Henry, accused of adultery by a close friend, became the world's favorite topic of conversation over breakfast. Chloe leaned forward and squeezed her friend's hand. Eunice gave her a tiny smile.

A man in the crowd shouted, "Tickets here! Five dollars will get you a seat!"

Henry shook his head, his eyes full of pain. "They held a lottery to dispense tickets," he said in a flat voice. "As of yesterday I still had friends asking me to get them tickets."

"Judge Neilson tried to ban women from attending," Moses said, "but the ladies from the church are determined to stand by you. They'll be there today."

Henry nodded.

Closer to the courthouse door, Chloe heard a man ask ten dollars for a ticket. She pursed her lips and looked away. Scandal made a person's life sensational.

When the carriage stopped, Henry emerged first and waved to the crowd, a nosegay of violets in his hand. He was greeted by cheers and jeers that elevated the noise level to an ear-splitting volume. Moses climbed out next and held the door for the women. Both men wore dark wool frock coats and trousers, though Henry's burgundy silk waistcoat was a nod to his love of flair. Chloe straightened her shoulders and lifted her chin into as regal a bearing as she could manage. Looking neither left nor right, she followed her husband and friends through a crowd reeking of tobacco and sweat.

A man with wild, impassioned eyes leaned toward them and shouted, "'Surely the day is coming; it will burn like a furnace. All the arrogant and every evildoer will be stubble, and the day that is coming will set them on fire,' says the Lord Almighty!"

"Malachi 4:1," Henry muttered.

Moses leaned closer to him and said, "I've heard you preach that those who have faith in Christ are declared righteous, and they have nothing to fear on Judgment Day because their punishment has already been borne by Christ on the cross." He put his arm around the reverend's waist and guided him up the courthouse steps.

Chloe kept her eyes on the courthouse door. What was it that made someone trumpet a fall from grace like the angel Gabriel himself? For years whispers had swirled around Reverend Beecher. His message of a loving God was too new, too different, for those raised on hellfire and damnation. She wished people could just trust in God's love on Earth and leave it to Him to pronounce judgment.

The courthouse door closed behind them, blocking out the noise and smells of the crowd. The four new arrivals found the correct courtroom without further drama. Chloe and Moses took a seat in the front row. Eunice sat in a wooden armchair in the spectators' section but apart from the crowd, facing the jury box with her head held high. Henry joined the defense team at their table.

At the front of the room, Henry greeted his six lawyers with a smile and a joke, laying his top hat and the nosegay of violets on the table. Chloe recognized the sunny mood Henry always brought forth when he was anxious. She worried about his reputation and state of mind. If the jury found him guilty, the decision would impact more than Henry Ward Beecher. Plymouth Church would lose its world-famous minister, and the scandal would ruin the closest of Beecher's friends, painting them with guilt by association and castigating their choice of religious leader.

Eunice Beecher sat in stoic silence, no doubt preparing to hear witnesses speak of the dreadful state of her marriage and philandering habits of her husband. Chloe sighed. She empathized with Eunice the most. The lady had already endured poverty, the deaths of four of her children, and a loveless marriage. Now she would have every detail of that marriage trotted out in public and examined. Eunice was drab next to the brilliance of her husband, and everyone knew it. Most people ignored her. From the time Chloe had met her, though, she'd felt it was her Christian duty, with maybe a touch of guilt, to befriend her pastor's wife.

At the prosecution's table, Ted Tilton sat on the edge of his seat. Even sitting, he towered over his team of lawyers. He wore his hair long in imitation of Reverend Beecher whom he'd admired for many years prior to recent events. Chloe acknowledged Ted's blond good looks, but couldn't put his spiteful words out of her head. Reverend

Beecher had performed the Tiltons' wedding and taken young Ted under his wing. Chloe knew what a talented writer Ted was. His political ideas were as progressive as Henry's religious ones. That was why they had become such close friends. Moses, Ted, and Henry were all ambitious men, drawn to each other like moths to a flame. But Moses no longer owned the New York *Sun*, Ted had been thrown out of the church, and Henry now faced losing his pulpit.

In the audience, Chloe spotted Elizabeth Tilton, wife of the plaintiff, wearing a black velvet dress and a short mourning veil. Chloe wondered if Mrs. Tilton mourned the death of her marriage or the alleged affair at the root of this case. Elizabeth was a petite woman, but today she looked even smaller than usual. As Chloe watched, Elizabeth preened a bit and dabbed at her eyes with a lace handkerchief, appearing timid and sentimental. She had to know everyone in the room would stare at her all day.

"I feel sorry for Mrs. Tilton," Chloe whispered to Moses.

"You're a good woman, Chloe Beach," her husband said.

She looked up into his eyes and saw the love that had been there since before she'd even heard of Plymouth Church or Reverend Henry Ward Beecher.

"But I'll never forgive her husband for this," Chloe said, waving a hand to indicate the lawyers, judge, plaintiff and defendant, and the audience.

"Some people can't keep their volatile emotions contained," Moses said. "Ted Tilton tried, but his righteous zeal wouldn't let the insult lie. He was compelled to make his allegations public."

"Distancing his wife, his church, and his friends in the process," Chloe said. She watched Moses clench his jaw, and she stopped talking. Her husband must be thinking of his own situation, his own choices regarding her relationship with Reverend Beecher. Chloe wondered how much the public examination of the Tiltons' marriage would affect her own.

As she did every Sunday at Plymouth Church, Chloe peered closely at Henry, trying to discern his emotional state behind the face he presented. He never shrank from having a public speaking platform, but he also didn't do well when high emotion was involved. Many times he had been criticized for speeches containing more of himself than God. The enthusiasm of a young boy mixed with the faith of a Christian man was what made him relatable, though. Henry had thickened about the middle, as had they all, over the years. His long, loose hair had grayed, though his chin still sported no beard. Chloe knew his kind blue-gray eyes held nothing but love for his fellow man and hurt over these entire proceedings. She'd known those eyes for twenty years. Chloe smiled and let her mind wander back.

ONE SUNDAY IN 1854, Moses and Chloe Beach had taken a ferry across the East River to attend Plymouth Church in Brooklyn. Moses held the hand of their seven-year-old son, Charles. Chloe had charge of five-year-old Emma. The family was not alone. Thousands of New Yorkers left Manhattan on that Sunday morning as they did every week, taking ferries to hear Reverend Henry Ward Beecher preach. Moses and Chloe were Episcopalians, so Reverend Beecher's Gospel of Love was different from the hellfire and brimstone of the angry God Chloe had grown up with. Although she'd never heard him speak, Chloe was suspicious of the reverend's ideas, believing them sinful and wrong. Moses, however, appreciated the Congregationalist preacher's progressive ideas and wanted to hear him speak.

In Brooklyn Heights, on a shady residential block, parishioners entered the church through three large double doors. Chloe stopped in her tracks, overcome by the size of the sanctuary.

"Over two thousand people can be seated here," Moses told her. He waved toward the walls. "And there are more benches along there, with standing room, too." His satisfied tone told Chloe that her husband approved of the reverend's ambition in designing a church that looked more like a magnificent theater.

"Where's the pulpit?" Chloe asked.

"He doesn't use one, I guess," Moses said.

A stage jutted out into the audience so that the preacher could be surrounded on three sides by his congregation. An armchair and small table graced the back of the stage. Chloe could see a stack of notes on the table as well as a bouquet of flowers. This wasn't like any church she had ever been in. They found seats and waited while the audience settled in.

Reverend Beecher came out onto the stage and welcomed everyone. Chloe saw not just a preacher, but a man. He wore a silk brocade coat over a satin vest, and his shirt was open at the throat. When he began to speak, Chloe felt as though he was speaking directly to her. Enthralled, she hung on his every word as he spoke of ending slavery and of embracing God's love.

"As individuals, we must rise above society's sins in order to dispel them," he said, moving around the stage as he spoke. "God gave us the ability to love and laugh. We must make the most of his gifts. If we don't, we risk damaging our health." His voice rose to fill the rafters. It echoed in Chloe's heart, resonating with her deepest faith. She sighed. Here was a charismatic leader, much like her husband. His restless energy, too, reminded her of Moses.

After the service, as they filed out, Reverend Beecher shook hands with Moses and welcomed him to Plymouth Church. He waved at a woman nearby and introduced her. "Mr. and Mrs. Beach, this is my wife, Eunice."

"Welcome," Eunice said. "What lovely children." She didn't have her husband's charisma, but she smiled.

Chloe thought she saw sadness behind Eunice's eyes. "Thank you," she said. She introduced the children then said, "We just had to come hear your husband's sermon. He's a wonderful speaker."

Eunice said, "You'll have to come again." Then she moved on to greet other parishioners, all in a very proper, if stilted, way.

Moses and Henry erupted in laughter over something they'd been discussing. They looked like they'd been friends for years. Chloe stood at her husband's side but didn't attempt to follow the conversation as she studied the preacher. Henry was not a classically good-looking man. He was heavy-set, and his lank hair kept falling in his eyes. The man's charm wasn't external though. Henry Ward Beecher glowed from within, as if illuminated by God's love. Chloe wanted to feel that love herself.

Later, on their way back to Manhattan, Moses couldn't stop talking about the wonderful church, the wonderful sermon, the wonderful man. By dinner time, he seemed to have run out of words. Chloe talked softly to the children, urging them to eat their dinner as usual.

Moses laid his fork alongside his plate with a sense of finality that made Chloe stop talking and look at him. "We should move to Brooklyn," he said.

"Move to Brooklyn?" Chloe asked. Her initial reaction was to protest, but her heart leapt at the idea of attending Plymouth Church on a regular basis.

"Today's sermon touched me." He placed a hand on his heart. "I must be near Reverend Beecher, be a part of his church."

"Isn't this rather sudden?" Chloe didn't deny she felt the same draw to Plymouth Church, but she had to think about what was best for the family.

"Brooklyn is growing. There are several suitable mansions on Brooklyn Heights that overlook the river and are close to the church. Henry gave me the address of a few to look at."

"Henry, is it?" Chloe murmured. She knew Moses would forge ahead with whatever he decided, and she knew she would follow. It was her job to make household transitions smooth for the children, which in turn kept everything in order for her husband. In this case, she was more supportive of the move than Moses knew.

Moses Beach said no more to her about a house on the heights. The family attended Plymouth Church for several more weeks, and each time they crossed the river to Brooklyn, Chloe felt like they were coming home to the warm embrace of the Lord. So it was not much of a surprise when Moses directed the carriage driver to stop in front of 96 Columbia Heights after service one Sunday.

"Behold!" he said with a sweep of his hands. "The new residence of the Beach family!"

Chloe admired the imposing mansion. They went inside, and she enthused over the chandeliers and intricate moldings even as she planned the move. In the front parlor, she said, "Here is where we will hang the painting of the children." She'd just commissioned Irish painter James Shegogue to paint Charles and Emma. Maybe having their likenesses in the house would make the transition easier for the children.

Chloe had no regrets about leaving Manhattan although she didn't want to admit to Moses how right he had been about Plymouth Church. Reverend Beecher's loving God resonated with her in a way her parents' vengeful God never had. Reverend Beecher possessed a keen perception and empathy toward the daily moral struggles of the people coupled with innate common sense. He understood when a person stepped off the path of righteousness, and he was the first to admit he wasn't perfect, either. Preacher and parishioner worked together to stay in the glow of God's love. It was a heady experience.

The first guests the Beaches entertained at their new home were Henry and Eunice Beecher. At Henry's request, Chloe invited Theodore Tilton and Elizabeth Richards. The young couple was also new to the church and would be married by Henry Ward Beecher in the fall. Chloe only saw another man like Moses and Henry, and another quiet woman.

Chloe knew that her husband's friends considered her enigmatic and reserved because she rarely revealed her feelings to anyone but Moses. Eunice Beecher was quiet because she was not a critical part of Henry's world. Chloe empathized with her, befriending Eunice in spite of Henry's indifference. Elizabeth Richards was too young to speak her own mind, maybe too young to know it. Chloe watched Elizabeth simper at Theodore and dismissed her.

OPENING statements in the Tilton-Beecher trial took several days. Chloe sat next to Moses every day as they staunchly supported their friend and pastor, Reverend Henry Ward Beecher. Everyone knew the details of the complaint from the newspapers, the gossip, and the church investigation the previous summer. Mr. Tilton alleged that Reverend Beecher had engaged in an affair with his wife, Elizabeth Tilton, and he asked for one hundred thousand dollars in compensation. Chloe nearly choked at the amount. Moses squeezed her hand and released it.

Last summer had been called the scandal summer by everyone associated with Plymouth Church. The church convened an investigative committee to look into the matter of the preacher's behavior with his female parishioners. Although the testimony was not open to the public, daily reports leaked out. Moses had taken Chloe to Europe to avoid gossip and speculation, but Eunice wrote letters. So Chloe heard about Mr. Tilton speaking of his once happy home, of the faith in God once shared by him and his wife.

Rumors of an affair had tarnished the marriage, his reputation, and his career. So now the audience was restless. No one wanted to hear more rehashing of allegations that had been circulating for several years. Even Chloe struggled to suppress a yawn. Moses took her hand again and this time didn't let go.

Chloe looked up at him, seeing a tightness to his lips and tension in his cheek. Was he thinking about her own relationship with Henry Beecher? She knew Moses didn't like how fast she'd gone from disliking Reverend Beecher's ideas to completely embracing God's love. Moses had even moved them out of their new house in Brooklyn, back upstate to the country, shortly after the birth of their second daughter. Chloe had withered there, though. Two years later, Moses capitulated and brought his family back to Brooklyn Heights. Now Chloe presided over the house and children while Moses took the ferry to Manhattan each day to take his place in the business world as owner of the New York *Sun*. It was natural for the reverend to visit Chloe Beach and bring little treats for the children, just as he visited other women whose husbands worked in the city. She'd actually joked with Henry on one occasion that he must be the only man left in Brooklyn on a weekday.

For ten and a half days, the trial moved at a glacial pace as a member of the church's investigative committee was examined by the prosecution and then the defense, detailing their investigation from the previous summer.

"Can't they just skip to the part where they found Henry blameless?" Chloe asked Moses.

"Blameless? I'm not sure I'd go that far. Not guilty at least." The tension in her husband's jaw created a tic near his mouth. He wouldn't look at her.

"Moses," she began, wanting to know what he was thinking. But then the judge called for silence and the testimony resumed.

In February, two weeks after the trial began, Moses and Chloe woke to ice on the East River. No ferries could cross the river. Some brave souls walked across, but surely fancy New York lawyers wouldn't attempt such a stunt. The trial was delayed for four days.

Chloe dressed eight-year-old Violet in her warmest clothes and took her to skate on the river. Her other children were all older, busy with their own plans for the day. Chloe convinced Moses to join them. Before long the three of them were laughing at their bright red cheeks and noses. Chloe's heart felt lighter than it had since Theodore Tilton had first made his accusations public. Moses was such a good father to Violet. He always had been, despite the girl's uncanny resemblance to Henry Ward Beecher. Two years ago, Henry had commissioned a portrait of himself with Violet. At that time, although rumors abounded, no one, even Moses, said a word where anyone could hear. Nowadays, it seemed every glance and smile needed to be reported to the newspapers and every affront magnified to a court case.

Moses was a good man. She loved him. Chloe never denied that she loved Henry, too. Reverend Beecher taught that God's love should be shared with everyone as the Lord intended. Chloe embraced the notion that God wanted His children to love each other unconditionally. Reverend Beecher preached that God's love multiplies and is never divided. That rang true. As she'd had more children, her love had increased. She didn't have to split a finite supply of love between them.

When the river ice broke up and ferries could once again reach

Brooklyn, the trial resumed. Theodore Tilton was called to the stand and examined by both teams of lawyers. Chloe peered closely at him, looking for evidence of lying, but could only determine that whatever the truth of the situation, Mr. Tilton believed his story to be fact. He spoke of a trip he'd taken in November of 1866, leaving his wife and children behind and asking Reverend Beecher to check on them from time to time.

Chloe would never forget that winter. She'd been pregnant with Violet. Moses had been so ill the previous spring that he must have known with certainty that the baby couldn't be his. Tense conversations danced around the subject, punctuated by the hurt in his eyes and the anger in his pursed lips. Those outside the family whispered with wide eyes about the preacher's frequent trips to the Beach house in those months, comforting the wife of the very sick man. Then Moses recovered. Chloe stayed inside to hide her growing belly and to silence whispers of scandal.

In her uncharitable moments, Chloe begrudged Elizabeth Tilton's closeness with Henry Ward Beecher. Chloe believed if she hadn't been pregnant, Henry would undoubtedly have continued to spend most of his time with her instead of Elizabeth. After Violet's birth, though, that had changed. Henry resumed frequent visits to the Beach home. Even now he was besotted with Violet and brought her gifts. Moses continued to welcome Henry into their home and didn't protest Henry's closeness to Violet. If sometimes her husband's lips seemed pressed together too tightly, his jaw clenched, only Chloe noticed.

The trial continued with pointed cross-examinations of Theodore Tilton, who had been accused of having his own free love views, at odds with his work at a religious publication. He claimed it was the same viewpoint espoused by Reverend Beecher. Chloe knew better, though. Reverend Beecher was indeed progressive in his views, believing joy and pleasure were gifts from God. Free love, though, went too far. Henry didn't approve of a man indiscriminately loving many women in a physical manner. When his own relationships crossed the line, he was overcome with remorse and prayed for forgiveness.

Although people chose to focus on Reverend Beecher's physical love of women, he loved everyone. He was an advocate for women's rights and had even drawn the Tiltons into the American Equal Rights Association. During the Civil War, he'd used Plymouth Church as a stop on the Underground Railroad while he worked to abolish slavery. In April of 1865 President Lincoln had decreed that on the anniversary of Fort Sumter's fall, the Union army would raise the same flag over the fort once again. The president invited Reverend Henry Ward Beecher to speak at the event, and Henry had invited Chloe.

TEN YEARS AGO, on April 8, 1865, a sunny day that shone with God's approval, the *Arago* left New York packed with influential passengers bound for Charleston, South Carolina. Military personnel were aboard, like Brevet Major General Robert Anderson, the officer who had lowered the flag over Fort Sumter on April 14, 1861. In today's ceremony, he would raise the same flag back to its rightful place. The abolitionist William Lloyd Garrison was there, as were politicians, wealthy merchants, intellectuals, and reporters. Henry Ward Beecher had only eighty tickets to distribute to friends, family, and supporters. Eunice was there, of course, as were Chloe Beach and Theodore Tilton.

Chloe leaned on the deck railing the first night of the journey to South Carolina, admiring the stars in the clear sky. The rampant exhilaration of the leave-taking from New York had subsided to a thrum of anticipation that left her smiling.

Beside her, Eunice sighed. "Tiring day. I know Henry, though. He'll be too excited to settle down and write his speech."

Chloe laughed. "He's good at last-minute speeches, though. This trip is a celebration of a major victory for the Union, and I know he's honored to be the one asked to commemorate it."

"I'm proud of him," Eunice said. "He's being asked to give lectures all over the country, and he's starting to write his first novel. I just wish he would spend more time in Brooklyn with his family."

"He soaks up attention like his precious flowers soak up rain," Chloe said with a smile. "And this speech is important. He wants the world to know that the United States went to war with its own people to defend liberty and morality."

"The Southerners hate him," Eunice said, her tone glum.

"The passion of righteousness is on his side," Chloe said, laying a hand on her friend's arm.

"He needs to walk a fine line between celebrating the Union victory and promoting the reconciliation of the nation," Eunice said. "Everyone who hears this speech will be listening for something. Some will want to hear that Henry is abandoning abolitionism, or insulting the South, or that he has some sort of hidden political agenda. He can't please everyone. He may end up pleasing no one."

"We can't help him with that," Chloe said. "All we can do right now is enjoy this beautiful night."

On April 14, Chloe and the other passengers awoke to a hot breezy day. The *Arago* had anchored just outside the shallow bay at Charleston. Standing on deck with the Beecher party, Chloe watched a converted blockade runner come to transport them to shore. As it pulled alongside the ship, Chloe could see a flurry of activity on board. The sailors were shouting something, waving their hands and dancing around as if possessed. Her heart clenched, fearing the worst.

Henry Ward Beecher leaned over the railing to hear what was being said. He turned back to his friends as joy suffused his face and raised his arms above his head. "Hallelujah!"

Before he could say anything more, Theodore Tilton shouted, "Lee has surrendered!"

A momentary frown flashed across Henry's face. Chloe felt sorry for him. Henry hated to have his thunder stolen. But no one else seemed to notice. The entire ship had broken into a joyous din. The smile returned to Henry's face. He leaned toward Chloe, eyes shining, and said, "I feel as though every man is my brother and every woman my sister. What a wonderful omen for our event today."

The distinguished visitors crowded aboard the smaller ship that would take them to the fort through a jumble of ships draped in flags and bunting. The crowd of *Arago* passengers had pushed Chloe and Henry together, separating them from the rest of their friends.

"So serious, my dear friend?" Henry asked with a teasing smile. He slipped his arm around her waist to keep her from being brushed aside by others. "Your beautiful eyes are so mysterious. Unlike so many others, they never reveal the depths of your thoughts. Are you not happy that the war is over?"

Chloe turned to look back past the *Arago*, toward the ship *Oceanus*, anchored nearby. When Henry's followers became indignant about not being chosen to accompany him, one of them chartered the *Oceanus* and filled it with most of Brooklyn. Moses was aboard the *Oceanus*. "Of course I'm pleased," she said. "I just wish I could share the moment with my husband."

"I'm sure he would want you to express your jubilation none-theless," Henry said. "Human beings spend too much time bemoaning the errors in our lives. I know that I am guilty of that. When a joyous occasion arrives, we must embrace the feeling like we would a small child, with no reservation." He squeezed her tight for a moment before loosening his grip, but he kept his arm around her waist.

A soft and warm gladness spread through Chloe. She refused to feel badly about not being with Moses when she was with such an inspirational man. Henry always understood exactly how she felt.

The visiting dignitaries disembarked and walked up wooden steps over the wall of the ruined fort and down onto the parade ground. They were accompanied by drum and fife, and by four thousand people who had gathered for the event.

Chloe hung back and waited for Moses, who was among the first to disembark from the *Oceanus*. They'd been married so long that a smile and quick handclasp expressed their feelings about being together, the Union victory, and sharing this momentous occasion.

They found a place where they could see Henry Ward Beecher speak. As soldiers raised the flag over Fort Sumter, Chloe saw tears running down Henry's face. She knew they were tears of joy, but her nurturing instinct wanted to take him into her arms and wipe the tears away. Moses would never let himself be so vulnerable in public. They presented a stoic front, Moses and Chloe, and sometimes forgot to put it aside when they were alone.

Ted Tilton stood near them, and Chloe's heart froze as she heard him say, "I don't know why Reverend Beecher was chosen to speak here today. Everyone knows his sermons aren't as good as they once were. The scandalous rumors about him cause more comment than his ideas about love." He laughed, and Chloe missed the response of whoever Ted was talking to.

It was true that when someone reached a pinnacle, several more people gathered to knock him off. Those striving for the top picked at the political and religious statements of someone like Reverend Beecher and attributed meanness where only generosity was intended. Chloe pushed away the heartache caused by Ted's words and focused on the words of the speaker.

It didn't matter what Henry Ward Beecher said that day or how he said it. The Union had prevailed, and euphoria elevated the crowd.

THE TRIAL HAD BEEN in progress for almost three months when Henry Ward Beecher took the stand on April 1. His supporters had taken to sending bouquets of flowers every day, so much so that the defense's table was buried in them. Judge Neilson banned the flowers, calling them a distraction to the proceedings. So when his lawyer called Henry to the stand, he carried only a fresh nosegay of violets.

Chloe, with Moses beside her as always, watched Henry draw himself up tall as if getting ready to preach a sermon. "He looks very dignified," she whispered to her husband.

"He is a prosperous man, well-known, and well-loved by his congregation. His friends are powerful and wealthy. I would expect him to conduct himself with dignity."

Chloe shook her head at his frosty tone. "He is your friend, Moses."

Her husband's jaw tensed. "Yes, we've been friends. But Chloe, this trial has ramifications far beyond the man on trial. Henry is accused of destroying the Tilton family, dishonoring Elizabeth and causing Ted to be thrown out of the church. If Ted prevails, Henry is ruined, too, as well as his family and all of Plymouth Church. A lot of people would lose their connection to God."

"If Ted had handled this privately, man to man, instead of going to the newspapers and pressing charges, he'd still have his family, his career, and his church." Chloe couldn't meet her husband's eyes. She looked at her hands, clasped in her lap, and tried not to fidget.

"Ted just couldn't accept that Elizabeth's feelings for Henry were an expression of God's love," Moses said in a flat tone.

"We love our parents, our children, our spouses, our friends, and our preacher all in different ways. The mistake here was Ted making something carnal out of it and provoking a scandal in the newspapers." Chloe kept her voice calm, refusing to let the subtext erupt.

They'd discussed this before, while she was pregnant with Violet. Chloe wasn't sure she'd ever heard the truth of her husband's heart, only the truth inspired by duty. It took a truly generous soul to allow his wife to love another man, to accept a mistake when that love expressed itself inappropriately, and to forgive. Moses tried. He really did. Ted Tilton, in the same situation, allowed his anger to boil over and had chosen scandal. Moses had chosen his marriage. Chloe knew the choice did not always sit easy with him.

"What about Victoria?" Chloe asked, shifting the topic. Victoria Woodhull was at the root of this scandal. The woman had made a name for herself as a suffragist, a spiritualist, and the first female candidate for president. She had accused Henry Ward Beecher of his affair with Elizabeth Tilton in an article printed in the magazine she owned. It was the beginning of a series of events that culminated in Ted Tilton bringing this case to court.

"I don't understand why she hates Henry so much," Moses said. "Victoria's a close friend of Henry's sister."

"Henry is progressive, that's true, but Victoria goes too far. He believes joy and pleasure are gifts from God, but draws the line at the physical free love Victoria supports."

"I will not sit here in this courtroom and discuss free love," Moses said. "A preacher plays at being God when he thinks his own efforts can change the world. Henry's my friend, but I know he dances close to that line. It's not appropriate for a man, especially a preacher, to continue crossing the line and begging for forgiveness."

The bailiff approached Henry with the Bible. The courtroom fell silent, preventing Chloe from saying anything else. Her husband's words were as close as he'd ever come to chastising their preacher.

Henry took a deep breath and struck a dramatic pose. "Young man," he said to the bailiff, "I have conscientious scruples about swearing on the Bible."

Confused, the bailiff looked to the lawyers, then the judge.

Moses whispered to Chloe, "What is he doing? There's truly no point in delaying this any further." Annoyance clipped his tone.

She knew the emotions in Moses, whirling like a storm about to break, had more to do with her own relationship with Henry Ward Beecher than with this trial. She said nothing.

At the judge's nod, the bailiff swore Henry in using the presence of God rather than the Bible itself. Henry's lawyers came forward and questioned him on charges from undue familiarity to carnal inter-course. Henry denied everything, maintaining a positive attitude throughout. He was modest rather than confrontative, with a self-deprecating humor that made the audience clap wildly. Judge Neilson stopped the questioning several times to warn the audience against unseemly applause.

When the defense rested, Moses said to Chloe, "That should be good enough to bring this trial to a close."

Chloe knew Moses had wanted Henry to confront his accusers earlier. Chloe admired Henry's performance, but ached at the necessity for such a show.

But when the lead lawyer for the prosecution began the cross examination, Henry's entire demeanor changed. His answers were clipped, with none of the casual humor he'd used previously. Eyes lowered, Henry evaded questions or claimed not to remember. The prosecuting lawyer forced Henry to recant claims he'd made in the church investigation the previous year. Chloe twisted her hands in her lap until Moses stopped her by putting his hand over hers.

For three more weeks, Henry Ward Beecher made a poor showing of withstanding the prosecution's attack. When the lawyer stated that it had been clear for five years that Tilton was accusing him of adultery, Henry protested that he believed the accusations meant nothing more than causing dissent in the Tilton marriage. Letters written by Henry revealed sorrow at his behavior and threats of suicide.

Hearing that, Chloe reached for her husband's hand. No matter what had tried to come between them, he loved her. His warm hand encircled hers, as it had for thirty years, and gave her strength.

Finally, the prosecuting lawyer gave a dramatic wave of his hand and said to the judge, "There is generally not much done, sir, after the sermon but the benediction."

Chloe's eyes opened wide. Surely he didn't believe the judge could bestow a blessing upon the prosecution in the middle of the trial.

Still in the witness box, Henry laughed and said loudly, "There has been no collection taken up!"

Chloe kept her head up. She did not want other audience members to see her cringe at Henry's misplaced attempt at humor. The past weeks had erased the brilliant orator she knew and left a broken man. For the first time, Henry Ward Beecher's mistakes shone brighter than his religious devotion.

As the audience filed out, exhausted from the testimony but looking forward to new witnesses the next day, Chloe and Moses remained seated. They'd learned it was easier to fight their way through the ever-present crowds outside if they were among the last to leave.

If anyone understood Elizabeth's position, it was Chloe. She, too, had been enveloped in God's love while in Henry's arms. Elizabeth had miscarried a child that most likely was the reverend's, but Chloe had Violet. Forgiving Henry's transgression of the line between a pastor and his flock had resulted in Violet, her gift from God. Was it possible Elizabeth had never forgiven Henry so her own gift was never born? Chloe found herself imagining a world where Moses reacted like Ted to her relationship with Henry. If Ted won his case, she might yet feel open hostility instead of whispers about Violet's parentage. If Ted won his case, her own marriage might be ruined.

AFTER TRAVELING to Fort Sumter in the spring of 1865 with Reverend Beecher's retinue, Chloe could not get enough of Henry's preaching. He visited her almost daily, bringing treats and gifts to the children and talking with Chloe about the benevolent God she wanted so desperately to embrace. On occasion, a few of Chloe's friends were present during one of Henry's impromptu talks. Chloe insisted vehemently that no one stand up to leave while Henry was talking, and she didn't hesitate to rebuke anyone who did.

That fall, Moses told her he could stand it no longer. He sold the house in Brooklyn Heights to his brother and moved his entire family out of the city for the second time. "Your association with the preacher is dragging me into despair," he told Chloe. "The one aim of my life has always been to love and cherish you, to bask in your affection. But now that affection is directed elsewhere and I can no longer tolerate it."

"I love you, Moses, and have no desire to cause you anguish," Chloe said.

Distance from Plymouth Church didn't weaken Chloe's faith, but she missed Reverend Beecher's sermons with an ache that she couldn't heal. Eunice wrote to her of church doings, but that only made Chloe think of Henry even more. Moses slipped deeper into melancholy. One day he wouldn't get out of bed, and Chloe called the doctor.

After examining Moses, the doctor joined Chloe in the hallway. "I won't sugarcoat this, Mrs. Beach. Your husband is seriously ill with typhoid fever."

"Typhoid fever?" Chloe repeated. She thought of the strong man who had whisked her out of New York scant weeks before. He didn't resemble the gaunt man now confined to bed.

"Has he been worried over much?" the doctor asked.

Chloe nodded. "He has."

"The mind is powerful. If it is afflicted, it can affect the body."

Chloe furrowed her brow. "His melancholy caused the typhoid fever?"

"No, it wouldn't cause it. But his mental state surely weakened him. I will return to check on him tomorrow."

All winter, Moses hung at death's door and Chloe never left his side. She sponged his painful rashes and helped him through bouts of intestinal distress. When the winter ice began to melt, Moses rallied. By the time the apple trees were in bloom, he could sit at the window and admire them. In March of 1866, mostly recovered but still weak, he sat Chloe down for a talk.

"I know I nearly died," he said. She began to protest, but he forestalled her with a raised hand. "I would have gone willingly, but for you. My love for you means I must protect you, but it also means I must do what makes you happy. I've repurchased our house on Brooklyn Heights."

Chloe was stunned. "Oh, Moses." Her heart soared. Not only was her husband well again, but she would soon be back in the bosom of Plymouth Church. She kissed him and said, "Thank you, my love."

The Beach family slipped right back into their old life in Brooklyn Heights. Henry Ward Beecher resumed his daily visits, bringing God's word to Moses and God's love to Chloe. If Moses looked despondent, Chloe blamed the illness that continued to fell him with bouts of intestinal distress.

One day in April, Moses went to lie down for a short rest. Chloe sent the children out for the day with their tutor, hoping the peace and quiet would help Moses sleep.

Henry arrived only a few minutes later.

Chloe said, "Oh, Henry, Moses is in need of your guidance today but he is sleeping. Can you stay a while?"

"Of course I can," he said.

Chloe took him into a sitting room at the back of the house and sat on a small couch. "My husband's melancholy overwhelms me," she said. "He suffers so, and he cannot seem to put this illness behind him."

Henry sat down beside her on the couch and took both her hands in his. "Chloe, God commends your love for Moses. If I can help you regain your spiritual strength, I will do so."

His eyes were filled with an earnest passion. Chloe felt her tears well up, and one slid down her cheek. Henry's words filled her with peace. He understood her turmoil and wanted only for her to be enveloped in God's love. "Oh, Henry," she said as her tears spilled.

Henry leaned toward her and lifted a finger to gently wipe away each tear. Chloe barely felt it when he kissed a tear from her cheek. As he kissed her eyelids, Chloe's heart nearly burst with joy. She hadn't felt such happiness since before Moses had snatched his family out of New York the previous year. Turning her head slightly, she caught Henry's next kiss on her lips. He deepened the kiss, inflaming every inch of Chloe's skin. She trembled as they pulled apart.

"This is wrong," Chloe said, turning her face away. She still struggled with merging Henry's view of God's love with society's expectations of a married woman.

Henry kept hold of her hands. "God's love exists beyond the ties of family and tradition, dear Chloe. We must embrace our natural soul affinities, those connections that exist on a higher plane. God encourages us to be true to our desires without guilt or fear."

Chloe whispered his name as his hands caressed her body. She pushed guilt and doubt out of her mind and surrendered to the euphoria that suffused her body.

Afterwards, she was surprised to see tears on Henry's cheeks. "I am weak," he said. "I cannot love without guilt, no matter what I preach."

"God forgives you," Chloe said, "and so do I."

By late summer, Chloe could no longer hide her swelling stomach. Moses narrowed his eyes when she told him they'd be having a baby after the first of the year. The children had gone to bed, and they were sitting in the parlor as they did most evenings.

"Immaculate conception, was it?" he said. His tone dripped with sarcasm. "I was pretty sick last spring. I don't recall moments intimate enough to produce that." He pointed at her stomach.

Chloe didn't want to admit her relationship with Henry Ward Beecher, which had continued while all of her husband's energy was expended getting to work in Manhattan every day. She also was incapable of lying to this man she loved. They'd never kept secrets from each other. Even so, he would see this as society did—a major rejection of her marriage vows. Her heart twisted. When she was with Henry, it felt like being in the arms of God. It wasn't wrong to want such joy for herself. Society's laws, however, were undeniable. In the court of public opinion, she had done wrong. "It might be Henry's." She braced for his reaction. It wasn't what she expected.

Moses dropped his head into his hands and his shoulders slumped. "In wanting you to be happy, I have delivered myself into eternal Hell," he said. After a long silence that chilled Chloe to the bone, he said, "The child will, of course, be raised as ours."

A pang of guilt struck Chloe. She pushed it away. Henry insisted she had a right to love whoever she wanted, that their love was God's love, so how could it be wrong?

Henry was delighted when Chloe told him about the baby. "I will acknowledge this child in my heart of hearts," he promised her, "even though the world will see Moses as the father."

In January of 1867, a daughter was born to Moses and Chloe Beach. Chloe named her Violet, after Henry's favorite flower that symbolized a hidden gem and innocence. Chloe adored her, and Henry showered the infant with gifts. He told Chloe that Violet was evidence of God's love and approval. Chloe believed God had given her Violet because she'd forgiven Henry for the act that created her.

When Violet was only a few months old, Moses took his oldest daughter, Emma, on a five-month cruise to the Holy Land.

NEAR THE END of Henry Ward Beecher's time on the stand, the prosecutor questioned him about a letter he'd written to Theodore Tilton that was filled with guilt and apology. The prosecution referred to it as the Letter of Contrition. On that day, the author Mark Twain came to see the reverend testify. Henry Ward Beecher, Moses Beach, and Mark Twain were old friends. Even so, the author's attendance sparked excitement in an audience growing numb from days and days of detailed interrogation.

Moses Beach nodded to Mark Twain before the trial began for the day, and afterwards exchanged a few words.

"Henry seems at ease," Mark Twain said. "Innocent and unafraid, at least."

"He's holding up well," Moses said.

Mark Twain scratched the back of his neck. "I must admit his style of speaking doesn't measure up to what I know of him, though."

Moses said, "He spoke better when he made his statement. The cross-examination has rattled him a bit, I think."

Mark Twain nodded and made his way out of the courtroom.

The next morning, Moses read the *Sun* over breakfast as he'd done since before he sold the newspaper. Chloe sipped her tea and scanned the society pages. A sharp laugh from Moses brought her head up sharply.

"Oh, that's rich! I don't know whether to laugh or cry," he said.

Chloe shook her head, not understanding.

"The *Sun* reporter didn't recognize Mark Twain. They mistook him for Ted's friend, Frank Moulton. I'm glad I'm not in charge anymore. How embarrassing for the paper."

Chloe said, "Both men have red hair and handlebar mustaches. I suppose it's an honest mistake."

Moses laughed. "It's a joke on Mark Twain, actually. He despises Frank's appearance."

His laughter faded long before he and Chloe had collected Henry and Eunice and proceeded to the courtroom.

With the conclusion of Henry Ward Beecher's testimony, the

public began insisting that Victoria Woodhull and Elizabeth Tilton be brought to the stand.

"Will Elizabeth testify?" Chloe asked Moses. She already knew that lawyers for both sides considered Victoria to be too unpredictable to put on the stand.

Moses shook his head. "She wants to, I hear. The injunction against spouses testifying doesn't really apply since it's not her husband who is on trial. His lawyers, though, shouldn't let her speak. She's changed her story so many times no one will believe anything she says."

That morning, Elizabeth Tilton rose from her seat, looking like a pale wraith. "Your Honor, I have a communication which I hope you will read aloud." She handed a piece of paper to the bailiff, who gave it to the judge. He glanced at it but didn't read it.

Judge Neilson banged his gavel. "Take your seat, Mrs. Tilton."

Elizabeth Tilton sank into her chair as if she was melting. After the day's testimony, newspaper reporters mobbed her.

"Soon everyone will know her current version of the story," Moses said with the satisfaction of an old newspaperman.

When it was published, Elizabeth's statement did nothing more than attest to her innocence. She expressed a desire to tell the whole truth, including how she was compelled to lie in previous statements.

Moses threw down the morning paper in disgust. "Whatever is the woman thinking? She's made so many confessions and retractions that no one cares about her anymore." He looked up at Chloe, sitting across from him at the breakfast table. "Closing arguments begin today. God willing, we will be finished with this soon."

Finished. The decision of the court had the potential to end Henry's career. Ted and Elizabeth's marriage was already broken, but if the court ruled for Ted, they might be able to mend it. This decision could even validate or ruin Victoria Woodhull. Moses had been wonderful, but she feared his determination would dissolve if faced with open disapproval of his handling of Violet's parentage. Society believed Chloe's love for Henry to be immoral. Until now, she'd been able to live with her core belief that their love transcended any earthly restrictions. If that relationship was publicly dragged through the mud, Chloe's marriage would be broken like Elizabeth Tilton's. The end of this trial would be a day of reckoning for more than just Henry Ward Beecher.

For twenty-five days, the prosecution and defense teams presented their closing arguments. Both sides claimed to be on the side of righteousness and decency.

The lawyer for the defense said, "Our social structure of marriage and religion is false to the core. Do we believe there is no connection between character and conduct? That vicious men hide behind the cloak of sanctity? Henry Ward Beecher lives his life as he preaches. He believes all humankind should strive to see the world as God does, to love and forgive others as God does. Humanity is full of conflicting desires and mixed motives, so it is especially important to find strength of character in refuting false evidence. Let people be judged by the good they do, not who others say they are."

That sounded right to Chloe. Henry was first to admit that he was human and made mistakes, but that God's love surrounded him always. God always forgave the sinners. She knew, after this was all over, that no matter the outcome Henry Ward Beecher would forgive Ted Tilton for what he'd done to bring this scandal to light. She prayed for her own strength to forgive.

At one point, the prosecution said, "It all comes down to human nature. Do you truly believe it is possible for a man to hear his wife confess betrayal, then forgive her and continue to live with her, even if he is miserable?"

Chloe felt ice fill her veins. Her ears filled with a roaring noise that had nothing to do with the courtroom where she was sitting. Was this it? Was this where someone accused Moses of being a more patient version of Ted Tilton? She had entertained doubt many times in the past few years, believing she didn't deserve the love of such a good man as Moses Beach. She doubted Reverend Henry Ward Beecher's promise that God encouraged expressions of love. She knew Henry blamed his human weakness for taking God's love further than he should have. But God had given them Violet. No better proof of God's approval existed. Few, if any, in this courtroom understood that.

Moses kept looking straight ahead, as if the lawyer's words were more legal minutiae that made a lay person's head swim. His hand found Chloe's though, and they held each other tightly. Whatever the world thought, their marriage worked for them. Or had until this point.

After six months of testimony, the case was sent to the jury. That night, June 25, Henry Ward Beecher held his usual Friday night prayer meeting. Despite being in the midst of the first heat wave of summer, the church was full. The meeting started with the choir singing "Praise God From Whom All Blessings Flow." When Henry stood to address his congregation, Chloe thought he looked so tired he might be ill. The case had taken a toll on him.

Henry said, "The world is wide and will not be destitute of opportunities. As long as there is a champion needed for the downtrodden, so long as any need God and can't see Him directly, they will see Him reflected in me if God gives me the power to go on."

The rousing support seemed to cheer him.

The next day, Henry left for his farm in Peekskill for a much needed rest. Eunice stayed. She would send word when the jury returned with a verdict. Moses and Chloe Beach waited at the courthouse with Eunice.

"Twelve retail merchants," Eunice said of the jury. "Head juror is a flour merchant." Her tone was disconnected, dazed.

"We can do nothing now but wait," Chloe told her.

"Thank you, Chloe," Eunice said. "You and Moses have been dear friends."

For eight days, the jurors did not leave the building. Neither did Eunice Beecher.

"I will stand vigil until my husband is cleared," she said.

"We will stay with you," Moses said.

They watched as two old mattresses were taken upstairs for the jurors to take turns sleeping on. Food and clothing changes were carefully inspected by Judge Neilson before being sent up. The heat intensified. Chloe could hear the jurors upstairs moving from one side of the room to another to avoid the sunlight coming in the windows. It was stifling in the courtroom. Upstairs it would be even worse.

Outside, the circus atmosphere had given way to a grim vigil. People crowded nearby rooftops to peer into the juror room. Some even rented rooms that faced the courthouse.

Inside, Chloe could feel the sweat pooling beneath her breasts and sticking to her back. She had given up holding Eunice's hand for support. It was too hot to touch anyone. Chloe's mind ran over every testimony that had been given over the past six months. The jury could render a decision that would validate Henry Ward Beecher's entire pedagogy. If that happened, both Tiltons would be forgiven. Knowing Henry, he might even welcome Ted back into the church. If Henry prevailed, future scandals over his relationships would cease to be a threat. Chloe could rebuild her husband's trust in their marriage.

If Theodore Tilton prevailed, Henry would feel as though the world was against him. Chloe knew how much Henry had strayed from the hellfire and brimstone preaching style of his father. Henry ardently believed in his gospel of love. It would ruin him to be denied. And it might well ruin her own marriage as well.

By the sixth day of deliberations, everyone was exhausted. Henry Ward Beecher returned from the country and resumed his seat at the defense's table without even greeting Eunice. Chloe ached for her friend, who had stood by her husband despite the loveless state of their marriage. Just before lunch time, the jurors came into the courtroom. Despite the heat, Chloe took Moses's hand.

The head juror stepped forward, his hair damp with sweat and his collar stained. Chloe remembered Eunice identifying him as a flour merchant. He said, "Your Honor, after fifty-two ballots we are unable to reach a verdict."

Judge Neilson reached for his gavel in a courtroom stunned into silence. As he closed the trial on a hung jury, however, the room erupted into cheers and applause.

"Congratulations," Moses said to Eunice.

Chloe's mouth had dropped open into a very unladylike expression. She snapped it closed and looked at Eunice. "Not as satisfying as an outright win," she said, "but better than a loss."

"He's been found not guilty if not innocent," Eunice said.

Chloe considered her remark. A verdict of not guilty would have sent the message that the jury believed Henry Ward Beecher had been innocent. Eunice was right. By not delivering a verdict, they told Henry that they didn't have enough evidence to convict. They were not saying they believed him innocent.

It was a legal technicality. To the world, Henry Ward Beecher had won.

Henry turned to face the audience, and in his best preaching voice, said, "As it says in Malachi, 'For those who have faith in Christ, Judgment Day will be the day of final salvation when they are rescued from all of the adverse effects of sin.' Thank you for your support, my friends."

HISTORICAL NOTES:

Elizabeth Tilton watched as her marriage was dragged through the mud. With no verdict, the public believed Ted Tilton lost the case. After publicly admitting the affair, she was dismissed from Plymouth Church. Consumed with embarrassment and guilt at this public airing, she filed for divorce. Ted, dismissed from the church before the trial, was unable to make a living in New York after the verdict and moved to Paris.

Victoria Woodhull was ruined. Once well known and respected as a suffragette and writer, her vicious attacks on Henry Ward Beecher backfired and she was shunned by everyone working for women's rights, including Henry's sisters. Victoria was the whistleblower condemned for bringing it all out into the open.

Eunice Beecher had been taken for granted for most of her marriage. She valued Chloe's friendship, and considered the Beach family, including Violet, as part of her own family. Eunice's unquestioning support of her husband paid off. No verdict meant she could continue the life she'd become accustomed to, imperfect as it might be.

Chloe Beach felt relief at the verdict. Her own marriage was safe. She and Moses continued attending Plymouth Church, and they bought a farm in Peekskill next door to Henry Ward Beecher. Chloe couldn't shake the image, though, of Henry being broken by the prosecuting lawyers. He was most often just a man, after all, not a man of God.

FOR MORE ABOUT Moses and Chloe Beach, and their daughter Emma, read my novel *Innocents at Home*.

ABOUT THE AUTHOR

Linda Ulleseit, an award-winning writer of heritage fiction, has an MFA in Creative Writing from Lindenwood University. Her books, including the most recent *Innocents at Home*, are the stories of women in her family who were extraordinary but unsung. She has also written a young adult historical fantasy trilogy and several stories for anthologies. Linda is a founding member of Paper Lantern Writers and member of Historical Novel Society. She is a retired elementary school teacher who now enjoys writing full time as well as cooking, leatherworking, reading, gardening, spending time with her family, and walking her dog.

THE TENTH COMMANDMENT

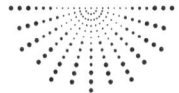

BY JONATHAN POSNER

Thou shalt not covet thy neighbor's house, thou shalt not covet thy neighbor's wife, nor his manservant, nor his maidservant, nor his ox, nor his ass, nor any thing that is thy neighbor's.
The Tenth Commandment (Exodus 20:17, King James Version)

ESSEX, ENGLAND, SUMMER 1515

T he stag staggered to a halt in the forest clearing.

It gave a deep snort; a cloud of breath bursting from its flared nostrils. A dark eye flicked left and right, seeming to search for the men who had been pursuing it across the sunlit parklands and into the dappled light of the trees. It raised its head and sniffed hard, as if seeking the men's distinctive scent. But none seemed to reach it, and with a small grunt it dropped its head and began stripping and eating the leaves off a sapling.

Sir Andrew Fox watched the beast as it finished the first sapling and moved to another, seeming now to be off guard. He moved behind the thick oak trunk he was using as cover and rested his back against it. He slipped an arrow out of his quiver. With another quick glance round the tree to check the beast was still unaware of his downwind presence, he fitted the arrow to the string of his bow and took three deep, steadying breaths.

He was about to swing round and shoot, when a movement caught his eye. It was no more than a shadow changing amongst the trees. He looked again, but there was nothing.

Then it came once more, and this time he recognised it as another hunter, slipping from one tree to the next. Andrew frowned, concentrating hard, ready to still the man with a raised hand so as not to alert the beast.

This one is mine, he thought. *I will not have another rob me of the kill.*

There was a further movement and the man emerged. A shaft of sunlight flashed across his face before he slipped behind a new tree. Andrew's frown deepened. It was someone he did not know; someone who had been brought as a guest by one of the other hunters when they were forming up earlier at Marchington Manor.

The man emerged again, and this time Andrew took his hand off his bow and held it up, glancing back over his shoulder at the stag. The other hunter seemed to understand; he nodded and became still.

Andrew took a deep breath, then slid round the trunk so he was again facing the clearing. The stag still had its head down, and was close enough for Andrew to see the neck pulsing as the blood coursed through the beast's veins. Andrew held his breath as he drew back the bow, aiming for the heart. For a moment he kept his aim as the beast continued to eat.

As if the stag seemed to sense Andrew's presence, it stopped grazing and lifted its head with a grunt. Andrew kept as still as he could, as the stag swung its head around.

It gave a small snort as it turned towards Andrew. Its eyes narrowed and it let out a deep bellow. It had seen its hunter.

Andrew let his arrow fly.

He had aimed to kill the beast outright—but his shot missed completely. With an enraged bellow, the stag dropped its head and charged. As the animal thundered across the clearing, Andrew knew he could never outrun it. Instead he tried to draw another arrow, but in his haste, he fumbled it.

The ground was shaking as the stag got closer. It was nearly on him, bellowing again. Andrew decided he had to run. Just as he jumped away from the tree, a figure stepped into his path with bow raised. There was the whoosh of an arrow almost in his ear.

The stag screamed.

At least that was what Andrew thought it sounded like as the beast crashed to the forest floor. The scream of a creature felled in a single moment of agony. Undergrowth and branches were tossed aside like chaff in the wind as the great beast came tumbling to a stop.

Andrew staggered to a standstill against another tree and looked back, breathing hard. The stag had its forelegs out and its head was down. The great antlers with their evil spiked tips were pointing forward. The thought of those horns goring him in the back made Andrew almost vomit. The other man stepped past him and walked over to the stag.

"Is it dead?" Andrew panted.

The man prodded it in the side of its neck. "I would say so," he replied. He took hold of the antlers and, with some effort, pulled them back. The head came up, to reveal the shaft and flights of the arrow buried deep into the beast's chest. "I warrant my arrow pierced its heart directly."

He let the head fall back again and rubbed the dirt off his hands.

"Sir Reginald de Courtney," he said, sweeping off his cap with a small bow. "I do not believe we were introduced earlier." He replaced his cap and straightened up.

Andrew drew himself to his full height, but found he was still looking up at Sir Reginald. The man's thin stature made Andrew feel as if he were an ungainly pudding. "Sir Andrew Fox," he muttered, giving a perfunctory bow without removing his cap. "Of Marchington Manor."

Reginald looked him up and down, a small smile turning up one side of his mouth. "That was good fortune," he observed. "Had I not been able to loose an arrow, we would even now be picking pieces of you off those fearsome horns."

For a moment Andrew was tempted to damn the man for his

impudence, but he resisted, swallowing hard. "I must thank you, Sir Reginald," he said. "Your quick action saved my life."

Before Reginald could reply there was a rustling in the undergrowth and several other men appeared. The first one walked over to the stag, looked all round it, then came up to Andrew and put a hand on his shoulder. "By Heavens, cousin," he said, "that is a fearsome beast. Is it you to be congratulated for shooting the arrow that felled it?"

For a moment, Andrew hesitated. Could he actually claim credit for the kill? All it would take was a strong denial when Sir Reginald protested. Then to call this thin stranger out as a liar.

There was every chance Andrew could make it work. His cousin, Sir Richard Fox, was unbearably honest and always ready to believe whatever he was told. But then Andrew remembered that every man's arrows are different, and it would be easy to identify the one in the stag's chest as Sir Reginald's.

"Nay," he replied, shaking his head. "It is Sir Reginald here who is to be thanked for his quick action. He loosed an arrow of his own, after mine failed to kill the beast as it was coming for me."

Richard bowed to Reginald. "Then I must give you my heartfelt thanks, sir, for my cousin's deliverance. I, and the rest of our family, are most grateful."

Andrew made a grimace. Who was Richard to act as if he were the head of the Fox family? That was his position—his right as the eldest, even though it was only by a few months. He had held the position ever since the death of their grandfather a few years before. Grandfather Fox had taken over the upbringing of his grandsons after both their fathers had fallen fighting the Cornish rebels at Deptford Bridge when the boys were infants. Grandfather had treated them as if they were brothers, although it had always been clear to Andrew that the old man favored Richard. Grandfather's death had come just as both boys had become men. But because Richard was now taller, slimmer, and more manly, people seemed to assume he was naturally the head of the family.

Andrew scowled. "Thank you, Richard," he snapped. "We must have the carcass taken back to the kitchens. See to it, will you?"

THE HUNT OVER, the men mounted up and made their way back to the house. Richard and his companions set off at pace, leaving Andrew and Reginald riding slowly behind.

Reginald drew his horse alongside Andrew's, and they rode together for a few minutes in an uneasy silence. Then Reginald said, "I warrant you were seriously considering claiming the kill as your own back there, Fox."

Andrew shook his head. "Nay, you are mistaken," he said in his most innocent tone. "I would ne'er do such a thing."

They rode on. Andrew took it that his denial had been believed, so further conversation on the subject was unnecessary. He glanced across at the other man, sitting tall and slender in his saddle. The fellow must have seen how he had given serious, if momentary, thought to making the claim. Andrew made a small curse below his breath. He must learn to control his expression better. How could he hope to assert himself over his upstart cousin if he could not scheme undetected?

For scheme he must, if he was ever going to achieve his greatest ambition: to win back the heart of Eleanor—the girl he loved more than life itself. The girl Richard had stolen from him.

His thoughts were interrupted by a sudden comment from Reginald.

"I would."

"You would what?"

"I would have considered claiming the kill if the positions had been reversed."

Andrew stared at him. What in the name of all that is holy was the man saying?

"If I could have succeeded in the falsehood; if it had been my word against yours, I would have claimed the kill, had you been the one to make it."

Andrew could not think of a single thing to say. To have his own deviousness reflected back by another man was a new, and somewhat disconcerting, experience.

"I believe we are very much alike, you and I," Reginald continued with an easy smile. "But you are, I believe, easier to read. Your face tells your story like the open pages of a book." He gave a small chuckle. "For example, I can see you dislike your cousin. Why is that? He seems a pleasant enough fellow."

"It is complex," Andrew muttered.

"Tell me, then. I might be able to help."

Andrew bit his lip as he considered his response. Should he share his deepest concerns with this man? A man he had only met this very morning? Although one who had saved his life...

Throwing his usual caution to the wind, Andrew said, "I do dislike him." He paused. "No, I do not dislike him; that is not the case. In truth, I hate him!"

"You say this with great feeling," Reginald said. "How is it so?"

Andrew took a deep breath. "For many reasons. He was the favorite of our grandfather, who raised us as his own. And all men seem to think him head of the family." He paused. "For all that is my position, not his."

Reginald leaned forward in his saddle. "But all this can be solved by you simply asserting your rights and your position?"

"Perhaps. But there is one thing that cannot be so asserted."

Reginald raised an eyebrow. "And that is?"

"He stole the girl I love, married her, and has three sons by her."

They rode on in silence again, each considering these words hanging in the air between them. Eventually Reginald frowned, then said, "If this is so, you must have held this grudge for many years. How old are his sons?"

Andrew thought a moment. "Richard is around six years. Edward is, I think, a year younger. There is an infant called Henry in his third summer."

"And you have never found a wife yourself?"

Andrew gave a rueful shake of his head. "Nay, for I cannot while Eleanor stays under my roof, and smiles and makes kisses at him like an enchanted angel. How could I countenance another woman, when she is so close?"

"They smile and kiss? Then it was a love match, not arranged?"

"It was arranged to start, but…" Andrew stared hard at Reginald. "But the arrangement was not with him." He shook his head. "It was with me."

Andrew paused and had to take a breath before he could continue. "She is from the Peshall family of Shropshire, who were looking to build their influence further south."

"I see. So she was betrothed to you, but he took her?"

"Yes. She was brought down and we were introduced. A girl of but seventeen years. The moment she lifted her eyes to mine, it was as if my heart was captured by her beauty. I knew then that I loved her, and would love her for all my life. So, I was happy with the forth-coming marriage, and told Grandfather that I was well pleased to make the match." Andrew gave a small sigh. It was good to say this to another man; something he had kept to himself for the last eight years. It had been eating him up from inside, like an evil canker.

"So, what was the problem?" Reginald asked.

"Richard," Andrew snarled. "He was the problem."

Reginald nodded. "I see. She met with Richard, and he made his suit for her?"

"Aye, and he waited not a minute, either." Andrew paused. Here was a chance to lance the canker by pouring out his story. "It was immediately after I had first met her. She was talking to me, and we were making ourselves acquainted, when Richard came in. I could see she was shocked—to be betrothed to the cousin who was short in stature, well-covered in flesh and socially awkward, while the other man was tall, slim and carried himself with such charm and grace. A charm I have never been able to master. It was clear she felt she had been allocated the wrong cousin." He sat back in the saddle feeling almost lighter, as if it was a weight off his mind.

"But there was an arrangement," Reginald asked. "How was this broken?"

"Richard made it his mission to steal her from me. He started by being most attentive to her, making sure he was always at her side. He looked to her every need. Every time I approached her to talk about our wedding, he was there, like he was her guardsman."

"And she welcomed this attention?"

"That she did. Because no matter how hard I tried, I could never match his ability to make her laugh and smile." Andrew scowled. "It was not long before Richard had convinced her that she would be better with him, not me."

"You heard him say this?"

Andrew considered a moment. "Not exactly. But he must have said it at some point—for why else would she have agreed to break the arrangement?"

"And her family?" enquired Reginald. "Were they content with this?"

Andrew shrugged. "I take it they were, for Grandfather impressed on me that the connection between the families was the same, whichever cousin she wed."

"I see." Reginald nodded, and again there was a silence as they continued to plod home.

After a while it was Andrew who spoke. "Grandfather took me aside, and said that the arrangement had changed, and for the good of both families he would be pleased if I accepted it. He said that Eleanor would always hold me in the highest regard, but her preference was for Richard. Would I therefore step aside and be her loving cousin, not her husband? What must I say? Of course, I protested, but Grandfather told me that if I refused, Eleanor would not marry either cousin, but take her dowry back to Shropshire. After the deaths of both of his sons, our fathers, he seemed in need of the money, so I had little choice."

Sir Richard Fox scooped up his youngest son and sat him on his knee.

"How is Henry, my mighty little prince?" he asked, giving the boy a playful bounce. "Papa has been chasing great stags across the countryside. Have you been up to mischief while Papa was out hunting?"

The little boy looked up at him with big solemn eyes. "No, Papa. Mama says I been good. Edward and Richard been practicing fighting with their swords and Mama let me watch."

Just then his wife Eleanor came into the nursery with their other two boys, one holding on to each of her hands. "By Heavens, Rich," she exclaimed, stopping in the doorway, "you are covered in mud and dust!" She grinned. "Begone and change your clothes this instant!"

"I will, presently," he replied. "But I would have a little more time with my boys before they lay down to sleep." He placed the child carefully on the floor and addressed his other sons. "Henry says you two have been practicing your swordplay."

Edward let go of his mother's hand and rushed to his father. "Yes, Papa!" he exclaimed, putting both arms round Sir Richard's waist. "I touched Richard with my blade twice!" He unpeeled himself and patted the middle of his chest. "Right here! I touched him right here!"

"Is that so, Richard?" his father asked with a serious frown. "Did you let down your guard?"

The eldest boy hung his head. "Yes, Papa." He looked up, and held his father's eye with perhaps a little too much intensity. "But I let him, for you said he must learn from his successes as much as his failures."

Sir Richard chuckled, delighted to hear his own words repeated back. He ruffled the boy's hair and said, "I am pleased, Richard. But I must see these moves."

"Oh, my lord!" Eleanor said. "They must lie down to sleep. It is too late for swordplay!"

"Yes, my love," acknowledged their father, "I know. But just a few moves, and they will be even more ready for their beds."

"Just a few then," she agreed.

Both boys pulled their wooden swords from their belts. Sir Richard and Eleanor moved back to give them space. Sir Richard looked on with a critical eye as the boys bowed to each other, then engaged. A couple of times he paused the fight and gave critical instructions, but mostly he made calls of encouragement; recognizing good parries, successful blocks, and expert thrusts. At one point, Edward proved his point by touching his blade to Richard's chest, and their father was strong in his praise.

Eventually, the boys were visibly tiring. Eleanor clapped her hands. "Enough!" she called. "To bed!"

Richard and Edward put their swords in a chest by the wall, and, together with Henry, each gave their father a big hug. After wishing them all a good night, he went to the door, then stopped and turned back. "I will get changed and see you down in the hall," he said to Eleanor before leaving the nursery.

A short while later, she joined him by the fire.

"How do you fare, my love?" he asked as she eased herself into the chair beside him. "You seem a little pale."

She fixed him with her clear blue eyes. "I fare well, husband." She paused and whispered, "And with good reason."

Richard's heart leapt. He had seen that look before, and it was one she used when she had something of the greatest importance to tell him. And what could be more important to a woman than... ? He raised an enquiring eyebrow, inviting her to tell him more. To confirm what he suspected.

She nodded. "I am again with child."

Richard felt a warm glow rise from his toes right up to the crown of his head; a glow that was nothing to do with the fire. He moved over and knelt at her feet, then took her hands in his. "My love! That is the best news!" He gave her a broad smile. "We are truly blessed by the Lord." He moved his hands to her belly. "Perchance it will be another boy?" he asked.

She shook her head. "This one is different." She put her hands over his. "We will have a girl, Rich, I know it. A little sister for the boys."

"A girl!" His smile broadened. "Our own daughter!"

"Yes."

"She will be the most beautiful in all Christendom," he said. "The very image of her mother." He moved one hand up to cup Eleanor's cheek. "She will have your bright eyes, as blue as cornflowers, and your hair, as fair as a field of summer wheat."

"And your steadfast spirit," Eleanor added. "A blessed child indeed."

Richard stood and poured himself some wine from the bottle on the table. "Mary," he announced. "We will call her Mary, after Our Lady. She shall be truly blessed." He raised his glass. "To Mary Fox! May she be healthy and hearty. May she be forever loved by all!"

SIR ANDREW GLANCED along the table to where Eleanor sat beside his cousin, picking daintily at her food. She looked truly radiant this evening; her eyes glowing as if lit from within. She leaned across her husband and made some comment to Sir Reginald, who had been invited to dine after his exploits at the hunt a few days earlier.

Andrew frowned. How could his hated cousin have a wife such as her? Why must Richard have all the joy, and leave him with nothing more than the sight of a thing he could never have? To be left forever wondering what it must be like to hold her? To touch her?

Andrew shifted in his chair as if the seat was suddenly burning him.

How would it be to caress Eleanor? To kiss her neck... His eyes narrowed... Just there, where it rose up to meet the soft curve of her cheek... To have those beautiful eyes gaze up at him, just as they had for that one brief, glorious moment all those years ago. To run his hand from her neck down her velvet-soft skin to those glorious, bounteous...

He slumped in his chair. Truly, the Lord had forsaken him, to place such beauty within reach, yet to deny it to him for all time. While allowing it to his odious cousin instead.

A sudden hand on his shoulder made him start.

"By Heavens, Fox," a voice hissed in his ear, "you look at your cousin's wife as if you would eat her for pudding." Andrew glanced round. Reginald had come to stand beside him. "And you look at your cousin as if you would gladly do him to death. I would you have more of a care for the look on your face. Once again you are an open book."

"Later, Sir Reginald," Andrew whispered back. "We shall talk of this later."

They met in the rose garden after the meal had ended, strolling together by the light of the summer moon. The lights of Marchington Manor flickered behind them as they walked.

"It burns me up, Reginald," Andrew muttered, once he was sure they were out of earshot of anyone inside the Manor.

"So I could see," observed the other, with a dry laugh. "That is your failing."

"Then what must I do to conceal my thoughts?"

Reginald stopped, his angular face taking on a wolverine grin in the blue light of the moon. "Practice, my friend," he said. "Be aware when you have dark thoughts and practice keeping your face still." They walked on until they passed out of the rose garden and into a patch of open grass. A well stood in the middle, its dilapidated roof making it look like a small tumbledown house in the moonlight. They carried on over to it. "Tell me," Reginald said, "what do you think when I talk of...icy stillness?"

Andrew frowned. "I know not," he said, unsure where this was going.

"How about if I say 'frozen'? Does that bring an image of something that moves not?"

"I venture it does."

"Good." Reginald sat on the side of the well. "Then I want you to think of that word whenever something makes you angry, or upset." He crossed one slim leg over the other. "Your cousin has taken the girl you love? How does it make you feel? Frozen. A stag escapes you on the hunt? 'Tis no matter, for you are...frozen. This is how you think to keep your face still. To give naught away. You are frozen, and it serves you well."

"Frozen, eh?" Andrew looked at the word from every side, considering how best to make it work for him.

"Aye. Remember it. And when you feel anger, or frustration, still your face. Make it frozen."

"That I will. I thank you Reginald. This is good advice."

Reginald stood. "Try it," he said. "Let us make a scenario. You walk in and see your cousin making passionate kisses across his wife's face. You wish it were you being so loving to her. How do you feel?"

Andrew scowled. "I would wish him dead," he muttered.

Reginald gave a resigned sigh. "By all means, wish him dead," he said. "But show it not. How is your face to be?"

"Frozen?"

"Yes. Good."

Andrew made a real effort to relax his face, as Reginald studied him carefully. Then the thin man jumped up. "And there it is! Now you give naught away! Remember it well!"

Andrew allowed himself to crack a small smile. "Indeed I will."

ELEANOR CLIMBED into bed next to Richard and drew the hangings closed, so she and her husband were together in the darkness. He moved towards her, putting his arm around her shoulder and drawing her close.

"I saw Father Michael today," she said. "He has agreed to say the blessing and prayers this coming Sunday for safe delivery of the babe. Then we can tell the boys they are to have a little sister."

"I warrant they will be most excited," Richard observed. "It will be a new experience for them."

"The first girl child in the family," she agreed.

There was a silence. Eleanor let it go on for a moment, then asked, "Your thoughts, my husband?"

He pulled her closer. "I was thinking it is a shame Andrew has not married, nor been blessed with sons himself. Or daughters," he added quickly.

"I am sure there are plenty of families looking to make a good match who would have a daughter for him to wed," she responded.

"My Blount cousins have a girl of marriageable age called Elizabeth who would be ideal."

Richard gave a mirthless chuckle. "I do not believe he would look at her," he said. "Whenever the subject of marriage arises, he puts on a face like a bull in pain and finds a different subject immediately." There was another silence. Then he said, "I warrant he has never truly recovered from Grandfather letting you marry me instead. I see the way he looks at you sometimes. It is as if he has taken a blade to the heart."

"I know," Eleanor agreed. "I also see his looks. In truth they concern me, for they speak of a man who is not the master of his emotions. A man who has a temper that ill suits him." She snuggled her head onto Richard's chest. "Unlike my dear husband, who is more even-tempered than any man I have ever met."

He stroked her hair. "Only because I have the loveliest wife any man could wish for."

She raised her head and her lips found his. "When this girl is born, we will be the perfect family. Three boys and a girl. Maybe with more girls to come." She kissed him again. "They are lucky to have such a father."

He kissed her back. "Children need a father. Girls need one so they know how a man should behave." He emphasized this point with another kiss. "Sons need one to be shown how to be a good man." Another kiss. "Andrew and I both lost our fathers as infants. We were lucky to have our grandfather in their place."

She sat back, and tried to see him in the darkness. "But do they need one who lets them practice swordplay when they should be going to sleep in their beds?"

"Ahh, yes, that is because a father knows that skill with a sword is of the highest importance to his sons. There is never a bad time to practice."

THE SUMMER LEAVES were turning brown and falling in drifts across the parklands, as Eleanor's pregnancy became ever more obvious. A range of gowns that she had last worn when carrying Henry were retrieved from their chests, and even these needed to have their lacing loosened as her belly swelled.

Richard helped where he could, spending more time with the boys as she started to become too tired. He shooed away the servants who flustered around the nursery so he could have the boys to himself. He gave his sons more and more instruction in swordplay—even little Henry, who would wave his wooden blade at his brothers in an effort to be included in their learning. Richard also took them riding, finding small ponies for the two eldest, and an even smaller one for Henry.

As the weeks wore on and her belly swelled ever larger, Eleanor found her energy slipping away. It became harder and harder for her to do anything more than struggle down to the hall for meals; and once they were over, she wanted nothing other than to go back to bed.

"I know not why this babe demands so much more of me than any of the boys did," she said to Richard one day. "I have little energy, and every day I must suffer strong headaches that will not let me alone." She squinted at her husband. "And I am seeing two of everything. Including you."

"Is that not twice as good?" he asked.

She gave him a small, playful punch on the arm. "Nay, silly." She lay back and closed her eyes. "Unless it is good that you are both difficult to see clearly. As if through a piece of thick glass."

"For sure this babe, 'tis a girl," he observed, "that she must make her mother suffer so." He leaned forward and laid his hand on her forehead. "Does that help with the headache?"

"Oh, that is nice," Eleanor said with a small smile.

A few minutes later, he tried to take his hand away. Immediately she gave a small groan. "No," she said. "Do not remove it." He put it back and sat beside her on the bed. "It was hurting my arm," he muttered, adjusting his position.

"Mmm. But it eases the pain for me."

Eventually, she must have drifted off to sleep, for when she opened her eyes again, he was gone.

Over the next few days Richard did all he could to keep her spirits up. He brought her hot broth if she wanted to stay in bed throughout the day, and would often sit with her, his hand on her forehead.

"You are my angel," she said one time as he put down a tray of broth and bread. "I could not do this without you."

"I am here, my love," Richard said. "Each and every day, until this babe comes." But the next day, it looked as if Richard might not be able to keep his promise, for he came down with a sudden fever.

At first it was just a slight morning cough, which he dismissed as "nothing much." But it became worse throughout the day, until by the evening he was bending over with paroxysms that left him breathless. Then, after a particularly bad bout, a bright red gobbet of blood landed in the rushes. So, like Eleanor, he also took to his bed.

A barber surgeon was called, who prescribed a foul concoction of herbs that had little effect, then shuffled out, muttering darkly about 'God's will.' By the next day, Richard was lying in a sweat-filled bed, slipping in and out of consciousness.

For Andrew, this was a time of mixed emotions. In part, he could think of no better outcome than his hated cousin, the man who had done him such wrong, breathing his last. But then, he could see how the reports of Richard's deterioration were so desperately upsetting Eleanor. His love for her meant that he could not prevent her pain becoming his pain, and he knew he must do whatever he could for her. So he decided to become her 'angel' himself, and take over the care that Richard had been providing.

He sought out Marion, Eleanor's maid, and accosted her at the foot of the stairs leading up to Eleanor's chamber. She was carrying a tray of broth, bread, and some ale.

"I will take that up," he said. She handed it over and dropped into a small curtsy. "How oft do you bring this?" he asked.

"Three times each day, Master," Marion replied. "An hour past dawn, midday, and an hour before sundown."

"Then I will meet you here each time, and take it up for the mistress myself," he said.

"As you wish."

So three times each day he brought the tray in, and used this as an excuse to spend time talking with her as she lay in bed. He even put his hand to her forehead when she asked, holding it there for a few minutes—or at least as long as it took before his arm started to protest.

"I must thank you, Andrew," Eleanor said when he came in on the third morning of Richard's illness. "I feel so helpless. I should be tending to my husband and my children, but I can do none of these things, for the babe lies so heavy in my belly. You are being most kind."

"I am pleased to help," Andrew found himself saying. "And while I see to your care, the servants do the same for Richard. They take it in turns to tend to his needs, feeding him a little broth and changing his bedding when it becomes too soiled with sweat."

"How does he?"

"There is little change. But he gets no worse. The doctor says that every day he remains with us, the chance increases that the fever will break.

"I pray every minute that it does," Eleanor whispered. "I cannot bear the thought my sons will have no father, and this babe will never know him. Every day, I pray for his deliverance. I am beseeching sweet Jesus to intercede with the Lord, for if Richard has done anything to incur God's wrath, surely he can atone for it."

"I am sure the Lord will hear your prayers," Andrew said.

Frozen.

She sat up and searched his face. "There is something different about you, Andrew," she said with a frown. "Although I am not sure what it is." Then she nodded. "I have it. I usually know exactly what you are thinking, but now I do not." She lay back. "Belike this babe dulls my senses."

"I am sure not," he replied, putting his hand on her forehead.

Frozen.

"That is nice," she murmured. "In truth, you are being very kind, Andrew. Perhaps I have misjudged you."

The next morning it seemed as if Eleanor's prayers worked, for Richard's fever broke.

Andrew came in with her food and set it down carefully. "Your husband sits up and takes some bread and ale," he said. "There is reason to believe his illness is gone."

Eleanor let out a small cry. "Oh, Heaven be praised! The Lord has heard me! Oh, Andrew, is that not the best news we have heard?"

"Indeed it is, Eleanor."

Frozen.

"Send me Marion please, Andrew. I would get dressed and see to my husband. It has been torture for me not to be with him these past days."

Frozen. Frozen. Frozen.

OVER THE NEXT TWO WEEKS, Richard's recovery progressed well, until he was sure he had regained all his strength. This seemed to help Eleanor also, and as her pregnancy moved to the next stage, it seemed that she too had found new energy.

Now that things were back to some level of normality at Marchington Manor, Andrew sent word to Sir Reginald de Courtney, inviting him to visit. It had been some months since he had last joined them, and Andrew looked forward to enjoying the man's companionship once again.

Reginald came a few days later, and agreed to stay for a week or so.

On the first night, Richard and Eleanor retired to their chamber soon after they had all dined, leaving Andrew and Reginald to play chess by the fire.

They were well into their third game when Reginald surprised Andrew with an announcement.

"I was wed a couple of months ago," he said in a conversational tone, "to a woman by the name of Cecilia."

Andrew paused in the act of moving a pawn and looked up. "By Heavens Reginald, you kept that quiet!" His face remained impassive while a more obvious—and concerning—question came to him. "And why was I not invited to the wedding?" He put the pawn down on the board.

Reginald took it with his knight. "Checkmate."

"Eh? What?" Andrew glanced down at the board. "I suppose so." He looked up. "But what is this about a wedding?"

Reginald shrugged. "Cecilia is the daughter of a wealthy Colchester merchant, so she came with a good dowry." He paused. "And, with something else…" he made a curved motion over his belly.

"She is with child?" Andrew gasped. "And you have wed her? I assume it is yours?"

"No, it is another man's. A fellow she was seeing in secret from her family, but who, unlike your cousin, died of the sweating sickness. Her father looked to me to rescue the family's honor." He gave a dry chuckle. "Or such honor as a merchant might have." He paused. "So, once we had agreed upon a considerable dowry, I obliged."

"But…" Andrew struggled with the idea. "But, you have accepted another man's child as your own?"

Again Reginald shrugged. "Why is that so bad? The child will know only me as its father, and I will raise it. This obsession with being the natural father makes little sense to me. Especially as that man is dead and gone." He poured himself some more wine and topped up Andrew's goblet. "But, as she was fallen, you will understand why we had the smallest of ceremonies. No guests."

"I do understand, but…" Andrew shook his head. "A fallen woman, Reginald!" He looked up. Reginald was giving him a sly-looking smile. "What is it?" he demanded.

"I am impressed, Andrew."

"You are…what..?" Andrew felt this conversation was becoming stranger by the minute.

"I am impressed. When I told you my news, your face gave nothing away."

Suddenly all became clear to Andrew. He had been tested—that was all. And he had passed. "I understand," he exclaimed. "You were seeing only if I could keep my emotions from my face. There was no truth in this story of a wedding."

"Actually, no. It is wholly true. I am wed to Cecilia and she is with child. But it was good to see for myself if you can maintain your composure. And you did."

Andrew shook his head. "I know not whether we come or go in these conversations."

Reginald laughed. "Then I will make it clear to you." He settled in his chair and swirled the wine round inside his goblet. "If I have wed a woman already with child." He circled the goblet once more. "Then so can you."

For a moment Andrew thought he had misheard. But the words were there—he had not mistaken them. To marry a woman already with child? What in the Lord's name could Reginald mean?

"I know not such a person," he protested. "And how can I marry some fallen woman, when I have forsworn all others? If I cannot have Eleanor?"

Suddenly Andrew's jaw dropped. He stared wide-eyed at his friend. With all thought of staying frozen leaving his head, he leapt to his feet, knocking the board and sending some of the chess pieces rolling off the table. "What are you proposing? Have you taken leave of your senses?"

"Certainly not." Reginald said. "Listen. As we dined this evening, both you and Sir Richard were full of the tale of his fever, and how close to death he had come." He took a sip of his wine. "And Lady Fox was most concerned to make it known how helpful you had been while her husband was abed, as if standing in as his proxy. She seemed to think you have changed, and are better in control of your temper." He gave a thin smile. "Which I take it is not the case; you are simply better at masking your thoughts?"

Despite his shock, Andrew felt a small swell of pride. "I have been using the method you suggested."

"Good. And it has worked. So now she sees you in a different light; no longer the short-tempered cousin, but instead a man who has the necessary qualities for fatherhood." He paused. "Should her husband have been carried off by the fever."

"But he was not. The shame of it is that he has recovered fully."

"Indeed he has." Reginald picked up the white king and put it upright on its square. Then he reached down to the floor and came back up with the white queen and the black king. He put them on their own squares and looked up at Andrew. "What if a way is found to do what the fever failed to do?" He leaned forward and put his finger on the white king. Without breaking eye contact, he pushed it over. "What if the king were to die? What then?"

As Andrew stared in stunned silence, Reginald moved the black king onto the white king's square, right beside the queen.

"His queen would need a new consort."

THE NEXT DAY, Reginald and Andrew met by the well.

"Do you have a scheme?" Reginald asked. "Have you devised a plan to achieve your aim?"

Andrew took a breath. "I have," he said, glancing round to make sure they were alone. "Now he is recovered, Richard is keen to hunt once again." He leaned in closer, and whispered, "This is where the deed will be done."

"And how exactly?"

Andrew explained his plan in some detail. Reginald asked a few questions for clarification and nodded as Andrew gave his answers. He also made some suggestions of his own, and they debated these until they were both in full agreement.

Reginald then set out the moves they would each need to make, and the order in which they would make them. Once they were both agreed, they made their individual ways back to the Manor.

As he crunched across the pebble path towards the house, Andrew felt as if he was floating on a cloud. It was really going to happen! Finally, he would have the woman he loved as his own! Of course, it would never have been possible without Reginald's instruction in masking his emotions. That simple little word that now came unbidden into his head any time he felt anger, frustration or impatience, stilling his face into an implacable mask. Before it, how he must have shown every angry thought as if written across his face.

Andrew stopped suddenly with his hand on the door latch as a thought came to him. Was that why Eleanor had been so ready to abandon him all those years ago? To switch her favors to his odious cousin? Because she could read him too easily, and did not like what she saw? Well, now he had changed. He had presented himself to her as an even-tempered alternative to Richard, and she had fallen for it.

When Richard met his end, she would come into his arms willingly.

He'd allow her a short period of mourning, and would initially deny any intent to wed her. But once any possible suspicion of the truth of Richard's death was settled, he would present a wedding as the best option for Eleanor and the children.

Andrew could not stop his face breaking into a big grin as he imagined all the happy years they would have together. The boys would grow into fine young men under his instruction, while this new babe—which Richard had said was certain to be a girl—would be ideal for creating an advantageous alliance through marriage. And Eleanor still had many more child-bearing years left. There would be further sons of his own, and more girls to find good marriages.

And the best of this? That he would have won out over his cousin! He would have proved himself a better man than the one Grandfather so obviously favored.

He was Sir Andrew Fox; the older cousin, and not to be trifled with.

THE FOLLOWING morning the hunt formed up in front of the Manor.

It was a crisp, clear day, with the breath of the men and their horses rising into the air as they made ready to mount and set out across the parklands.

A servant placed a mounting block on the path. Sir Andrew climbed up, swung his leg over and settled himself in the saddle. The servant pulled away the block, then offered it to Sir Reginald. Reginald shooed the man away and mounted unaided. He walked his horse over to Andrew.

"All ready?" he murmured, so quietly that Andrew could only just hear. Andrew gave the smallest nod.

Reginald looked round at the group of fellow hunters who were all now mounted as well. Richard was not among them. "I see your cousin is not here," he observed in his normal voice, loud enough for a couple of the nearest men to turn in their direction. "Has he been taken unwell once again?"

Andrew gave a small conspiratorial grin. "Not at all," he replied in the same loud voice. "Thank the Lord for his mercy; my cousin is back to the finest health."

"Heaven be praised indeed."

Just then Sir Richard walked out from the house, pulling on leather gloves. "My apologies, gentlemen," he said. "But my usual horse Lucius has suddenly been taken lame. My groom has needed to saddle up my other horse, Griseo, in his place."

Andrew leaned down. "That is indeed unfortunate, cousin," he said, adding just the right amount of sympathy.

Richard looked up. "Aye," he agreed. "I am told that Lucius was in the best of health last night, but when the groom went in to make him ready this morning, the horse was lame."

There was the sound of hooves crunching on the pebbles, and the groom came round the building. He was leading a muscular grey destrier, who tossed his head and snorted as he walked.

Richard walked over and the groom held the horse while his master mounted unaided.

"I had not realised how pale is this Griseo," Reginald murmured to

Andrew. "But 'twas a good idea to force the change. That beast has a most distinctive color. You will have no problem identifying your cousin at a distance, even in woodland."

"Aye," Andrew agreed. "Lucius is a roan, just like all these other mounts."

Andrew glanced round at the other men, and held up his hand. "Are we all ready?" he called. There was a cheer in response. "We will make for the woodlands on the east side," he announced. "The huntsman has completed his quest, and tells of a hart there with ten points on its antlers. We will hunt *par force* with bows rather than using dogs to make it run. So I want to be sure you are each well stocked with your own arrows, so we can attribute the kill?"

Again a cheer.

"Then let us proceed." He dropped his hand and led the hunt onto the parklands. As they rode, Andrew dropped back to ride beside his cousin. "I would have you take the lead when we spy the quarry," he said. "I know how you have missed the hunt while recovering. You deserve it."

Richard nodded. "I thank you, cousin," he said. "I would like that very much."

"Good. Then let it be so."

"I see a change in you, Andrew," Richard observed. "You have been better able to keep your temper these past few months."

Andrew glanced across. "Do you say I was unable to keep it before?" he asked, arching an eyebrow.

Richard looked down a moment, then sighed. "Indeed, that is so." Then he smiled, and added, "But I do understand, Andrew, truly I do. Life has been hard for you since Grandfather died. You have had all the responsibilities, while I have had only the care of my wife and sons."

"That is the prerogative of the younger," Andrew replied, his teeth gritted.

"Indeed, but mayhap I can be of assistance? Relieve you of some of your responsibilities?"

Take a breath. Stay frozen.

"Why so?"

"I wish to be more help to you." Richard paused a moment as they rode towards the woodlands. "You were so good to me when I lay sick. You looked to Eleanor's care with love and devotion. It was much appreciated by us both."

"You are most kind to say this," Andrew observed, trying hard to make his voice sound sincere.

"I know we have not been the best of cousins at times, but your kindness, and your change of temper, have assured me that you are a better man now. I would we were to become closer, and I know Eleanor feels the same."

Andrew shifted in his saddle. For sure he planned to become closer to Eleanor—but not in the way Richard meant.

ANDREW HELD up his hand once again, and all the hunters halted behind him. He surveyed the woodlands, then withdrew a goose down feather from his bag and cast it to the wind. "The breeze comes from the west," he said softly. "We approach from the east, to stay downwind of the beast." There was a rumble of assent from the men. "Walk your horses with care, lest it hears us coming."

The hunt rode to the east side of the woods, with just the slightest creak of leather or clink of a bridle, while their hoofbeats were muffled by the soft ground. Andrew rode at their head, stopping when they reached the eastern edge of the trees. Without a word, he indicated where each man should position himself, spreading out on either side of him. He placed Richard on his left, with Reginald on his right.

At his signal, the hunters rode towards the thick woodland. They had only gone a few yards in amongst the trees when the light seemed to be doused, turning from the bright sunlight of the parkland into the dappled green and browns of the trees. An occasional shaft of golden sunlight beamed down through the canopy. Andrew shivered;

it was as if these were the eyes of God himself. Looking down. Judging him.

He took a deep breath to steady himself, then looked across at Reginald. His friend was picking his way through the branches and roots. Reginald seemed to be aware that he was being observed, and looked back at Andrew. He gave a small nod, as if of reassurance. Andrew returned the gesture, then switched his gaze to Richard. His cousin was sitting tall in his saddle, his grey destrier showing up clearly against the changing colors of the forest.

Richard's sight remained fixed on the path his horse was taking. He did not seem, like Reginald, to sense his cousin's attention. Andrew allowed himself a small frown. Every move of Richard's body, every arrogant tilt of his head, set Andrew's teeth on edge.

At least he would soon be free of the man. Free to take back the woman who was rightfully his.

The hunt progressed through the forest for a few more minutes, without sight of the hart. Andrew scoured the way ahead, seeking to understand every shape, every shadow, to determine if it was a trunk, a bough—or a beast.

His eyes narrowed. There was a shape, up ahead and to his left, which had the look of a curved haunch. He fixed on it as he rode, unsure if it was what he sought. Some rooks cawed in the trees, and the shape moved. It was the hart.

Richard must have seen it at the same time, for he raised his hand, then pointed. Andrew nodded, then waved the hunt forward.

As if one man, they all urged their mounts on. Now they were moving faster through the forest, their horses picking expertly through the trees. The quarry lifted its head, then skittered round and ran before them, jumping past trees and leaping over roots in order to escape his pursuers.

Andrew had not moved. He unhooked his bow, carefully selecting an arrow from the quiver by his knee. The men were now thundering away from him, with Richard taking the lead.

Andrew fitted the arrow to his bow, then urged his horse forward. With one hand on the rein and the other holding the bow and arrow, he let his horse find a clear path, keeping his eyes fixed on the distinctive grey horse ahead. Waiting for his moment.

Then it came, as the other huntsmen all loosed arrows of their own at the beast.

As the shafts flew through the forest air, Andrew pulled his horse up. The very moment it stopped, he took careful aim at the broad back above the grey haunches, and let his arrow fly. Then he quickly selected another arrow and loosed it at the beast.

He kicked his horse forward. Crouching low over its mane, he thundered up behind the rest of the men. Pulling up beside them, he leapt down from his horse and ran towards where Richard now lay. The other men were dismounting and coming over as well, shock on all their faces.

His cousin was face down. The arrow was buried so deep in the centre of his back that Andrew knew there was no point in turning him over.

He looked up, into the bloodless face of one of the hunters. "An accident," the man gasped. "A dreadful accident."

Andrew nodded, but did not reply; words were not needed. The man moved back to a respectful distance.

Reginald came over and put his hand on Andrew's shoulder. "This is dreadful," he said loudly. "My condolences for your loss, Sir Andrew." Then he leaned down. "That was a fine shot," he breathed into Andrew's ear. "A fine shot indeed."

FIVE WEEKS LATER, Eleanor walked up the aisle in Marchington Manor's small chapel. Andrew was waiting for her at the altar.

Eleanor's progression was slow; it was now a month since the babe had quickened and walking was not easy for her. She made her way past all the pews of friends and family, who looked concerned rather than happy for her. She accepted that she was indeed lucky to have Andrew offer his hand. For as her father had made clear, there was no possibility of her raising four children alone.

But when the subject of how best to support her had first been discussed with Andrew, he had protested that he was not worthy to step into Richard's place. How could he countenance such a thing, he protested, so soon after the dreadful death of his beloved cousin? Even with some impassioned pleas from Eleanor, he had still refused, despite her saying it would be his duty to support his cousin's family in their hour of need.

The matter had still lain unresolved when the inquest was held. As was the custom, it took place in the nearest manor house—which, unfortunately on this occasion, meant Marchington. Eleanor looked on in horror as the Coroner, his clerks, twelve jurors and many of the local people all crowded into the great hall.

But the Coroner had been most considerate of Eleanor's situation, offering her his deepest condolences. He vowed that he would make a thorough investigation and establish the truth of what happened. She sat uncomfortably for two days as he called all the men from the hunt to the stand, as well as a fletcher and the groom from the Marchington Manor stables. The story that emerged of that fateful day chilled her to the bone.

The whole hunting party had surged forward when Richard had spotted the quarry. They had all loosed many arrows at the beast at the same time. One of these must have mistakenly hit Richard as he rode ahead.

The Coroner spent much time considering the arrow that had so tragically pierced her husband's heart. Eleanor could not bear to look, as the dreadful thing, still rusty red, was shown to each of the huntsmen. Each denied that it was his, producing one of their own in order to demonstrate how theirs were made differently.

The fletcher confirmed that the individual maker of an arrow could be determined from the size, barb and flights. Then he asserted that the fatal arrow was not made by the same fletcher as any of those carried by the huntsmen on the day.

The Coroner came to the conclusion that it was a rogue arrow, one that could have somehow found its way into any one of the quivers. As such it was not therefore possible to establish who had loosed it.

By the afternoon of the second day, the Coroner said he had no alternative but to record a verdict of a tragic accident, and the jurors all agreed.

Once the Coroner and his court had left the Manor, Eleanor dismissed all her ladies and took to her bed. For the first time since she had heard the dreadful news, she allowed herself to weep for her husband.

She wept for Richard—a man of honour and integrity who should not have died so soon. She wept for her three sons, that they had lost a loving father who would have raised them to be the best possible men. She wept for Mary, the babe that kicked in her belly, who would never know her father. And she wept for herself, that she had lost a friend and a lover; a man who made her feel truly special.

Eventually she could weep no more, and the tears dried. She managed to raise herself up in the bed. *Andrew is my only hope*, she thought. *Now he has become more even-tempered, and even loving, I must look to him as my protector. I may never love him as I loved Richard, but he will look to my interests, and those of my children. He must agree to the wedding. I will make sure it happens.*

After offering up a prayer for the success of her mission, Eleanor called her ladies and got ready to go down to dine.

Andrew was alone in the hall when she came in, sitting before the fire with a glass of wine.

"Andrew," she began, but he held up a hand. "Shh, Eleanor," he said, rising from his chair and coming up to her. He took both her hands in his. "I have given it much thought," he said, "and now that awful inquest business is over, I have realized you were right all along. It would be the best thing I can do in memory of my dear cousin, that I take on his duties as a husband and a father." He got down on one knee before her. "So I would give you my troth. Let us be married as soon as we can, and start a new life together."

AND NOW THE wedding had finally happened. As they emerged into the winter sunshine as man and wife, Sir Andrew allowed himself a small smile of satisfaction. He had succeeded! The woman he loved was now his, and he could look forward to a lifetime together. There would be cozy nights by the fire, laughter in each other's arms, and of course, nights of passion. Eleanor Fox would raise her eyes to his with a look of love, just as she had that day all those years before. The day when he had lost his heart to her. The day when she had been so cruelly taken from him by his odious cousin Richard.

Well, that period of her life was mercifully over. Now, she could begin again, as the wife of the older Fox, rightful owner of the Marchington Manor fortunes.

Andrew took her hand in his. "Come my love," he whispered, "let us go inside for the wedding celebrations."

TWO MONTHS later Eleanor went into her confinement, ready for the birth of her daughter. She was accompanied by her ladies, and it was made clear to Andrew that he was not welcome under any circumstances.

"God willing, I will be out in four weeks," Eleanor said, "and we will have a fine daughter. Pray for me, Andrew. Pray for a safe delivery."

"I will, my love," he replied.

But sadly God did not hear his prayers. One night a month later, it was not his wife, but Marion who came out. Her eyes were red with tears.

"What is it?" Andrew snapped. "Is the babe born? Is it a girl, as Lady Fox said?" He frowned. "Is the babe not well?"

"The babe is indeed a girl, Master, and she is very well," Marion replied. "It is the Mistress."

"What of her?" Andrew gasped. "How does she fare?"

"I am sorry, Master, but she has a fever, brought on by the birthing."

"A fever? But she will recover?"

Marion shook her head. "I have never before seen a childbed fever strike as fast and as hard as this. I do not expect a happy outcome."

"Where is she? I must go to her." Andrew pushed past the maid and marched into his wife's chambers. It was dark, with heavy drapes across the windows, and only a few candles to give any light. A wetnurse sat beside the fire in the anteroom. She held a swaddled babe in her arms, suckling at her breast.

Andrew marched into the bedchamber and ripped back the bed hangings.

The woman lying with her eyes closed on the sweat-soaked sheets was hardly recognizable as his wife. Her hair was stuck to her fore-head in thick, dank tendrils, and her face was deathly white.

He leaned in. Her breath was coming in short, labored rasps. "Eleanor?" he said. "Eleanor?"

Slowly her head turned, and her eyes opened, but he could tell they were not seeing him. It was almost as if she was looking at something just behind him. He glanced back, but there was nothing there.

"Richard," she breathed. "Is that you?"

"No, it is Andrew... ."

Eleanor's breath slowed. "I am coming, Rich, my love," she whispered. "I am coming... ."

Then she let out a long sigh, almost as if her spirit was leaving her body, while her eyes continued to stare past him.

Only now they were staring into eternity.

Andrew stumbled back into the antechamber. The wetnurse was laying the babe in its crib. It was snuffling and mewling softly as she tucked it in. She looked up. "The mistress?" she asked.

But Andrew could not answer; the power of speech had left him. He just shook his head and ran. He ran from the body that had been his new wife. He ran from the babe who had killed her. He ran from the future life he had longed for, and fought for.

He emerged into the corridor to be stopped by Marion, who must have seen from his face what had happened.

"The Lord has taken the mistress?" she asked, her face ashen.

Andrew nodded.

Marion crossed herself. "And the babe? Mary Fox? She must be cared for."

Andrew found his voice. "I want nothing more to do with that mewling thing," he snarled. "It has killed her, and God help me, I would do it the same service."

"But she is your daughter...."

Andrew rounded on the woman like a wounded bear. "Nay!" he yelled. "It is the spawn of Satan! It is not mine and never will be! I will have nothing to do with it, do you hear?"

"But...."

"Keep it out of my sight! That thing you call Mary Fox—if God spares it, I will make it suffer each and every day for what it has done to me!"

He stumbled away and passed through room after room, until he found himself by the door out of the house. Hardly aware of what he was doing, he pushed it open and staggered out into the moonlit night. Continuing through the grounds, he soon found he had reached the old well.

No longer a husband, a father, or even a man, he grasped the bricks and leaned forward. The blackness of the void seemed to suck him down, while his face contorted with rage.

A long, blood-curdling scream of pain and hate echoed down the well.

And into the future life of Mary Fox.

AUTHOR'S NOTE:

When I first wrote *The Broken Sword*, a full-length novel that introduced us to the seventeen year-old adventuress Mary Fox, I gave her a wicked stepfather called Sir Andrew Fox, with a sinister side-kick, Sir Reginald de Courtney. They both had evil—but not fully explored—motivations. In *The Tudor Prince*, I started to fill in more of Mary's back story, particularly the wider family's suspicion that it was Sir Andrew who was behind the 'accidental' death of her true father.

But this story existed only as a series of references in Mary's later adventures. How great then, to go back and tell it in detail! When this anthology came along, with the theme of 'destiny becoming due', it seemed the perfect opportunity.

I have worked back from all the references, drawn the various threads together and woven them into the story of the momentous events leading up to Mary's birth. In doing so, I have discovered more and more about Sir Andrew's hatred of Mary, as well as the motivations that drive his, and Sir Reginald's, actions in the later books.

ABOUT THE AUTHOR

Jonathan Posner writes action adventures set in Tudor England. *The Broken Sword* introduces Mary Fox, a feisty Tudor heroine, who discovers what it takes to survive – and succeed – in a man's world. She goes on to have further adventures in *The Tudor Prince*, and Jonathan's forthcoming adventure, *The River of Fire*. He has also written *The Witchfinder's Well* trilogy, a Tudor action series which begins with a girl time-travelling back to Tudor England from 2015. For more about Jonathan visit his website, or follow him on Facebook, Instagram or Goodreads.

THE WIDOW MORGAN DON'T
TAKE NO MOONSHINE

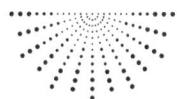

ANA BRAZIL

Ida Morgan was the very last person in Gettysburg to see the photograph of her dead husband. If the National Soldier's Cemetery had not been consecrated on the third Thursday of November 1863, she might never have seen her beloved's likeness at all. But cemetery consecration or not, Ida had been planning, since July, to fire her single-shot derringer into the heart of the photographer Otis C. Cooper.

The day before the consecration, the widow next door informed Ida that a photographer from Washington City had arrived with a crate of battle images. He set himself up at the Eagle Hotel, in the very rooms that Brigadier General John Buford himself had used as headquarters. The photographer charged five cents to view his images and the line went out the hotel doors. The widow next door had seen the photographs herself, and she was sorry to say that one of the dead men in one of the photographs was most certainly Ida's husband Amos.

Within hours, five more people stopped by Morgan Stables, their whispers to Ida strained by outrage. *It's Amos all right. Lying in the dirt and dead as night. A rifle by his side.* And then, *We knew you'd want to know.*

Ida listened intently to each inflection of horror, fighting hard to keep her meager breakfast down. The day she had long waited for was finally here. Still, she kept steady at her work. Horses never brushed themselves, did they? And stalls needed constant shoveling.

With the influx of visitors to Gettysburg that week—*The Adams County Gazette* posted broadsides stating that thirty thousand people were coming to hear President Lincoln dedicate the cemetery—Ida worked through supper, stabling the horses that were ridden in from Philadelphia and Washington City. Hours after sunset, with the stable doors closed and fifteen horses and six mules bedded down for the night, Ida stood over an open barrel filled with rainwater. She swiped the cake of horse soap with a stiff brush and scrubbed her face and hands clean.

She put on her Sunday dress, a once-splendid stiff silk with delicate pockets, the same dress she'd worn to marry Amos four years ago. It had been a lavender-and-brown plaid then, a lovely complement to her blue-violet eyes, but today it was a mottled black, dyed dark after Amos's death.

She removed her derringer from the pocket of her work apron and placed it into the right pocket of her dress. The gun fit snugly, so that there was little risk it could be accidentally cocked, but there was room enough that Ida could grab it quickly. She bundled herself into her coat and bonnet, blew out the lanterns, and bade the animals goodnight.

All of the thirty thousand visitors predicted to visit Gettysburg seemed to assemble about the Eagle Hotel that evening. There were town folk and strangers, dignitaries and newspapermen, veterans and soldiers. And of course, there were widows, many with children by their sides. Now and then Ida recognized someone she did business with: a tanner, a carriage maker, a glueman. And wasn't that Tommy Braun, the smartest scamp of the Widow Braun's red-haired brood, wearing a longboard around the front of his thin body? Fighting the darkness that settled around her, Ida tried to read the lettering on the board, but all she could see were the largest words: BATTLEFIELD PHOTOS!

She stood in a long line outside the Eagle Hotel for an hour, waiting to enter the photographer's rooms. Men wearing top hats and women holding fur muffs were admitted directly into the hotel while locals like Ida stood out in the November cold. She poked a finger through the largest hole in her coat pocket until she could feel the fabric of her dress. She traced the bulbous handle of her gun, and a surge of satisfaction ran through her.

Only one bullet, she reminded herself. As Amos said when he pressed the derringer into her hand the night before he marched away from her forever, *There's only one bullet, so pick your range—four to ten yards should do—and make it count. Don't take no moonshine, Ida Morgan. Protect yourself and shoot straight to the heart.*

Ida was willing to wait all night to see the photograph that might be her Amos; willing to wait all night to shoot the heartless photographer.

But first, she had to relieve herself.

As she stepped out of line and walked away from the hotel, two townspeople doffed their hats. Ida stumbled slightly at the recognition, but continued on.

A little farther down the path, Elizabeth Thorn, whose husband Peter enrolled with the 138th at the beginning of the year, leaving pregnant Elizabeth to take on his job as caretaker of Evergreen Cemetery, joined up with Ida. Elizabeth, not yet recovered from the birth of her fourth child just weeks earlier, entwined her arm with Ida's and leaned lightly on her. The two women walked side by side, with Ida keeping Elizabeth to her left, away from any possibility that the derringer would discharge near her.

Ida had no family remaining on this earth, but she did have Elizabeth. The women did not meet often, since work took most of their hours, but they shared a comfortable camaraderie.

Just then a high, young voice—Tommy Braun it was—blurted out, "See every inch of the battlefield! Do not miss this astonishing show! Only five cents a visit!"

The battlefield! Ida pulled Elizabeth to her, as if to shield herself from all memories of the battlefield.

"You'd think the war had ended." Elizabeth leaned harder into Ida as a drunken man sloshed toward them. "People are just beside themselves tonight."

"I've got a full stable; had to turn away four teams."

"Business is good then?" asked Elizabeth.

"For tonight. You?"

"They're still dying to get in." Elizabeth attempted a grim smile as she repeated her husband's response about managing Evergreen Cemetery.

They reached an outhouse and Elizabeth stood guard while Ida completed her business. Ida returned the duty.

On their way back to the hotel, one of the men who had greeted Ida earlier offered news. "They turned us away, Missus Morgan, Missus Thorn. Closed up for the night. Photographer said he needed to prepare for the show tomorrow."

Ida looked at him roughly, her heart beginning to beat quickly, now that her opportunity to end the photographer's life was lost.

"Come away then," said Elizabeth to Ida. "There's nothing to see tonight."

Despite the thinning crowd, the boy with the board continued to shriek out his litany. "BATTLEFIELD PHOTOS! See every inch of the battlefield! See how the dead of Gettysburg will live forever!"

FOUR AND A HALF MONTHS EARLIER, on July first, the first day of the battle of Gettysburg, Ida had turned over the Morgan house and stables to a pair of Union doctors for use as a field hospital. The soldiers hauled her piano into the yard and pulled her curtains from the windows. They brought in tables and saws and hammers and wedges, and ransacked her cupboards and drawers. Her petticoats became bandages, her sheets were tangled into slings, and Amos's baskets broke from the weight of sawn-off legs and arms.

Soldiers who did not perish during surgery were carried to the stable. Recognizing the severity of their wounds, the hopelessness of their recovery, Ida did the one thing she knew to be right: she offered each man the final comforts of a good death.

She sat on the floor next to their blankets, clasped their hands in hers, and listened as they shared their last hopes or confessed their final sins. She nodded at them as they called her *Ma* or *Sis* or *Sarah* or *Jewel*, and before each dead soldier was carried to the burial wagon outside, she closed their eyes and blessed their souls.

ON THE THIRD day of battle, the day that Amos Morgan of the 141st Pennsylvania Volunteers was shot dead, Ida's heart twisted violently. She staggered backward, clutching her chest, collapsing onto a bale of hay.

She imagined she saw Amos before her, calling her *Ida, Darling Ida* and she reached out for him. She called his name and called his name and called his name until finally his strong arms enveloped her. He begged her to hush, he begged her to sleep, and slowly, she did both.

She awoke on the floor of the stable, her arms and legs wrapped within a scratchy, bloodstained blanket. She remained quiet for a few moments, tempted to stay inside the blanket's firm binding, solemnly accepting that she would not see Amos again until they were reunited in Heaven.

But Ida would not stay quiet for long, she would not stay down. She emerged from the blanket and took in the jumble of bandaged bodies surrounding her. She gently slipped her hand into the grasp of a barely-breathing man who lay next to her.

"I'm here for you, soldier," she whispered. "I'm here."

TWO DAYS after the battle ended, Elizabeth Thorn's buckboard stopped in front of Morgan Stables. Elizabeth climbed down and limped to the open doorway. She cradled her small, swollen stomach with both hands and leaned against the door, saying nothing, but keeping her gaze on Ida.

Ida took a few moments to adjust a cloth on a soldier's forehead before coming to Elizabeth, who, despite being with child, was almost as thin and dusty as any man lying in the stable. Elizabeth's Evergreen Cemetery, located just south of the city and featuring a high ridge that any general would envy, had become part of the battlefield. Once the rebels retreated, Elizabeth had been tasked with digging graves and bringing men inside for their final rest. There was only one reason Elizabeth would leave her hard work at the cemetery today.

"You found Amos," declared Ida softly. She had yearned for this moment with all of her heart, yet her chest filled with fear.

Elizabeth turned away from the men who lay suffering on the stable floor, as if she could not bear to see more soldiers who might soon need burial.

"I found a dead soldier near the peach orchard," she said. "Right around where the 141st was said to be fighting. He's missing part of his little finger." She looked at the small finger of her right hand, as if her finger, like Amos's, was missing the top joint. She curled her dirty fingers toward her palm before saying, "He's got that burn mark on his right cheek, too."

Ida staggered out of the stable, her breathing rapid and raw, her heart beset with sorrow and rage. Elizabeth limped toward her friend and led her to lean against the buckboard.

"He's still at the orchard. I wasn't strong enough to carry him." Elizabeth looked down at the lump in her belly, as though she were ashamed at how weak her pregnancy made her. "But you need to know...I wasn't the first to find him."

Ida's thoughts flashed to the angry snippets she'd heard over the last few days. *Johnny Reb scalped him just like an Indian. They branded him like a horse. They dug the shot out of his chest for a soo-ve-near.*

Ida put a hand on the buckboard to steady herself. "Was it...was it rebel scavengers?"

Elizabeth shook her head. "No. Not that."

"Then what?"

250

"A Union photographer from Washington City," replied Elizabeth. "Soldiers said that a white-haired man was taking likenesses of soldiers during the battle. And afterward, after the retreat, he stayed to photograph the dead. And...and he was *posing* them. Laying them out on the ground, or against a wall, or against a fallen horse. He was trying to make the battle look a certain way." Elizabeth fell silent for a few moments before continuing. "But the soldiers also said that the dead rebs were so badly shot up, the photographer couldn't pose them. Instead, he dressed our boys up like the rebs. Just for his photographs!"

Ida steadied herself against the buckboard, fighting to silence her raging heartbeat, fighting to understand exactly what Elizabeth said.

"A *Union* photographer desecrated my Amos? Dressed him in gray, just like a rebel traitor?"

"I'm so sorry, Ida." Elizabeth caught Ida just as she slumped and slid down to the ground. Ida landed on her rump against a wheel, tears streaming down her cheeks and chin, both hands braced against her heart. Elizabeth stooped down as best she could and put her arms around Ida's trembling shoulders.

Ida drew her sleeve against her nose and mouth. "I want to bring Amos to Evergreen, but not wearing gray."

Elizabeth stretched out her dirty hands and helped Ida rise to her feet.

"Take me to Amos," said the Widow Morgan. "Take me now. And then, tell me everything you heard about this photographer."

DEDICATION DAY in November dawned cold. Ida pushed through the crowds that were gathering to watch the grand parade, which was set to march right past the Eagle Hotel. Once inside the hotel, she stepped confidently through the lobby and up the stairs to the second floor, where she found a sign on a door: BATTLEFIELD PHOTOS. To the side of the sign was a *carte-de-visite* showing a white-haired man with a large camera at his side. Ida felt for her derringer and knocked on the door.

A man's voice shouted out, "Tommy, is that you?"

Ida knocked again. The door jolted open. She looked from the man standing before her to the man in the *carte-de-visite* on the wall.

"Yes?" The man stamped his bare feet and glanced at the untucked tails of his shirt before acknowledging the *carte-de-visite*. "Although you have caught me at an unfortunate moment, I am Otis C. Cooper. The *gallery*," Cooper's words dripped with reverence, "is closed until this evening. Later today, I'll be taking photographs of the President and the speakers. And in the cemetery, if the crowds can be kept out. Photographs of the event will be available around Christmas time."

Ida peered past Cooper to view the huge photograph that hung on a false wall parallel to the door.

"My Imperial portraits," said Cooper, "such as you are looking at now, always make an impressive Christmas present."

Bigger than any likeness Ida had ever seen, the Imperial showed two men in plain clothes standing in front of the Gettysburg train station.

Cooper turned to admire his work. "That was before the battle, of course."

Ignoring the photographer entirely, Ida stepped through the doorway and into the room. She had never been in a gallery before, but she understood the natural flow of the false walls. Before the photographer could protest, she walked deliberately to the next image (soldiers standing hearty and whole in front of a grove of trees) and the next (rows of white tents with no one in sight) and the next (scores of dead Union soldiers lying on their backs in a field, arms crossed over their chests and stocking'd feet exposed, looking like cut-down logs left out to dry).

Ida panicked for a moment, and despite the autumn chill that ran through the room, she began to sweat. She walked on, realizing that she was circling back to the gallery entrance. She approached what appeared to be the final image slowly, her heart beating wildly in expectations of seeing her husband once more.

Then there he was: alone on the ground, sprawled out to his full length with a rifle by his side, clothed in light-colored pants and a ragged gray jacket with a sharpshooter's insignia—vile pieces of Confederate clothing that Ida had burned to ash in July.

The photograph even had a title: *A Southern Sharpshooter.*

Ida had a slight awareness that the photographer was advancing toward her…. *Now* would be the time to end his life, but she could not turn away from Amos, her Amos. Her ungloved hand stretched out to touch her husband, to caress that lock of hair away from his forehead, to play the back of her hand against his.

But before she could reach Amos, Ida crumbled to the ground.

A JOLT of ammonia salts revived her. She opened her eyes and realized she'd been carried out of the gallery. From the large box camera aimed at the elevated platform in front of her, she reasoned she must be inside a photographic studio. An open trunk overflowed with pieces of clothing and an upholstered chair sat centered on the platform.

She checked her pocket; her derringer was still there.

Something stirred behind her and Ida turned sharply. Large sheets of canvas had been fixed to two of the hotel walls, creating something like a soldier's tent in the corner of the room. The noise had come from the tent, whistling or whispering or some such waste of breath. Then she saw the gallery through a connecting doorway.

A red-haired boy waited by Ida's side with a cup of water.

She took the cup and sipped. "You're Tommy Braun, aren't you?"

"Yes ma'am, Missus Morgan." The boy's voice cracked twice. "I know you too, from when you came to see Ma, although my name's Tom now."

"And you work for this photographer?"

"Since July, ma'am. He came through town and Ma begged him to take me since Pa—" The boy stopped abruptly and gnawed at his lip.

One of the canvas flaps opened and the photographer emerged, a surge of sour chemicals clinging to him. He had tucked in his shirt, buttoned his vest, put on his boots, and tied a small black cravat around his neck. He'd oiled back his white hair, but the odor coiled around him was not sweet Makassar oil, it was something strong and bitter.

Ida frowned, and the boy replied, "That's the chemicals. To coat the glass to make the photograph."

Ida walked stiffly from the chair and anchored herself at the door between the studio and the gallery. She knew, after many years of working in a stable, just how to keep an animal from escaping.

"You should go," she said to Tom. "Go home to your ma. You're not a part of this."

"Part of what?" The photographer stepped toward the window, opening it wider before taking a breath of fresh air. "Part of what, Madam—Madam—Mad—"

"Widow—Widow—Widow—" Ida parroted back at the photographer even before he'd finished speaking. "I'm the Widow Morgan, and that man in that photograph in that gallery of yours is my husband, Private Amos Morgan. A proud Union soldier. Until you shamed and disgraced him."

"Madam, you are entirely mistake—"

She pulled the derringer from her pocket, aimed it at the photographer, and set her thumb against the hammer.

The photographer stopped protesting and put his hands up in the air.

An urgent knock sounded on the hotel hallway door. Elizabeth's voice called out, "Ida, are you in there?"

"Come in! Come in!" shouted the photographer.

Ida kept her derringer leveled. The photographer was three, maybe four, yards away.

Don't take no moonshine, Ida Morgan. Straight to the heart.

Elizabeth kept her voice low. "I know you're in there, Ida. Let me in. I'm not leaving without you."

Ida nodded toward the gallery room. "Let her in, Tom."

"Yes, ma'am."

Tom opened the door to Elizabeth, who came directly to Ida's side.

"God in Heaven, Ida! What are you doing?"

"Making things right, Elizabeth. Just like I vowed when we buried Amos."

Elizabeth shook her head. "You've already made things right. Amos is buried in a blue uniform in Evergreen. The preacher praised him for an hour and we sang his soul up to heaven. Amos has nothing more to worry about in life or in death."

"Except the shame of that photograph. Being dressed up as a rebel and having everyone see it. And the title! *A Southern Sharpshooter!*"

Despite Ida's aim at the photographer's heart—his vest, actually, because Ida was sure that he had no heart—Cooper found his voice.

"I did nothing! He was dressed like that when I found him. I didn't even touch him; I just took an image where he lay."

"Have you seen him, Elizabeth? My Amos? Go look and tell me I'm not right."

Elizabeth hurried to the gallery. She returned slowly and soberly, wiping tears from her eyes and carrying the large framed photograph against her chest.

"How many more of these are there?" she asked Tommy. "Of Amos I mean."

"Just that one. I'd swear to it, Missus Thorn."

Elizabeth set the photograph on a table, took the image from the frame, and showed it to Ida. Then she tore it in half and in half again.

"No!" Ida cried out, the gun quivering in her hand. "His face; give me his face!" Elizabeth handed three of the quartered images to Tommy. "Add these to the fire."

Ida sidled toward Elizabeth. With the gun still aimed at the photographer, she took the remaining quarter image from her friend, gazed upon the likeness of her husband, and tucked it into her pocket.

Ida's thumb tapped against the derringer's hammer. "Is that right, Tom? Was that the only photograph of Amos? None others?"

"Yes ma'am, that's right. There was only time to make that one Imperial before the show. But ma'am—" Tom attempted to look at both women but could catch only Elizabeth's eye. "There has to be a negative somewhere. You need a negative to make more photographs."

"Of course there's a *negative somewhere*," Ida spat out, the gun wavering slightly in her grip. "*To make more photographs.* Of course there is."

"Where would that negative be, Tommy?" Elizabeth asked.

"Back in the studio in Washington City."

Imperials. Negatives. Washington City. Ida could not endure any more delays or surprises. She had come to shoot a bullet through the photographer and she would do so. But with only one bullet to shoot, she needed to be sure.

What she did not need was Elizabeth distracting her. "Go on Elizabeth, and take the boy with you."

"Oh Ida, haven't we seen enough death?"

"The wages of sin is death, Elizabeth. Cooper sinned against Amos and for that he deserves to die. An eye for an eye."

"There's got to be another way." Elizabeth's eyes darted from Ida's stern focus to the stains on Cooper's upraised hands to young Tommy, standing tall next to the large box camera as though he might have to protect it from Ida. Elizabeth had an idea. "Can you work that camera, Tommy?"

"No, ma'am; I'm not even allowed to touch it. It's too fragile for the likes of me."

"That's not what I asked," Elizabeth scowled. "Do you know *how* to work it? Can you manage a photograph with it?"

"Of course I *can*," the boy bragged. "I been watching him for months."

"That's what we'll do then," announced Elizabeth. "Not an eye for an eye, but a negative for a negative. He'll have the negative of Amos in Washington City, but you'll have a negative of him here in Gettysburg. If we ever hear of or see another *Southern Sharpshooter* photograph, or if he tells anyone that we were here, we'll have copies of his negative developed and sent around to every newspaper in every city in the United States."

"What?" Ida, the photographer, and the boy asked at the same time.

"Take your clothes off," Elizabeth commanded, her voice ringing out with maternal authority.

"Never!" For the first time since Ida drew her derringer, the photographer looked away from her. "I would not lower myself," Cooper told Elizabeth. When his refusal met with silence he added, "You're insane. You're both insane."

Ida did not protest, for she had been wondering, more than occasionally, if she might *be* insane. She had surrendered all expectations of a happy life since Amos's death and dishonor, and now she cared only about shooting the photographer. If that made her insane, so be it.

And if making a negative of the photographer pleased Elizabeth and would remove her from the hotel room, so be it also.

"That's right," said Ida. "Take your clothes off."

To ensure that the photographer complied, she cocked her derringer.

"MISTER COOPER just finished preparing all of the chemical baths when you awoke, Missus Morgan, and the camera is set up and ready." Tom's youthful squawk seemed to disappear as he assumed the photographer's responsibilities. He had not protested Elizabeth's direction and seemed to relish his new role behind the camera.

Stripped down to his patched undershirt and discolored drawers, Cooper slouched with his hands around his groin. He glared toward the fireplace, which managed a warm glow in the November cold.

"Go stand in front of the chair." Ida motioned Cooper to the position she declared, away from the fire, and more importantly, the poker beside it. Reluctantly, he climbed the platform.

"You'll pay for this ambush," he barked. "You'll all pay. I'll see to that."

The boy disappeared into the makeshift tent. Ida and Elizabeth stood together, inspecting the photographer's pose as if they were horse traders.

Finally Elizabeth said, "Something's missing." And then she eyed the various pieces of clothing draped over the trunk. "He needs to put on one of those bonnets. And maybe...carry a fan?"

Ida nodded her agreement and pointed her gun toward the women's finery. The photographer swore mightily at both women but finally did as he was ordered, encasing his white hair in a red bonnet and picking up an ivory fan.

Tom Braun emerged from the tent, holding a small plate of glass that dripped liquid. He delicately placed the coated glass into a holder and then slid the holder into the camera.

"Stand up straight," the boy ordered the photographer. "Look directly into the camera and do not move or smile."

As strands of sunlight shot through the curtained window, illuminating almost every inch of the photographer's shame, Tom pulled the black cloth away from the camera lens. He counted softly to himself and then replaced the cloth. He removed the holder from the camera and hurried into the tent.

Ida kept her aim on the photographer while Elizabeth waited outside the tent.

It was some time before Tom yelled out, "I've fixed your negative. Do you want a paper photograph too?"

Now that Elizabeth had had her joke, Ida could spend no more time humoring her. "No. Just the negative."

Ida accepted the packaged negative that Tom gave to her and handed it solemnly to Elizabeth.

"You can get dressed," Elizabeth told the photographer.

"And you can go to hell. All three of you." Cooper dropped the fan to the floor and tugged off the bonnet. He grabbed the poker from the fire and lunged toward the women and boy. "Get out of my studio. Now."

Elizabeth and the boy staggered away from the photographer, and Ida, her derringer cocked, her finger against the trigger, and her heart still broken, had a clear shot at Cooper.

Holding the negative tightly to her chest, Elizabeth grabbed Tommy's hand and drew the boy closer. Ida's shot improved even more, but she hesitated, unwilling to force Elizabeth or Tom to witness yet another death.

Ida uncocked and lowered her gun. The photographer wielded his weapon at her again, as if the fiery poker was the devil's own demon. Ida turned to Elizabeth and the boy and pushed them both out in front of her, into the gallery, and through the hotel room doorway. Once Elizabeth and the boy were in the hallway, Ida shut the door after them.

Then she locked it.

Fists pounded against the door. Elizabeth shouted. "Don't you do it, Ida! Please don't do it!"

But Ida and her derringer returned to the photographer's room, where he was bent against a wall, scrambling to tie his bootlaces.

Ida Morgan, the very last person in Gettysburg to see the photograph of her dead husband, was also the very last person to see the photographer Otis C. Cooper alive.

ABOUT THE AUTHOR

Ana Brazil's historical mysteries feature brash American heroines, the more bodacious the better. Her latest heroine is vaudeville performer Viola Vermillion, featured in *The Red-Hot Blues Chanteuse*, set in 1919 San Francisco. Ana's debut novel, *Fanny Newcomb & the Irish Channel Ripper*, a New Orleans Gilded Age mystery, won the 2018 IBPA Gold Medal for Historical Fiction, and her short stories have been published in multiple crime fiction anthologies. Ana earned her master's degree in American history from Florida State University, and is a founding member of the Paper Lantern Writers. Meet up with Ana on instagram @ana.brazil or anabrazil.com.

ABOUT PAPER LANTERN WRITERS

The Paper Lantern Writers are an author collective focused on historical fiction of all eras. From Medieval Europe to Gilded Age America (and beyond), our books will take you on the journeys of a lifetime.

PAPER LANTERN
WRITERS

Find us at www.paperlanternwriters.com

facebook.com/paperlanternwriters
instagram.com/paperlanternwriters
youtube.com/@paperlanternwriters

ALSO BY PAPER LANTERN WRITERS

Unlocked

Beneath a Midwinter Moon

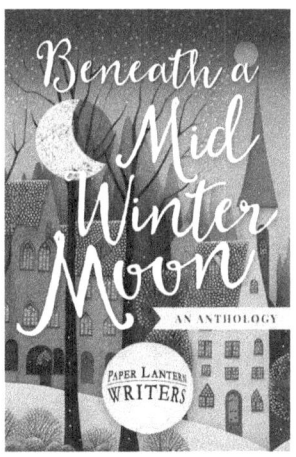

Find us at www.paperlanternwriters.com

www.ingramcontent.com/pod-product-compliance
Lightning Source LLC
Chambersburg PA
CBHW060625260626
47161CB00008B/2801